Chapter 1.

The best thing about screws make all the stupid Turk pour white spirit and varnish into his cup, and mix it up, and then throw it, I thought he was going to varnish his model ship, but he threw it over the old bloke's head and then set him on fire and it was too quick even to think about. I wrapped a blanket around the head and the hands flapping like crows but the Turk pulled it off and set him on fire again and laughed, fanning the flames, laughing like a demon. I thought he was dead. The screws took over, then, and banged us all up; and we never saw a thing, of course, while the old bloke went off to a burns unit and we waited for the old bill to come and ask us questions; it was a good time to be in the room. I wish I had a bolt on the door, but at least that Turkish bloke had been segged. Someone else might run through the door, but at least it would not be the Turk. I would have segged myself, rather than have to live with that.

It went on a bit. We could not go to work, the next morning. There had been a bit of trouble in the dorms, where the young blokes or short timers go. I have more than three years left, so I have a room. The dorms are terrible; tea bags all over the walls, everything running and brown, idiots every night, setting the place alight and messing it up for the rest of us. There is a lot of trouble; I try not to get involved, and most of us are the same. I hate swearing, I hate talking about women, I would rather not smoke. Inside it is a good idea to swear and smoke. After a while, it is all you do.

So the screws make all the decisions and you get up and go to work, after they have dressed up in their white coats and white hats and pushed the food trolleys from the kitchens to the wings and we have all queued up and eaten the food which was quite well cooked when it went into the trolleys but by the time we get it, has seen better days. Past its prime. Slop. Terrible. They go to a great deal of trouble to make us order the food. We have menus, and the idea is that if we "order what we want we will not waste what we get", as Mr. Davenport likes to tell us every time we throw the slop into the pig bin. Likes his W's, does Mr. Davenport. In fact, most of the blokes take the plate up to the room and then throw the stuff to the seagulls. Most of the seagulls prefer teabags to the food. They eat the teabags, but you throw them a beefburger and they'll drag it around the yard for a while and then leave it, the same for a mackerel fillet. Seagulls should like mackerel. The ones up here obviously do not recognise it as food. They take sedative syrup, soaked into bread. They swoop on it as you throw it from the window, and then perform aerobatics as the drugs kick in. It keeps us entertained, and the birds seem none the worse as long as they do not hit anything. They come and go, more when the weather's rough or in high wind; in fog or damp they come and sit on the yard or the sills, dripping misery. In sun, they wheel and scream, hanging against the blue with a speck of red at the beak and a slate grey back, and they look wonderful although the noise will put me off seagulls for the rest of my life.

We are not banged up. We have keys to our rooms and can go where we want. So, we stay in our rooms or on the wing, because where would we go? Two of the lads hid in a shrub in the garden, the other night. They missed them at roll call, and the whole prison was secured as they searched. The next morning the police dogs were brought in and the two lads came out of the bush, soaked and cold and tired. They'd had their fun, but they were shipped out to a bang-up nick immediately, one of them nearly lost his arse to a police dog, and they pulled all the shrubs out of the garden soon afterwards. It was a nice place to go and smell the flowers. The two blokes should really have thought on before staying out. It is not up to me to criticise the actions of other cons, but I liked those bushes. It's like the guitars. They had six, and the blokes stole them, so they bought another six and the blokes stole them and all. Then, the teacher said there'd be no more classes in music until they were given back, so the blokes on the wing got heavy with the ones who had nicked them, and they were sent back. Then they nicked the strings off them, took the machine heads off, and the keys, and broke one, and they shut down all the music lessons after that. They gave all the instruments to one of the screws and he set up a music club, and goes up there every night so that the lads can play while he sings. He's quite good but the teacher they used to have was a concert pianist, he could really play. The screw is not as good as the teacher bloke.

They went in to the head teacher's office, some of the lads. Shouting and swearing, giving the bloke a hard time. Quiet, fat little bloke, looked like he wouldn't say a word, he took it for a couple of minutes then really saw his arse and threw them out. Funny, the ones that gave him the hard time were the same ones who had stolen the guitars in the first place. Cons are mad, mate; I tell you. They take themselves too seriously. The sort that ends up in the teacher's room, anyway; they are musicians, not cons. In their own heads, they become something else. Instead of seeing themselves as a shabby dishonest sort of chap who has been stupid enough to be caught, they see themselves as one of the world's great musicians, fighting against society for the right to create and perform their art. A man wants a pencil and some paper; maybe he's seen someone else with pencil and paper, and so he wants some too. If they tell him it's not on, he'll make up some rubbish about his being an artist, he needs to draw a picture for some charitable purpose, to give to a school or to decorate an old peoples' home or he's promised the picture to a child in hospital. Then, he might get the paper and pen, and he'll do nothing with it, or ruin it, or sell it.

They had one the other day, stole a cheese wire out the pottery room, said he wanted to do some clay work in his cell. He didn't have any clay in his cell. The wire would have cut through steel. He wanted it to cut some poor bloke's head off, no-one in particular, just in case, so to speak. He had a spike as well. They put a Stanley knife blade into a welding torch the other day, got it red hot and then shoved it into the top of a plastic lighter. It melted in and set, so it made a good knife. Trouble was, the bloke plunged this other con and the blade came out, stuck up under the poor guy's breastbone, they had to take him to hospital to have the thing taken out and apparently it had got pretty close to the heart. They easily caught the bloke with the knife, he got an extra twenty-eight days. Laugh your head off at that on the out; it was definitely attempted murder, at least a section 18. They've got a bloke in here doing four and a half for putting three stitches in his girl's face, and this other bloke gets twenty-eight days for trying to kill his mate with a home-made shiv. It makes the poor sod doing four and a half feel really good, that does. It would do your head in, doesn't matter who you are.

Stupid, taking away the cheese wire. Ban dental floss if you want to stop people having their necks cut open. Ban sellotape, ban shoelaces. Better ban everything, because if you can make a weapon out of wrapping tape, you can make a weapon out of anything. There was one bloke made a television out of a computer game; another found where the prison telephone cables went and tapped into them with his Sega. He made a modem, used the fax, transferred money from accounts, no end of a laugh. They won't let anyone have computers, now. They won't let anyone have televisions, which is a shame. Tellies keep the lads quiet, and they've just spent hundreds of thousands wiring up all the cells after the riots, it was one of the recommendations, took years for them to get around to doing it, now the plugs are in but there are no tellies because they've decided prisons are too soft. Too soft? They'll soon change their minds. Give it a couple of months, and they'll all kick off again, and we'll see how quickly we get our tellies back. A minister said the other day that there hadn't been a riot for so long, they could make further cuts in staffing levels. Well, fine. No staff means no privileges. We can read, I wonder if they realise that. They want a riot we'll kick off a riot, but it seems a shame that they don't just remember the last ones. They weren't so long ago, after all, and all we want now are the tellies.

I hope there won't be a riot. You'd have to join in, even a bit, just for form's sake. Kick a nonce, or something, but not hang them, do a grass perhaps. Trouble is, there are a lot of people don't like me. There'll always be someone who doesn't like you, thinks you don't smoke enough, or swear enough, or you read too much or you are too polite to the screws. They'll get you in a riot, and they'll tell lies about you when the C and R boys clean the place up and trials begin. No joke, getting a long sentence for mutiny in a prison. It's the prison management's fault. They are giving the blokes a choice, riot or don't riot. They'll riot. Got to, haven't they? They may be cons, but they're still men. We may be forgotten men, but we're still men. Let them beat us down that much, and we might as well be dead.

There's a bloke with us, a robber. He's been a hard man, but only for the first six. If you are doing a long stretch, you've got to play hard for six. The first two get you your status, and then the next four keep it at a good level. Get nicked, say, 150 times in one year and they soon get the message. Famous cons get well paid when they get out. Kill a few on the out and a couple while you're in, beat up a screw and pull a section 18 if you can. You make a name.

Then, calm right down. They love results, but they measure them by returns. If they can say that a man has gone from 150 nickings a year to ten, or one, or none then they have to believe that something in the system is working and they'll give you a lower clearance. You'll go from A cat or a B, down to a C in a few years and then D in no time at all. D cats are easy. They let you out for college courses, home visits, town visits and all the good things in life. The clubs are better and it seems they get more money for education, music, drama and all the other activities that form such a ready source of paper, paints, access to computers and food. I know that school is a pain in the behind, but I would rather spend my day under the supervision of a teacher any day, than under that of a screw. That is not to say that many teachers are not worse than screws. They are quicker to nick, and what is worse, some of them like it. At least the screws are trained in how to treat cons. The teachers treat us as if we were kids, and impose the same penalties. They don't mean much to kids, but they do to us; a fine of 25p doesn't sound much unless you are used to earning four hundred a week and now you are down to £5.10p a week with all the canteen charges to pay.

I did nothing. Most of them here will tell you what they did, and a lot say they did nothing. I did nothing, though. The husband of the woman I loved (and she loved me) was working with me in an orchard, using a flail mower. We pruned trees and we were cutting back the brush. The flail mower got stuck in the brush and he put it in reverse. I heard him shout as the mower pushed him back onto a branch we had just cut. The mower has a cut-out in reverse, and he pushed the lever but it did not work. I told them all this. They tested it later, and it worked every time. It makes no difference now, but it did for the first few years. Then, the prison grew more important. No point in shouting about injustice if it gets up the nose of all the other blokes; they have done it, I haven't. It is better to belong than not, and they were offended because I wanted to be different. Innocent or guilty, what does it matter? You are in a nick, you've got to fit in. How much satisfaction will your innocence give you after six blokes with batteries in socks have been swinging at you for five minutes? The screws like it better as well. They train you to analyse your crime and express regret, and if you do well you get parole. It makes things difficult if the con refuses to admit the offence at all. Some do, of course.

I can forget parole for years, probably for ever; but I have admitted the offence now, and that is a start, at least. All I have to do now is keep my head down and do my time, whatever that time might be. It is not a good idea to think ahead.

I like music. I was in the music industry, of course I like music. The prison is full of musicians, they go on about their hands and fingers, and their skills wasting away as they do their time. Most of them might play a little but they are not pros, they've spent too long inside to be anything except cons. They are just cons who can play a few chords. You give them a guitar, though, and watch the change in them. It is their front, you see them change before your eyes. They pose and pout, and the head goes back and they look down their noses and glare and flounce in a way they would not dare use on the wings. They play a few bars and then argue, or they work out a routine and then storm out because the drummer was wrong or the microphone has not been mended. They have electricians, and road managers who love carrying amplifiers from room to room, and turning speakers so that the sound is balanced. Evening classes in the education department are drowned out by the racket these dickheads make. They play the same chord, or the same line, or they drain into a mike the words then again and again, until everyone knows them and dreads them. The final argument and the break-up of the music class is a relief to the whole wing. They fight, then, fight with the guitars, the axes. They break them up rather than let anyone else use them. They steal the strings and break the machine heads, like I said. The teachers think they will share the instruments, and rely on their sense of fair play. There is no sense of fair play. People with a sense of fair play don't end up in prisons in the first place. The bloke in charge of education had a death in the family, and it was the first time I saw him lose his usual temper. Nice bloke, he always calls us "Mister" when he talks to us, like "Mr. Yearwood" or "Mr Parry" and not just "Yearwood" or "inmate Parry" like one of the screws. Or "Convict Parry." The screw in question likes to stand by the serving counter, calling us all by our name, "Convict Smith, Convict Jones, Convict Parry..." he'll cause a lot of trouble in the near future. The music club screw gets his fun in different ways; he always wanted to be a singer with a band but was no good, so he has taken over all the musical instruments and formed a club. It only meets when he feels like singing and he tells them what to play. He's a big bloke and tough enough but he'll get a shock one day. It stops the lunatics taking over the club, though. They join, and hang around until they see it's a screw and not a teacher in charge, and they will either have to do as they're told or get nicked. Then, they go away.

Screws let you get away with quite a lot. You can push it, and they just go quiet and watch you for a while. Other cons, the younger ones, think this is good news, and push them as far as they can, and think they are getting away with it. Then, suddenly, they've gone. They find themselves in a van on the way to a dispersal prison, and they can spend twenty-three hours a day banged up thinking about how much better off they used to be. The news gets back to the long-term cons, who know how to behave themselves and keep their privileges. They will make a fuss, but they do it properly. They go to a solicitor, get legal aid, seek judicial reviews of judgements, and this is important to governors. They respect a fellow-professional, and they are trained to cope with professional opposition.

One robber on our block has got a Master's degree in the subject. He's doing years, sentence on sentence, some concurrent and some consecutive. He lost his claim to remand time, when they let hundreds out, frightened stiff in case the prison was sued for wrongful imprisonment; but he thought he'd win on the concurrent sentence issue. His appeal adjudication has been underlined to emphasise that his remand time has to come off his sentence, the second sentence he was given after he had started the first. It happens a lot. You get sent down for six years; while you are in prison you get charged for another offence, and the magistrate remands you while he hears the case. Then you get another six years; the prison system then puts the full amount on your sentence, probably because you serve your time in a nick and not on remand. The remand period for the second sentence should really be taken off your second six, and this makes a lot of difference for the serious cons. Some say remand should be taken off both sentences, although this would be hard on blokes who get bail...they only get one period of freedom while on remand. Now, it looks as if they are going to get their time, but if the prisons were not so full they probably would have been left in. They're only letting people go to make more room for the extra sentences that they are passing. Hard on crime, hard on sentencing. Someone should realise that if they go on like this for much longer they are going to have 100,000 prisoners in another three years.

Makes sense to lock up most of the ones I see. I have to say that. They know what to do in prison, and they do not know how to behave on the out. One bloke on our wing, messed up badly, works well in prison. They all say he's a good bloke. He was let out, and couldn't understand how people sorted themselves out. He tried for work but couldn't get it, he spent his giro as soon as it arrived, got into debt, had his gas and electricity cut off, the police kept hassling him. He lived near a family that had identical twins, and the girls used to do everything together. They left school and got a job with the same branch of a supermarket, and they walked to work every morning, dressed exactly the same. They worked in the same place, in the same uniforms, their hair was identical, when one lit a cigarette the other one did, too, they were synchronised. He watched them, followed them, saw them at work and at home. It seemed to him that they had life under control, they must be able to understand where he was going wrong. He tried to talk to them, and they laughed at him. Both at the same time. Both in the same laugh.

Their teeth looked the same when they laughed.

They were walking to work one morning and he ran one of them over. He had a car, no MOT and no licence, he'd found enough money for some petrol, he had bought the car to go on holidays as he had planned, when he was inside, long holidays in Wales on sand in the sun, nice holidays. He had never been able to manage one; his car had overheated about three miles from his home and he had been towed back by one of the locals who had seen him stuck. It was only a thermostat but he couldn't do it, and the car would only run for a few minutes before overheating. The pedestrian crossing was only a few minutes away, though, so that was all right. He waited until they left for work, then managed to get the car going, and when they crossed the road he managed to get one of them. They usually walked beside each other, but one of them was slightly in front when they crossed the road, and he got the one behind. She was killed, straight out; he was doing about fifty. I think he was happier just to have one of them. If he'd killed them both, they'd have died together, screamed together, bled together. This way, the one that was left has to make sense of life without the other one. She's wrecked. He makes no trouble inside, and the teachers and screws like him. He's the orderly in the Library, or one of them. I'd rather speak to him than most of them in here.

They let their trousers fall down low around their hips, but they pull their underpants up. Prison underpants are blue or pink check. They look really cheerful, bright flashes of colour, wobbling around like banners above the trousers. Most of the clothes are denim, made in another prison and sent here. They have a brand name, "Gaolers" or something, and a slogan that says something like "Made with security in mind." There is a denim jacket and trousers, and a blue and white striped shirt like a Marks and Spencers shirt but made from heavy cotton, they're good shirts. There is a denim jacket and jeans, and prison boots which are a bright orange plastic coated leather, socks, trainers, track suit top and bottoms, T-shirts with the number stamped on them small, near the neck somewhere; and the donkey jacket. It is just like any donkey jacket, except that the shoulder patch is not made of black plastic, but instead is bright powder blue. Originally they were meant for works parties, but now everyone gets one. They give us woolly hats and gloves. They even issue us with ties.

It's the same with lifers' coats. Lifers get a charcoal-grey duffel coat, and they wear them like a badge

We had one bloke who wore his track suit bottoms, too short for him really, with the underpants pulled up and sticking out of the top of his trousers, mostly out the back. He wore the denim jacket and a shirt under it, with the collar up and the collar of the jacket up as well. He was thin, and bandy-legged. He spent most of the day walking back and to along the corridor, with a half-rolled cigarette half way to his mouth, striding fast, and then stopping, turning, striding fast, and stopping. His trousers flapped, except under the crotch where the cloth was obscenely full. He visited each class in turn, and stayed for a while, and then left. Then, they found him standing outside the window of one of the classes, tapping on the window and beckoning to the teacher. He was tapping with one hand, and holding himself with the other, his trousers pulled down, his genitals cushioned on a sea of checked underpants.

The screws dragged him away, and locked him in the segregation unit, and shipped him out to a higher security unit the next day. They were laughing, the female teacher was laughing, the con was crying his eyes out and probably still is.

They shouldn't let women into men's prisons. Ugly women, old women, any women look good to cons, and the women know it. There is a probation officer who is very ugly who comes in at five to nine every weekday and she dresses in tights and a man's jacket, an open necked shirt, she has short hair cut like a man's high up her neck and short over the ears and her face is grey, long, like a horse, and lined. She has a deeply corded neck and a badly made up mouth. She walks into the gate, but instead of going straight to her office by the back path the same as most of them do, she walks down the back of the accommodation blocks and then around the block and up the main drag past all the blocks, walking very slowly, staring straight in front of her. She knows we're all looking at her, and she likes it. She knows that there is not a man inside who would give her a second glance on the out, but they all cannot take their eyes off her as she strolls to work every day.
She's a cow. Her risk assessments are vicious. She never recommends a man for parole, ever.

She is not the only one like it. There is a pair of teachers; they love nothing more than nicking cons in the classes, after they have wound them up. They get them going and then the con has to leave the room, and when he does he gets nicked. If a man gets nicked four times, he loses his C-Cat and gets shipped out. The teachers are middle aged and ugly, and again they love wearing tights and short jackets.

I know I said I was in the music business; I'm not a musician. I was a disc jockey. I knew the bands though, and I wanted to study music, so I went to the education centre to order a course. You can get grants for courses, and there is one from City University that teaches appreciation of music, and I like the sound of that. I went to see the bloke in charge, and he asked me a few questions about music. I told him, I was a disc jockey, not a musician. He said he was not going to spend his limited money on a course in musical theory for someone who would not be able to keep up with the course. I would have enjoyed the course, finding about how they make the chords, maybe learning how to play the guitar or something. I would have been into management, maybe. Not now, though; not if they won't let me even start the course, there are hundreds of pounds available for courses and cons all over the prison are studying for qualifications in chiropody, artwork, open university, but not me. It does my head in, really, I mean, really winds me up. I like the bloke in education, don't get me wrong, but he wouldn't help me. I had to walk out, I really would have done something stupid.

I am not a violent type of person, either. I run away from violence, always have. I know I'm a lifer, and it says that I took a life, but I've already explained that to you. It was just that he could have given me that course, and it could have changed my whole life when I got out. I know, lifers don't get out for a long time but when I do, on licence, because lifers get out on licence, then I might be able to stay out and work well in the trade. The music trade, like I said. Not a musician, but a disc jockey; but the job was great and the women we used to get, you'd never seen so many beautiful girls. Not like the hags. The women in a men's prison are all hags. They wouldn't take the job if they weren't.

If a dealer gets into prison with a kilo of heroin inside him, he can make four times its street value. Street value is about £50,000, so he can make nearly a quarter of a million pounds. The price for drugs inside is higher than on the street. It's worth doing some time, just to get to that sort of money. You would think someone would realise. The number of dealers who are disappointed when they get bail would make you laugh. They want to go to prison, want to make their money, and they find themselves having to waddle home with the stuff still inside them. It is harder than you think, getting into prison.

Many of the motiveless crimes that the press likes to write about are committed by people who need to get into remand centres with, let us say, a minimum of delay. The police in the cells and the charging unit can shake their heads and tut-tut as much as they like, as they put the bloke on the bus for the remand centre and they go home to their wives for beans on toast, the unfortunate con is in the bus staring at the immediate prospect of a profit of £150,000 for what will probably be eight months inside, if that. It is more than the Prime Minister makes. Not that they will see it; they probably owe it all to someone already. A user needs £100 a day for heroin or cocaine, and £300 to £500 for crack. That is £3500 a week; £182000 a year. It seems impossible, but there are thousands of kids who are making that amount of money and more, every year, year after year. The lad coming out of the remand centre will still be in debt even if he has managed to get his key into prison. He will have cleared some of the debt, possibly saved his mother or kid sister or wife or favourite kid having her face scraped off; and he will be in debt again by the time he comes out because he will have had a habit and his drugs will have been costing him four times as much as on the out. He'll have been using a lot, his possessions will be gone, all his phone cards will be used for drugs, he'll have segged himself to keep away from the debt collectors. Straight out, more drugs, commit offence, straight in again.

If they really want to break the cycle of drugs and crime, it's easy. Give them drugs. When they come to prison, open the cell door and shovel the stuff in. As much as they can use. Same on the out. It's not drugs that are evil, they're just stupid. It's what people have to do to get them, is evil. It's the fact that society allows government to lock people up who don't do as they're told, that's evil. If it's murder or rape, or theft, fair enough. They have always been offences, always will be, although there's theft and theft. But drugs? If someone wants to eat chemicals or drink alcohol or breath nicotine or cannabis, so what? The effects may be terrible, but you should see the effect a prison has on a person. You should see the effect that drug trading has on a prison, come to that. People with easy answers for the drugs trade, or for any other illegal activity, all have their heads up their arses. It boils down to the same answer, in the end. Take away the courses, the therapy, and it's the same old answer. Lock them away. What happens after they've been locked away? Not their problem? Well, it soon will be. The walls will fall down if many more end up inside. The walls are coming down anyway, it's just that they dress up the idea of release with tags and probation supervision and rehabilitation centres. The government will let them out, but only in such a way that they make money and jobs out of it, get people frightened and then milk their fear to ensure political support. Punishment for crime should have nothing to do with politicians. Courts, juries, police forces, that's different. The community will stop people from committing crimes; politicians just invent new crimes. They invent a policy, which nobody gives a hoot about, and then they make it important by saying that if people don't follow that policy, they'll be locked up. Then they take notice. The prisons are full of people who have disobeyed a political whim. One minute they are law-abiding, the next minute they're inside. They stick out like a dog's bollocks. Prison should be for criminals. If you don't know what a criminal looks like, leave it to those who do. Policemen know, judges do, so do screws and cons. We can spot criminals. We could tell you who should be in prison even before they commit a crime.

The drug free wings are coming in and the older cons like them. Lifers or armed robbers who do not use drugs like the wings, they are quieter and there is less need for searches of cells or people. Nobody likes having their cell spun. Mandatory drug tests are stupid, though. Cannabis shows up for weeks, but heroin hardly shows at all as soon as its been used. So, people use heroin rather than cannabis. The prison would say they should use neither, but to be realistic it would be better to encourage the use of the softer drug, and not the other way around. Now, the piss test shows up the drugs and a bloke who has promised to be drug-free will lose his place on the wing, possibly in the prison, if he is positive. So he buys someone else's piss, someone who is clean, who does not take drugs. He carries it underneath his armpit, and they don't watch when you give the sample. They are not allowed to, invasion of privacy. The clean piss market is like the tobacco market. Everything in prison comes down to smell, and dirt, and lavatories, and money.

I know I am going on too much about drugs. It gets to me, that's all. It is a vicious circle, and when I watch them going through it I wonder if anyone understands about these things except cons. It would be very easy to stop. Why not hold everyone in a cell for three or four days before they go to a remand centre or a prison? Check when they go to the lavatory, X-ray them, make sure they have nothing in their stomach or their rectum. That would stop a lot of the drugs, straight away. You see them, straight in the recess to swallow shampoo and make themselves sick, then cutting the stuff with sugar and the selling begins again. A holding cell with a lavatory in it would stop all that; then the only drugs would be the stuff that the screws bring in, and the works people, and the van drivers. They say that the police are not allowed to x-ray. Civil liberties. Or the con will surrender to a judge, not to a police station; that way, he goes straight to prison. Any prison will do; the drug dealers are networked.

They sing a lot, tuneless chants like football supporters. It echoes along the wings. "Oh -- ohoohwoh" first high "OH..." then dropping lower "Ohoowoh"...It sometimes gets an answer from some other con, further on. The nick echoes chant after chant. It is not communication, but only that the first chant reminds another person that he can chant as well. He does. It is like yawning. There are some of the black lads who communicate through rap, singing pointless jumbles of words to each other and then stopping, and laughing, leaning over to laugh weakly and to hit each other in a friendly way, as if commiserating at the pain of creation. They laugh as if they have no energy to do anything else, as if the pointless song they have just made up has drained them completely. They look as if they will collapse. Sometimes they do, falling backwards to sit wide-legged, head low, shaking from side to side as they laugh, white wide laughter, pink mouth, black face. It is a game. Get them on their own and the honky-tonk blackman routine disappears, they sound the same as you or I do. We all play games. They have a group and they need to display certain sorts of behaviour to stay in it, to show that they are part of it. I like to stay on my own, but quietly. I walk on my own, and keep away from the others as much as I can. I do not like people, it is not just because they are cons, although there are some people it is best to avoid. If you find yourself alone with some of them, it scares the crap out of you. They have done it all, and it shows. They look at you as if you had no personality, no significance. It's as if, to them, you were just a target, a height, a mass, a width and a weight. They answer you, if you speak to them, and they eat and drink with you and appear to understand normal behaviour; but they're wild, and have no idea of restraint or self-denial, of fair play or patience or respect.

They're not all killers. Many of the killers are quite the opposite; kind men kill. The husbands, usually, have killed their wives. Then they grieve for their lost partners, even though they themselves killed them. One man had a wife who was drugged up all the time and he left her. She followed him, pestered him, gave him no peace. He was upset already having to leave his children with her, and then she started bringing them around to where he was staying and making a fuss and bother. He met her in the park for a quiet talk one day; she went at him, she had a nail file and stabbed at his face and eyes, and he grabbed her and the pair of them went over the back of a park bench. He landed on top of her, and she broke her neck. Then he hid the body, and ran away. He was lucky to get away with murder, although if he had not run away he might have not even been charged. As it was, he got seven years for manslaughter. He spends all his time helping others, learning languages, writing to his kids (who are not allowed to have his letters. They are with their mother's parents) and crying for his lost wife. He grieves for his wife. She was his best friend; they did not get along too well, but she knew him better than anyone else.

They have shipped out the big armed robber, Wales' public enemy number one, the man of the match award 1975. He was a hard man for the first few years. When he hit a screw in Wormwood Scrubs they kicked the crap out of him and smashed his teeth. He has been trying to have a triple crown and a bridge made ever since but the dentist would not spend all the budget just on him. The robber's attitude was that they kicked his teeth out so they should buy him some new ones. Then they agreed to do the work and he was running around crowing about it, and the day before he got his teeth they shipped him out to another prison, and he will have to start all over again. Someone up there must have a sense of humour. Now he's going to a semi-open, and he will probably get D-cat soon which means he will be able to go home in a couple of years. When he does, I bet he will still not have his teeth.

They are broadcasting the budget debate. I used to watch it on BBC-2, and make notes. Nothing now seems more irrelevant than the rate of income tax; come to think of it, it never made a great deal of difference when I was on the out. To hear the other cons you would think they used to pay their tax religiously. They are furious that income tax is set at such a high rate. They never pay it, have never paid it, and they owe no allegiance to the fairness of the society that they have outraged all of their working life; yet, they claim the right to criticise.
"They."
I suppose I should say "we."
I do not feel that I am one of them.
Neither do they.
That must be why they are so interested in the budget.
Have I been taught something? Has my sentence just taught me something? Am I addressing my criminal behaviour?
I do not know what accent to speak in.
I do not know what accent to think in.

The canteen is open by now, and I need some soap. I earn five pounds sixty a week, but the soap still costs the same as it did when I earned that every minute. If a person commits a crime he should pay the penalty, and the high prices in the canteen serve us right. If society agrees to the deal, then so do I. The con earns his ill-gotten profit, hides it away so it cannot be repossessed by an intervention order, and he spends a few years before he can rejoin society, find the money and enjoy the benefits it brings. That seems fair to me, and obviously the government agrees. Others might prefer a straight job and income tax, every pay day. Cons just pay it all in one go.

Armed robbers are the elite, here. The other cons admire them, or sympathise as much as a con is capable of sympathy. Most have no idea of what the word means. If you tell a con that your father has died, they will immediately begin talking about their own bad times. Most cons cannot feel sorry for anyone other than themselves. They see others as sources of benefit for themselves. If they cannot see somebody, then that person has no significance for them. If they find out that their best oppo is about to leave the prison, they will fear the loneliness or regret that their friend will no longer be available as a source of blow, or burn; but that will be the extent of their regret, and as soon as their old mate disappears into the van or out of the gate, they will forget all about him. Some of them think of their wives and kids in the same way. Their property means a lot to them, but it is in a locker in reception. They would be annoyed if they found that their wife was seeing someone, or that their kids were forgetting them; but only because they might want to reclaim their family when they get released, and until then they want the family to be kept in some form of locker, too. This might seem harsh; but you watch them when they get divorced. They do not grieve, they just get angry; they announce that they are over the shock when they stop feeling angry. There might be some sense of betrayal, but there is no soul-sickness, no loss or sorrow, not with most of them.

Armed robbers are not sex offenders and so are safe people to be seen with. They have long sentences, and give good advice about the system because they know it well, and they enjoy the status. It takes a certain type to point a weapon, real or otherwise, at a bank clerk and make them fear you enough to hand over the money. The ones I know are harmless, quiet, the sort that enjoy playing the piano or practising pottery. They tend to insist that they be allowed to play their piano, or throw their pot; and they are prepared to insist, and whinge, and demand their rights. They study criminology and write long letters to solicitors. Armed robbers tend to be determined people. They are intelligent and thorough; but utterly self-centred. It may be that this is why so many of them are caught.

One of them started because he was in debt, but under no pressure. He dressed in two sets of clothes and found a replica pistol, then ran into a bank and took the teller's till contents, about eight hundred pounds. Out of the bank again, he ran into an alley, took off the first layer of clothes and put them and the gun in a bin liner he'd brought, and threw them into a skip. Then, he bought a paper from a shop, and a Mars bar, and then leant against a bus stop and ate the chocolate, read the paper and watched the bizzies as they arrived at the scene. One of them pulled up beside him, looked him over and then spoke into the microphone, just said, "It's not," and drove on. The bus came along, and he got on it and was whisked away.

He put the money in a cupboard when the shock hit him. It always does. Unless the man has done it a lot, and this bloke had never done it, then they will wake up hoping that their memory of the raid was a dream. When they realise it really happened, the sick feeling spreads through their stomach and chest and they have to move, walk, run, go out, do something. They might go for a pint, and not be able to finish it, unable to sit there long enough to finish the whole glass. They have to move, to go. This bloke drove to Wigan. He doesn't know why he went to Wigan; he had never been there, knew no one there. Then, when he got there, he had to drive back because the money was still in the cupboard, two hundred miles to the south.

He told somebody. A petty burglar, someone he knew, was bragging and he enjoyed the thrill of the respect in the man's eyes when he told him he was an armed robber. Elite status.

If he had known how petty burglars stay on the street, he would have realised that it might have been better to tell the barman; anyone. Small time criminals are always being pulled. The police want information and they get it from small-timers. If they do not get enough, they have a lot of crockery from houses recently on the receiving end of high-value burglaries. The police push them around, then break the cup, preferably on their head, then tell them to pick up the pieces; they will. It is a lonely place, a police station, for a small time burglar surrounded by large detectives. The burglar picks up the bits; and the police have got his fingerprints all over a cup from a raid.

I do no know what happened to this particular bloke, but it would have been something like that. He needed information to keep himself on the street, and thanks to the Cisco Kid, he had just what they wanted. The armed robber went to Wigan again.

When you have done it, and the bizzies know you have done it, you have a big problem because they will immediately prepare as many other similar cases as they can and tuck you up to accept the extra cases as T.I.C's. The offences taken into consideration do not affect the sentence but they clear the crime lists for the police. It makes you think twice about surrendering to a police station. Cisco was running around in small circles wondering what to do, in Wigan. It is not a very interesting place; even Cisco laughs about it. He had left the money behind, he had not even the sense to take it and blow it on night life, instead he ended up using up his last few quid buying tea and cakes in some tacky hotel in Standish. In the end, he phoned his mouthpiece.

Cisco's solicitor was switched on enough to give him some very good advice; he surrendered to a court. You can still surrender yourself to a judge, and admit the crime. If you do, the judge sends you to a prison, and from that time the police can interview you only with the permission of the prison service. It saves you spending hours, days being pressured into admitting strings of hookey confessions, and when you come to sentence the fact you surrendered to a court will go well for you when Lionel up there on the bench waggles his wig at you and reads you your horoscope.

Cisco has had an easy time, really, and has only about eighteen months left to do. His marriage has gone, of course, and there is no money out there for him, but he's a good-looking bloke and clever, he'll be fine if he stays lucky; and keeps away from banks.

I never robbed anyone and I'll do longer than Cisco. That annoys me. I hate cons, I do not feel like a con and I do not want to eat with them, talk to them or live with them. I stole, but only scrap steel; it was scrap to the chemical company, anyway. All I had to do was scrap the steel but I found someone who would buy it as obsolete equipment. He could still get some wear out of it, so I sold it on. I gave the firm the scrap value; they were no worse off. I used initiative and made some money. I still have the money, and a couple of houses, and my wife is looking after the cars and the tools. I liked boats and aircraft, I liked shooting and hunting, and the whole lifestyle out there is still there and always will be, so I am fine. I have a long sentence, though, and they will want to try to get the money back if they can, but they will not be clever enough. They'll want my guns, and they will never let me have a gun again. I will have a gun, though. If they want to get it from me, they might have problems because I am never going to be in one of these places again, that is one thing that has changed about me. I used to be a quiet, respectful, co-operative type but not any more. Once you realise the absolute certainty that smacking someone on the nose gives you, you use it all the time. It is a lot easier than going on and on for weeks about things, discussing and niggling and losing your rag; it is going to end in a fight anyway. Just get it over and done with, and go in hard to start with. I do it now. They say it, I go in, bang, hard as I can. The message soon spreads, and they leave me alone. Cisco will be out before I am, though. I never robbed anyone.

I get coffee from people when I fix their stuff; officers, civilians who work in the prison, teachers. They know I am good at my work. I fix televisions, radios, anything that needs circuit analysis. They are usually happy, and when they pick up their kit they give me coffee or tea bags, or tobacco. I do very well, but there are some officers who use me a lot, and others who think there is a line to be drawn between cons and staff, and that nothing should cross that line. I have seen one officer who was watching a television recording and enjoying it, until he was told that I had mended the video recorder. Then he turned off the programme and walked out. Then there are times when they want me to fix electrical equipment in the wings, and save themselves operating costs. I do it, usually; but just as they begin to rely on me, take me for granted, I refuse. I just refuse to do it. They cannot do anything about it; most of the time they have no right to ask me in the first place. I go up to the room, and stay there for a weekend. They do not even know how to set the timers. The TV goes into frame collapse, and they will throw it away. They want to tell me how to amend my offending behaviour, and they send me on courses to address my feelings of aggression towards children; they try to make me feel small, and they cannot even mend a television, they do not know how to use an oscilloscope. They are stupid, ignorant people, and their skills all relate to the ability to turn a key in a lock. That is the beginning and end of their ability; they can push someone through a door, and lock the door after them. They know no physics, no electronics; they speak no foreign languages, they have no degrees, they cannot make pottery, they do not know how to paint. They spend as much time, almost, in a prison as we do, and they produce nothing, they create nothing. They draw their wages and they go home. They come from the same places we do; they went to the same schools, live in the same estates, know the same people, sleep with the same women. When we are on the out, we have better cars and better houses and better women. When we are in, they lock the doors for us; they know we have the cars and the houses; they know we have the women, and even if they women go off, we will soon get other women and they will be just as nice, and just as much better than their women as the last ones were. We go to race meetings and spend more than they earn in a week, we go abroad, we hire planes or helicopters, go pheasant shooting, see our kids being taught in private schools...they go to work and lock doors. They clank around the prison with their black trousers and white shirts, the chain hanging from their belt down their leg, then back into the pocket where the bunch of keys are. They wear out the cloth with the chain. They love their keys and chains; I know people

in this prison who recognise the tangs and pawls on the keys and who know enough to copy the keys from
memory. Cons know more about everything than they do. They are turnkeys, and we know even more than they do about keys and doors.

I know; I know.
We are locked in, and they do the locking, when it comes right down to it.

Chapter Two.

Hail Ford Prison was a pentagonal fort that stood on a promontory at the end of a peninsula that was almost an island, joined to the mainland by a thin causeway that often flooded. The prison was at the very end of a spur of rock that jutted into the North Sea. It was stone on rock, and had a fierce beauty especially when the weather was clear and cold. Brian Thatcher was a governor grade works manager, and glad of the fact. He had spent years as an instructor, and had loathed it. He dealt with stone and cement, wood and wire, and not with people. Bad enough to have to talk to staff and contractors; cons, though. He shook his head, very slightly, and the thought fell out of his mind while he opened his eyes wide, threw his head back and stared at the sea. He breathed in, his nostrils flared slightly, he blew the unpleasantness of the prison away and replaced it with the air and sight and smell of the sea.

He stood on the top of the parapet wall, a flat expanse thirty feet wide, grass covered and pitted with the remains of anti-aircraft positions that had defended the naval port below during the Second World War. He had watched them, filling the air with stars, killing the Germans who now lay in the Naval cemetery under their ugly, heavy German tombstones. He knew their names, familiar as friends. In front of the wall a sheer drop overhung the harbour itself, and he stared out in one direction to the old east coast convoy run, dotted with ships carefully negotiating the wrecks of the last war's convoys, and in the other along the sweep of the east coast towards the North. The prisoners saw none of it; the prison wall blocked the view from the accommodation blocks.

They were rigging razor wire. It was essential to stop any more of the inmates from escaping, not so much because of any danger to the public as the need to pass the security inspection. The prisoners that escaped did so to avoid a beating; they would be in debt or in trouble, and had no choice but to seg themselves or run. Often, especially the debtors, they would be in the last few days of the sentence. That was the time that the debt collectors became most insistent; and when they were recaptured they had to serve another year.

Thatcher watched the two men unroll a second bale. "Watch that stuff, Tom" he warned. "Where's Williams?" The workman pointed along the parapet to where an inmate was rigging wiring to a series of aerials along the edge. Thatcher walked over to him.
"Learn that in the Navy?" Williams was a local, and Thatcher had known him years before. Williams had been one of many scrawny, anonymous kids brought up on the Island, as the locals had called it. His mother had gone away with a construction worker. She had been a pretty kid; frightened. Silly. He shook the thoughts away, breathed deeply and glared out at the sea.
"Learned a lot of things in the Navy, Guv." Thatcher shrugged. He remembered the bravery this man had shown as a child, the optimism and the brightness, and he searched the man's face for a sign of what had once been there. It had gone. It must have been buried by what had happened since. Thatcher never expected much from cons, but he liked to be civil. A con would always let you down, did not matter what you did or how you treated them. It did not matter, as long as they were in the prison. They could live in any way they liked. If they were out, they would have to begin making decisions again and they would always make the wrong ones. Crime was simply making the wrong choice; prison simply made the decisions for them.

Thatcher admired the inmate's skill, though. The hands were quick, and the work was precise and neat. He watched the man make a series of faultless repairs and then some quick circuit checks. Thatcher remembered; a stone with a slight crack in it, then the thump of the hammer, a crack, a fossil exposed or a stone discarded. The boy used to look up, and smile. Williams looked up now, and just stared. He seemed defensive, and Thatcher reacted from long habit and deep knowledge of the ways of prisoners.
"What are these for, anyway?"
"Equipment in the micro-circuit lab, Guv."
Thatcher nodded. He knew nothing about the equipment. If he had, he might have realised that he was watching the inmate setting up the aerials of a radio transmitter, not a receiver. It would not have alarmed him, nor surprised him particularly.

The inmate worked fiercely, in the same spirit as men must have worked when they were in German POW camps, installing equipment that they knew would be forbidden. With it he would be able to have surreptitious conversations with fishermen or lorry drivers. It was hardly a significant ability, but it seemed to signify liberation; he had taken a decision, and achieved a level of individual freedom. Thatcher would not have cared unduly, but would have obeyed the rules as he always did, and would have prevented the broadcasts. Nothing was more important than the stability of the prison. He maintained that by obeying the rules.
Thatcher nodded to the workmen installing the wire, and jerked his head towards the inmate.
"I'm going down. Keep an eye on Williams, bring him down as soon as he finishes."
He stepped into the basket of the cherry picker and the operator lowered him to the yard.
Later, for no other reason than the many years of training he had absorbed, he stopped the prison officer in charge of Williams' wing.
"What's he like?" Thatcher asked.

"Seems quiet enough, and he likes to dream. He claims that he is in for manslaughter, or theft, but always he admits he did something but it was innocent, never his fault. The theft will always be something daring, and usually the only people to suffer are the directors of some greedy large company. Every time they try to get him on an offending behaviour course, he pulls out one of his stories. Robin Hood stuff; he knows he has to admit to guilt, but when you ask him about parole he claims he wouldn't take it if it was offered. Hard man, he pretends; but he spends most of his time crapping himself. It means he never addresses the offence he is really in for, and he is so convincing most of the people running the courses believe him. His file comes as a complete surprise to them."
"So what is he in for?"
"Killed one of his kids."
"How?"
"Buggery. The kid started screaming and he smothered the boy with a pillow."

Thatcher nodded. He was not particularly surprised, nor censorious nor shocked. Robbery or buggery or murder, it made very little difference. The man was an inmate, he needed feeding and clothing, and they had to lock him up and make sure he did not get out. When he had done enough time, they would let him go, and he would probably try to bugger some other kid as soon as he could after he was released. Thatcher did not mind; the man was in a prison and that was where he should be. If Thatcher ever saw him on the out, especially anywhere near his grandchildren, he would react in a totally different way. As long as he was in and stayed in, Thatcher was happy. He used to hate buggery, but it was legal now. He had found this confusing. The prison had a few inmates who had been banged up for buggery with men, and some with women. Now those who went with men were legal, those with women were still illegal. He gave a slight shake to his head, and inhaled, and stared out to sea for a moment.

He strolled outside the block and across to the gate. Parker was lying on the top of the brickwork class area, an old Fives court; Parker was an old soldier, a relic of the army. So was the Fives court, like all of the many Fives courts built by the British Army in various places across the world. Some sheltered goats, camels, tribesmen; this one had been enclosed as a classroom. Parker was fully clothed and wearing a duffel coat, but he lay at rest on the top of the wall, feet crossed, head pillowed on a concrete block, his eyes closed and apparently enjoying the wintry sun on what was a bitterly cold day. He opened one eye as Thatcher passed.
"All right, Parker?"
"Guv," Parker replied, in a gentle voice, that shocked coming as it did from the rangy, powerful body. Thatcher was a tall man, broad from a professional life of public works. He would have been able to give the young lad a run for it, a few years ago; not now though, he reflected as, head tilted upwards as always, he walked from the gatehouse and around the outer wall of the prison, down the narrow road and through the tunnel and arch, through which the sea and cliffs could be glimpsed; jewels, set in black and grey granite.

As he cleared the tunnel the view widened on either side of the arch, and from one of the highest parts of the island he enjoyed the sight of forty miles of the coast. Shipping sheltered at the foot of the rock, and individual fishing boats tried hard to cut a wake through the seething wind-driven seas, the foam gleaming briefly in the sun before being whirled into greyness. He checked his watch. If that boat was making in, it must be fourish; he'd be away soon, time for a pint.

He lived on the island, as had his father. He knew the coast as well as the coastguard; better, probably, after a childhood spent climbing and finding rocks for diving and fishing. He knew the waters as well as the fishermen, and the Island as well as any man on it. He knew the prison inside and out, but also underneath, he knew the underground passages and the siege water cisterns set deep into the old fort. He had dug up old swords, badges, buttons and equipment left behind by generations of garrison troops; he knew the island in places where even islanders could never go, and the prison better than any other man in it. One of the holidaymakers had told him that an engineer was originally a man who designed fortifications and engines for their destruction. It pleased him. He considered himself a true engineer in the original meaning of the term. He knew the thickness of every wall in the fort, which were structural, which were load-bearing, how they were jointed, drained and buttressed. He had worked on the prison accommodation units and their upgrading, and would have been able to quote the pattern and make of most of the roof components, pipework, fixings and fittings. He did not regard the prison with affection, but as part of his home island, and he was pleased that no part of the Island was barred to him.

He stood at foot of the outer wall and checked the skyline, nodding as he did so. No trace of the razor wire could be seen from outside the unit, which was as it should be. Williams' two aerials could be seen, but only if you knew where to look and even then they were so thin they could be mistaken for brambles or tall grasses.

The prison van was growling up the hill, and he cadged a lift back to the gate. He checked in the radio and keys, and took his chain tally, and walked back to the outer arch and crossed under it and strolled at the foot of the mound of the fort's foundations, past the old tunnels and gate arches towards one of the major moats that had been cut into the rock of the island. The sides of it looked sheer, but he knew that at one point the joints of the blocks running up the side of the moat were like a staircase for anyone with a good head for heights, and they led onto the old track that ran from the prison's south gate over the downs towards the small town centre. It was a fine day for the walk. It took him less than an hour and gave him an appetite for the first pint. He smiled, threw his head back to better sniff the air coming over the moor from the tide race, and stepped out towards home.

The track ran over the old stone quarries, past a small inlet behind a hook-shaped harbour wall. He stood on the cliff edge and enjoyed the sight of the waves which crashed into the coast edge with enough force to dislodge rock, while a mere few yards away, the waves were dispersed and flattened so that the four boats at moorings behind the wall floated safe from damage, rising and falling gently, allowing the big man on the stern of one of the boats to continue with his work, paint spraying deck gear and floats. Thatcher made his way down to the sea wall, where he sheltered out of the wind and waved to Ron Freeman. The fisherman waved back with the large tin of fluorescent orange paint he was using. Brian knew that the paint helped recover any gear that went by the board, either by design such as Dan buoys or pots, or by mistake. Fishing was too poorly paid an occupation to let such items float away without making some effort.

"Wash your hands!" Thatcher yelled. Ron cupped his ear. "Wash your hands!"

It was an old joke. Wash our hands before you go for a piss. It was the risk of having fluorescent private parts. Ron nodded, and grinned, miming a woman screaming in horror, unaware as he did so that the ear he had cupped would now glow in the dark. Thatcher mimed a man drinking a pint, and Ron nodded again. Thatcher walked on, back towards the village. It was going to take Ron half an hour to clear and stow his gear, and to row back to the slip.

He walked down from the quarry onto a narrow lane that had once been busy with horse carts and lorries hauling rock, but now was just a road leading from the town to nowhere. His cottage had been a quarryman's home, and now was where he lived with his daughter Ella and her son, Peter. The boy's father had been a young prison officer who had met her at a local dance. When she found she was pregnant, he arranged a transfer to Manchester where he was now a Senior Officer, and at the thought of him, Thatcher breathed deeply and shook his head gently, and looked back towards the harbour. It was darkening, and the sea was ragged, falling in heavy blocks and chunks of water that were waves torn apart by the tide races off the shore, water streaming around the point of the peninsula meeting the up-channel currents from the Atlantic.

His daughter smiled, and for a second Thatcher felt excitement, almost panic, he loved his daughter so much. The boy looked up, nodded but said nothing, and then looked down again. Brian sat down for his tea, and relaxed, looking forward to his beer and then his tea.

"Come on, Williams. Time to get down."

The con put away the tools and packed the case into the workbox. He could just see the Governor from the works department. He had watched him go out of sight along the tunnel, and then much later had made him out coming up into sight from the outer moat, and strolling off towards the town. Williams imagined the governor's home, and he paused as he thought about a warm room, a fire, tea tables and a pretty young woman, spooning sugar into a large blue cup. He looked towards the tops of the roofs, just visible from the top of the wall. He imagined the inside of the house, warm and comfortable. Down the road was probably his local, a few shops, the local school. Williams decided he would go there, when he had finished his sentence. He would pick up his kit and walk out of the gate, down that tunnel and find out where to climb the trench, and walk across the moor the way the works governor had gone. He would find that town and go to the pub, and have a pint or two until the money they gave him ran out. He thought about this as they stepped into the cherry picker and lowered it to the ground. He put the tools away, took the tally and hung it on the pegboard next to his name. Then, he carefully stepped past the instructor who held the door open with the key in the outer keyhole and the key chain stretching from it to his trouser pocket. Williams knew he could take that key with the chain, and holding the chain in both hands, wrap it around the instructor's neck, twist and pull, and that would be the end of the man. He looked at the instructor who stared calmly back at him, just as aware of the chain and the man, and the threat that they both presented.

"Thanks, Guv."

"Good night," said the instructor. Williams walked fast to the block, head down almost so that his chin touched his chest. He was walking very quickly and swinging his arms to let anyone watching know he had once been in the forces. He was wearing a thin T-shirt in the biting wind, and tracksuit bottoms, and trainers. His chin was dark with two or three days' stubble, and his hair was disordered from having been on the wall top for the afternoon. It had been a good day.

Chapter Three.

"Evening, Maggie."

Thatcher deliberately changed his expression to one of slight pain as the landlady used his nickname. They all had them. The fishermen in the corner were called Klaxon and Digger; nobody knew why. Their boss, Ron, owned a couple of boats, and was a well-set up man in his early thirties whose good looks were spoiled by the bite taken out of his left ear. He would gently rub the ear sometimes, if he had drunk enough, and grin at Thatcher. He would smile, and mutter in his heavy local accent, "Done some hard times, Maggie." Thatcher would smile, gently. He remembered Ron as a boy, and had watched him grow into trouble, prison, prison again; Ron had been a brawler, and had worked in the quarries with Thatcher's father. It had been the young Ron who had pulled Brian's father's body from the cab of the rock-truck when it tipped over; it had been Ron who had brought the news to Thatcher's home. The boy had grown up, that day; he had built a boat, worked it, and finally bought two more.

The pub had a few rooms for holidaymakers and lodgers. The education manager was staying in one of them, and he came into the bar for his evening meal. He was a fussy little man, particular and finicky as he ate. He inspected every forkful, carefully ensuring enough salt or sauce covered the mouthful, and mixed parcels of the different types of foods which he then carefully lifted to his rat-trap of a mouth. Watching him eat was a painful but fascinating business, and he ate, and the pub watched. His name was Arthur Higgins, and to meet him was to dislike him intensely.

"Your man was fitting some aerials on the wall, Arthur."

Thatcher waited for Higgins to reply; it was an unexpected question, and Higgins liked to think out his response. He fiddled with a chip, some fish, a couple of peas, a dab of tartare sauce, and delicately nibbled the food from the fork, and chewed.

"My man?"

"Williams...he was up there with us today, setting two aerials onto the wall. He said they were for the micro-electronics workshop. Know about them?"

"Oh yes, I know about them. Micro-electronics." Higgins knew nothing about micro-electronics. "He is a very good type, Williams. Ex-Royal Navy, knows what he is up to."

"As long as you do, that's all that matters."

Higgins inspected a chip.

"I know what he is up to; I do not, of course, teach the micro-electronics course. That is done by a prison instructor. However, I administer the course, and yes, I do know what Williams was about, roughly. Have you any problem with the aerials? Are they in the way?"

"No problem. As long as the instructor knows about them, I have no problem at all."

Higgins chewed. "Well, then..." he sounded satisfied, smug. He ordered a pint of bitter, wiped his mouth as he finished his meal, and then sipped carefully at the beer. Ron swallowed two-thirds of a pint in one long gulp, and turned to Higgins.

"You let them do that, then?"

Higgins was never very comfortable talking to Ron. "Sorry?"

"You let cons put what they want up on the wall, do you?"

"Only if they are working for the instructor..."

"Was he, then? Working for the instructor?"

"I assume so, yes."

"What's an instructor want aerials for? "

"Testing televisions, I suppose...radios, perhaps."

Ron nodded, and finished off the pint. "Ah," he said, concluding the conversation.

Higgins thought he detected a note of agreement in the last "Ah." Emboldened, he expanded on training in micro-electronics. He was too stupid to realise that the conversation was ready to move on, to football or the next darts fixture, or fishing. The pub was quiet, half-listening, half embarrassed. The landlady carefully polished a glass.

"The course is designed to teach them circuits...computers, televisions, radios...they can repair radios, or computer ignition systems for cars, anything..."

"Clever buggers, then."

Higgins hesitated. "Some are very intelligent, yes; many are quite well trained, technically."

"And you teach them?"

"Not every subject, no."

Thatcher smiled. Higgins was in charge of clever and painstaking men and women who spent their days teaching maths and english to adults who could not count or read; professional instructors taught welding, circuits, wiring, motor vehicle mechanics and so on. Higgins administered the budgets and looked after examination registrations, but he had no practical skills. Despite this, he enjoyed being called "Sir" by any instructor stupid enough to fall for his front. Thatcher listened to Higgins expound on micro-electronics, and enjoyed the amusement. Then, as he always did, he finished his third pint at about nine-thirty, and walked home.

The next day he went to see the electronics instructor.
"Why was Williams setting aerials yesterday?"
"Aerials?" The electronics instructor was slow, Thatcher decided. "Aerials?"
"Were they for televisions?"
"Probably. Did they look like television aerials? If they were television aerials, it would make sense. We've got a lot of television work in at the moment. Williams is a good man, he virtually runs the section, very well trained."

Thatcher looked at Williams, working in the small side-office. The man's head was down over a circuit board, and he was freeze-spraying terminals and testing components to find a circuit break. He stopped occasionally, to answer queries from inmates on the course. "Does he instruct?"

"Some instruction, yes. Very good instructor, too, when he wants to be. Gets bad-tempered sometimes, not reliable. He does all the television repair in the prison, though. Runs the video club."

Thatcher decided he had better take the instructor up to the wall in the cherry picker. "See what they are for yourself, will you? I'm not very happy about them."

"Probably television aerials, I don't care for those lifts, too dangerous. I'm not paid to go climbing around walls, that's your lot's job. Nobody pays me to break my neck, falling out of a cherry picker."

Thatcher shrugged. The instructor was coming up for retirement; probably applied for VERSE, the redundancy package. Brian was finishing soon, too, but there was no need to let the end go just because it was the end of your time. More important to do a good job, in many ways. NFI...no flaming interest.

I found the break. As soon as I sprayed it, the transistor worked, until the spray wore off. Just clear the solder off and re-make it, and the board will be as good as new. The ignition control circuits on a car are about three hundred pounds. I could make one for about five quid. Not a bad line to get into when I'm out. I'll sell this one back to its owner for a jar of coffee or some tobacco, and he gets three hundred pounds'-worth of work and I get a couple of quid.

Thatcher has been snooping about. I knew he was too interested in the aerials. He walks around looking like a camel with his nose stuck up in the air as if he was sniffing the wind all the time; he's not as stupid as he seems, though. Not like old Barney, the electronics instructor. He should have retired when they got rid of diode valves. He spends most of the time in his office, and that means asleep. I do more teaching than he does; half of the bastards have no right to be on the course, anyway. That Nigerian; says he has got a degree, and he wants me to show him how to build a circuit. Four years' work, in a couple of months? He had to be joking. I gave him a circuit diagram and the components and a soldering kit, and he's been gluing it to the workbench ever since. Bastard.

The VHF works well. I crack on to be a bored naval rating and call up fishing boats on emergency, then chop and we can talk all day. I had a warship the other day, very pusser! "This is Warship Camberley, station calling identify..." I nearly jumped to attention, straight up. Training I suppose.

Helicopter control frequencies would be interesting, but I don't seem to have any luck with them, probably need a better aerial or a UHF set. Never spent any time with the air world; I know they have a guard frequency but I cannot remember what it is. Been in here too long. The VHF does me nicely, anyway. It is nice to talk to people who aren't cons. Better still, when the nick doesn't know I'm doing it.

The trouble is, getting caught. If they make a fuss about it I'll end up on the wrong side of an adjudication, for sure. Might lose remission; might even be prosecuted. Is there an offence of operating a set without a licence? Oh, bugger it, there is! They could add weeks on; years...I could be looking at staying here even longer. I might even lose my C-category, and be shipped out to another nick.

That bastard Thatcher.
That bastard Thatcher.
I might get shipped out to another nick.
B-Cat?

Dartmoor, or Blakenhurst, or Channing's Wood, or Albany oh shit oh shit oh shit, how the fuck can I get those fucking aerials down before they see them, oh shit, oh shit...
bastard Thatcher.
No harm, it was just for fun.
Could I get Barney to say he had asked me to put them up?
Higgins?
Higgins!

"Mr. Higgins?"
"Can I help you?"
"Williams. I'm the orderly on micro-electronics." The inmate stepped carefully into the education office. It was an enormous room, vaulted, part of the old fort.
"Mister Williams." Higgins always called the prisoners "Mister" this or that. It would have been a pleasant change if he had been able to use a different tone of voice, but the way he spoke it always sounded condescending, as if he knew he was doing them a favour and could not wait to enjoy their pleasure and surprise at being addressed as a human being.
" I'm afraid I've made a bit of a mistake, Mr. Higgins. It is about some aerials."
Higgins remembered something about aerials. What was it? He tried to remember and could only think of fish, chips and peas. Aerials, aerials...

" I was under the impression that our instructor wanted me to set up two aerials, and I went up with the work party the day before yesterday to do it...I am really sorry about this but I have set up the wrong ones."

"Oh dear," Higgins looked serious.

"They should have been TV aerials, you see. I set up whip aerials, quite the wrong ones. I am very sorry. Would you be able to sort out the cherry picker again, so I can take them down?"

"Take them down? Good heavens, that seems a bit of a shame. Can't you use them for anything. Er...to do with the course?"

"Well...as long as there is no problem about them being there.."

"Problem? Why, they're not going to damage the wall, are they?" Higgins was attempting to make a joke. Williams laughed, over-long.

"No, I suppose not."

"Leave them where they are, then. They'll not eat anything, will they? Cherry pickers cost money, you know."

Williams fawned.

"Would you mind clearing it with Mr. Thatcher, then? Just in case there is any trouble...I need to keep my nose clean with the Governors, you see. I might have a parole board coming up..." Higgins expanded. "Now look here, Mr. Williams. I have approved them being there, and that is all we need to tell Mr. Thatcher or anyone else who asks. I administer your course, you know; not the Prison."

Williams left, and Higgins phoned Thatcher. "Those aerials...yes, I know all about them. I have just had a word with micro-electronics. They are part of the equipment, is that all right with you?"

"Does Barney know about them?"

"Yes, he must do."

"Fair enough, Arthur. As long as you're happy. See you tonight, I expect."

"Of course." Higgins put down the phone, and walked out of the building over to micro-electronics. He wanted to be seen visiting his domain, and Barney liked to be visited. They could talk about his budget allocations, and what he planned to do with his redundancy money.

Higgins was employed by the local college of further education. The Home Office once had its own education group, which was later taken over by the local education authority and finally had been contracted out; the old system of providing useful education for inmates had aimed at correcting illiteracy and teaching useful skills in the hope that the students would be less likely to offend. Since contractorisation, education was provided to reduce the non-employed labour figures in the prison, in accordance with education standards set by the Home Office that were so low as to be out of sight educationally, and the standard of representation and management that the dedicated individual teachers worked for was so low that this cheapening of the quality of education provision in prisons was allowed to proceed unchecked. Under the new stringencies of a monetarist economy, education made insufficient profit for the colleges, and from the prison side, many governors had new budget cuts imposed on them so strictly that they either scrapped classes or turned off the electricity. A fine tradition of prison teaching, which in the past had stabilised the prison and redeemed many offenders, had been allowed to slide into disuse and abuse by the new breed of managers, like Higgins, experts in contract management, redundancy negotiation and tribunal procedures but as teachers, untutored and ignorant. Higgins walked through the industrial workshops pleased to see that the Health and Safety notices were correctly displayed, that the floors were clear of hazards and that the correct groups appeared to be in the right places at the right times; but he knew nothing of the subjects being taught and was unable to appreciate how many worthwhile results were being achieved despite the poor materials and the inadequate teaching spaces.

The micro-electronics shop had twelve inmates and one tutor, plus the instructor, and as Higgins let himself in by his suite key, he was pleased to note the silence of the workshop, spoiled only by a hissing coming from two large speakers that Williams, the tutor, was testing. The students stood at workbenches around the room, soldering components onto green boards in accordance with circuit diagrams and testing the completed boards with oscilloscopes. Higgins watched a Nigerian prisoner he knew, one who had asked to be enrolled for an Open University course in electronics. The idea! Hard enough to find that sort of money for a British inmate, let alone a foreigner. It was a puzzle to Higgins why drug dealers were kept in a British prison at all...send them back. Get rid of the Columbians and the Africans. What was the point of teaching them subjects just to make them a better drug dealer? £24,000 a year per inmate it cost; why flood the prison with foreigners? The Nigerian tested a component with the oscilloscope, rapidly tuning the gain and setting the wave band to the required patterns, and Higgins watched as if he understood what was going on. The Nigerian nodded in satisfaction and so did Higgins, and then he moved on; while behind him, the student shook his head ruefully, tore the component from the board and started again. "Barney!"

"Hello, Sir." Barney had no need to call Higgins anything, but he remembered when the Education Officer had ranked alongside junior governors, and old habits were too much trouble to change, especially now.

"Days to do, getting few, eh Barney? Looking forward to the gardening, eh?"

Barney had arranged to become an assessment consultant for the same college that employed Higgins, and at a much bigger salary. The new National Vocational Qualification had spawned a series of assessment and verification qualifications that meant very little but were difficult to obtain unless you were actually instructing a group of students in that system. Higgins had never been able to gain the certificates, being a manager more than a teacher. Barney, on the other hand, had them all.

"The garden, yes. Well, it has been a long time in one job."

"And a nice little nest-egg to fall back on." Barney considered the amount. He had never dreamed he would have more than £100,000 in one lump, unless he won the pools. Now, there it was, making his carefully-collected savings look like petty cash in comparison. At the thought of his bank balance a warm feeling seemed to fill the pit of his stomach and expand upwards into his chest. He nearly wept. Instead, he smiled, and poured milk into Higgins' cup of tea.

"Can't complain, Mr. Higgins."

Higgins took the tea, and sipped. Vague worries about his mortgage surfaced as they always did when he discussed money; his college had the contract for another year, nearly two; and he could expect at least one year's redundancy after that, if they lost the contract. They could well do so. Large regional prison education specialist groups were developing, with maybe a dozen prisons under contact, and they could afford to offer lower rates for instruction. Small contractors like his own were being squeezed out; and at his age, Higgins would never find another post as well paid as his present one; he would be lucky to find one at all. As a teacher he was worse qualified than most of those working for him. They sat and drank tea, one man so content he was close to tears, the other conscious of the unpleasant effect panic always had on his digestive system. Higgins sipped the tea, gratefully. He gulped, even when he was not drinking, and swallowed a lot of air. He began to talk about the department, his meetings, the conversations he had taken part in concerning cash allocation, prison security, inspection policy. Barney drank his tea, smiled and nodded, thought of his money and waited for Higgins to leave. Outside the cons soldered, tested, soldered, tested, until one day they would be allowed to go home. Williams watched the two men talking, hating them both and damning them to hell while inside him the fear of being

identified as a nonce grew and welled up and choked him with panic.
Later, Higgins sat with an orderly in his office in the education department. The orderly was pale, agitated, and spoke rapidly and continuously as he tried to convince Higgins of the need for music lessons. He was a pianist, and wanted some of the education budget spent on hiring a concert standard pianist to come in once a month to teach him enough for his next grade. Higgins thought this amusing; he said so, and the orderly then became extremely agitated. Higgins, by now thoroughly alarmed, became defensive.
The orderly, excitedly describing his offence, a complicated mixture of business fraud and pecuniary advantage, had begun complaining about the attitude of the authorities towards his parole applications. Higgins was tired of the conversation; he was also in need of bolstering his own feeling of importance. He interrupted the orderly.
"I have read your file, you know..."
The thin, pale face and the bluish lips stilled, and the orderly's eyes locked onto Higgins' face.
"I read them all; but especially if a man is going to work as my orderly. For obvious reasons."

The orderly struggled with his fantasy, his justifications and complaints, but the litany of accusations over his parole, which he so enjoyed creating and embellishing, died as the reality of what Higgins had just told him, sank in. The vague memory of his offence had become linked to the sexual abuse of the same nature that he had suffered when he was a child; he had managed to forget being abused, and had almost as successfully forgotten the abuse he had inflicted on his girlfriend's children. He stared at Higgins, his face and mouth working but unable to speak.

"Now, the truth of the matter, and I am very sorry that you have not had the confidence to confide in me, but still, be that as it may…you need to go to Albany and do the course, obviously. Then, you will have a chance of parole. Stop wasting everybody's time making up these stories, and own up to what you have actually done."

Higgins enjoyed the silence he had created. The orderly was transfixed. He prided himself that he knew when to stop delusions developing into a false reality. It was for the orderly's good, and one day the orderly would realise it.

"What would I do afterwards?" Higgins realised that once a prisoner had been to Albany he was marked in the system, as a sex offender. The orderly waited for help. He repeated the question.

"What can I do after the course?"
"Come back here, get parole, finish your time, go home. Simple as that."
"Would you have me back here?"
"Of course. You're a good orderly. Look, get off to the probation office, say you want to do the course at Albany and sort your life out."
The orderly waited for a while, and then suddenly stood up. Higgins flinched, but almost immediately the man left the office and soon afterwards walked past the office windows in the direction of the probation department. Higgins nodded with satisfaction at having solved yet another man's problems. He relaxed, and sat back in the cheap swivel chair, and looked around his office which needed cleaning, just as it always needed cleaning. He made a point of complaining about it to the officer on the door, every morning, and to the inmate whose job it was; and the inmate usually promised to do something about it and then promptly asked for a pencil, or a notebook, or some paint. Higgins had given out quite a lot of stationery to that cleaner, and still had a filthy office.

The walls were used to display the work some of the prisoners had done. There was a head, which stopped abruptly at the neck and glared resentfully from a dusty book case; and pictures in garish colours, a mixture of the limited choice available to the painter and the limited talent of the man who executed the picture. A series of excellent canvases had been prepared by one lifer with genuine talent and skill; Higgins had stacked them in the corner of the office where they gathered dust and rubbed gently against one another. They needed frames, and frames cost money. The lifer who had spent hours of meticulously detailed work on them looked at them every day, and his hatred for the Education Officer steadily grew. He spoke about it to his personal officer, an old screw who was very similar in appearance to the lifer, and the two of them often stared through the huge windows of the education block to see if the canvases were still there, under a desk, being kicked by those who sat at the desk or scuffed by passers-by. The officer remembered the hours of work, the number of times he had looked into the lifer's room and seen him repainting, correcting, cleaning, varnishing.

"It's a bloody shame, the way he's letting them just rot like that," the officer said forcefully.

"Not to worry, Mr. Weston," came the lifer's relaxed reply. The officer had spent nearly thirty-five years helping others control their anger. The lifer had, too; but he had not joined from the Service, but by killing. Of the two, the lifer was the gentler man, and by far the more intelligent.

Higgins spent most of his life with a feeling of unease gnawing at him. He suffered from dyspepsia, and was prone to pruritis if he sat for too long in one place. Fond of herbal tea, he had a selection of different sorts on a low table by his desk, along with carefully chosen cups and a neat tray. Now he fussed over the kettle and the cup, carrying out what could be the most cheerful of pastimes, but with an expression of strained misery. By the time he had the first sip, the pleasure of the tea had worn off and had been replaced by worry about what next he ought to do. By the time he had finished the cup, the windows in the upper floor of the accommodation block had exploded and as glass rained into the yard the air was full of sheets of music, books, personal possessions that hurtled down through the frame and smashed into the concrete walkways, and the head and shoulders of a man could be seen appearing and disappearing at the remains of the window, the broken glass cutting first at his face and arms, and then his back and shoulders as he managed to turn against his attackers, and flap at the edges of the frame while they tried to throw him from the window. Higgins watched as the man became redder and redder, and his arms appeared to grow suddenly weak, and he was picked up bodily and pulled horizontally backwards a few feet, the head swivelling desperately on the bloodstained scrawny neck as the education orderly screamed his loneliness and fear into the last moments of his terrified life. From the time he had been abused to the time he had abused others, he had known this would be the end. His father was beating him again, but before it had stopped before it destroyed him, and this time it would not. He felt hands punching, tearing, there was a sheet of agony as something gripped and tore at his testicles, he was being twisted, broken, and then he moved in the opposite direction, towards the window, and he knew that soon he would feel the rush of wind past his head and the stomach-lifting lurch and then great pain and...nothing? Endless torment? Would it stop? He wept years of grief.

The crash came, and he lay moaning on his back on the floor of the block, in shards of the window's glass, while feet scuffed around him and large men grunted deep in their chests, and across the yard in his office Higgins caught glimpses of wrestling heavily-clad bodies as the lifer and the prison officer pulled the orderly to safety and the other inhabitants of the wing attempted to kill him.

Higgins found later that instead of going to the Probation Office, the orderly had gone to his room. Having sat there for a few minutes, he had gone onto the landing, and in a loud clear voice had announced to the block that he was a nonce and was in prison, not for fraud, but for sexual offences against his stepson. He had needed to announce this only once. By the time the other officers arrived to help the murderer and the old officer save the life of the sex offender, a mixture of bank robbers, thieves of other descriptions, GBH merchants, car thieves, drug addicts and at least two other sex offenders who had to be the most vicious in case their own secrets escaped, had energetically and enthusiastically stripped and wrecked his cell and inflicted sufficient physical damage on him to ensure he would be in hospital for at least a fortnight; he was lucky not to be dead.

No inmate was charged for the offence against the orderly. The governor, quite rightly, was extremely annoyed. It had damaged the window as well as the inmate, and both matters had to be rectified. The prisoners had been locked in, losing production for the rest of the working day. Higgins was asked if there was any explanation he could offer to the behaviour of the orderly, but he was unable to help. Everything had been developing so well, he explained; only minutes before the incident, he had been giving advice to the man. However, now he looked back, it was obvious that his orderly had been depressed about something. Higgins said the same in the pub that night, once he had finished telling the young barmaid the details of the assault, which she enjoyed. Thatcher came in as he finished, and Higgins dared not continue, professional officers taking a dim view of any information from inside the prison leaching into their home lives. Higgins ignored the barmaid's wide-eyed interest and unspoken appeal for more. Disappointed, she flounced away, saying,

"Sex offender...bloody deserve it. Shame they didn't kill him."

There were many in the pub who had not heard the story but they did hear her comment. To a man, they agreed with her, and Higgins relaxed in the approval by proxy that he appeared to have gained. He ordered another pint of bitter, the mixed grill with onion rings, and hoped they would have some mustard and possibly some tomato sauce.

Higgins could have found out, had he been sufficiently interested, that eighty per cent of sex offences are unreported, and of those that are reported, eighty per cent go un-prosecuted. Of those that are prosecuted, three per cent are found guilty. There are very many members of law abiding society with a guilty conscience and who need to shout very loudly at every opportunity that presents itself to them to condemn sex-offenders in the strongest possible terms. Society is full of victims and perpetrators who do not want to allow the truth of their past to be discovered. He had unwittingly tapped into this wellspring of approval; he benefited from the same social approval as do most tabloid newspapers and many television presenters who like to campaign on safe bets. It is the source of much uncritical approval by the electorate for poorly planned government policy, and a useful catch-all justification for a series of reductions in civil liberty. When trial by jury is denied in Britain it will not be justified by some emergency, or enforced by a tyranny; it will simply be justified by reference to the unspecified but oft-repeated threat that emanates from sex offenders.

People like to be certain about some things, and one of them is that sex offenders deserve everything they get. The orderly deserved his cut back, scarred chest, dislocated knee and the bruising: and, as the nursing officer said when he straightened up and reached for the phone to call the ambulance that was urgently needed to take the prisoner to the nearest general hospital, "We won't have to worry about this one re-offending."

His colleagues smiled, grimly, but with considerable sympathy for the broken figure on the table.

Chapter Four.

Williams bit hard at the knuckle of his thumb, and paced the room. He turned without hitting any of the furniture, his head brushed the shelf, he then stopped just before reaching the door and turned and repeated the walk. He had heard of the orderly and his injuries, and seethed with fear. He had asked the duty screw about the orderly time after time; he couldn't ask again. It would start to seem odd. Time after time, he had heard the details of the injuries, and had almost forgotten to add the obligatory,

"Serves him right. Fucking nonce."

There was laughter along the corridor. He wanted to use the lavatory, but hated the idea of going to the recess. They might be waiting for him. They might know. They would do anything they wanted to a woman, most of them. Whether she wanted them to, or not. They would rob women, hit women, anything; but they were not in for sex crimes, they were in for high-grade, proper crimes, they might have stolen a woman's car, ruined her husband, robbed her bank, defrauded her insurance company, but they had not raped her. They were in for proper crimes, not nonsense crimes. They hated nonces, it was common knowledge. Read about it. Any paper would tell you, cons hate nonces. They cut them up, do what they can to them; and it serves the bastards right. We might be the lowest of the low, but at least we're not like those dirty bastards. What would we do to them? Anything we like, and we'd have the full support of society for what we did, too. The public are glad that these people have a hard time inside. It's what society wants. If you don't believe it, read the papers. Just read the papers.

The control room of the carrier was dark. The watch had been closed up in defence watches from the time they had entered the Total Exclusion Zone, watch on watch off for weeks. They had started making a paper flower garden. The kids on the plot were practising their co-ordinate control by drawing figure on the plotting screens...bicycles, patterns. The lights were warm, comforting, the place was full of half seen bodies, dark blue/black from the neck down, white from where the anti-flash started, long white gloves. They tried to move around the Ops Room as smoothly as possible, but their belts were full of torches, gas-mask case, survival suit, lifejacket...after the Sheffield they were taking no chances. Nobody wore nylon, it was all wool or cotton. They wore their trousers tucked into their socks, and "steaming boots." They waited for the codeword that meant Exocet carrying aircraft were on the way, and when it came they waited for the Etendards to pop up on the radar and release and turn away, then they were there, and gone, and once again they waited, their whole existence spotlighted by a few seconds of intense activity, counter-attack, chaff, launches, scrabbling at the electronic information to attempt some form of plot.

Williams had been there. He had been an operator and a good one; brave enough to go on watch every day, and as cowardly as many others who spent a great deal of time noting escape routes. If he put the mask on it would not let him breath any better but he would at least be able to see enough to find his way to a ladder, out of the Ops Room...unless they were hit in the room itself. His skin crawled when he tried to imagine a beam-on attack, the missile smashing through the thin skin at Mach 0.95, spitting burning fuel, its hooks grabbing at steel and people, the fire and the shock wave followed, as you burned to death, by the explosion. Probably it would be welcome by then. He had stood with the others, taken his chance, and as with most of them had never come close to danger; but was no less a Falklands Hero for all that.

Some had died, some had got medals, some had just gone home, had their neighbours pat them on the back, seen their family, seen their girls. He had not seen any street parties...they were the last back. The Queen had been on board, but he had been working too hard to notice. They got ashore after Prince Andrew had stopped messing about chewing roses, and he had been searched by the MOD-plod on the gate because some of the stewards had stolen champagne from the wardroom party. Gieves and Hawkes had donated a lorry-load, and some steward who had been away seven months and had been looking forward to being a hero in his hometown was in a cell facing prosecution for theft of champagne. What a laugh.
Williams still felt the injustice of that.

The reality of it caught him out at times, stopped him in mid-stride, took his breath away even now. The boy by the formica bulkhead. He had been a stretcher carrier and had seen the field dressings but later they had needed someone in the sickbay for a while, and he had seen them take the dressings away. The arm had gone, and the whole of the front of the lad's chest and stomach were shredded by razor-sharp fragments of Formica that had split away and then flown across the compartment, next to where the explosion had occurred. He had stared into the body, that still lived, and later had seen the lad survive the operations and leave the ship as a casualty. The man lived. He had made jokes, asked for "SAS" to be written into his documents, so he could pull the girls when he got home. Fun, courage, pain, all of it organised and they coped with it. It was almost normal. Men would be there one day and dead the next; ships would disappear. One minute there was a merchant vessel, picture-pretty and expertly manned, and the next it was a fire, just a floating blaze, and the people were dropping off it like its paint, into rafts and into other ships, and then it is as if nothing has happened and the ship has never existed. Life seems fragile, and unimportant, and very precious. Her had loved the life on board, in war; it was different from peace time Navy, different from his home.

He had gone to his stepfather's home. It had made the local paper and his stepfather, the stupid old bastard, wanted to play the great I am by taking his son up the pub, and Williams had wanted to have no part of it but he had still gone, and listened to the bull while in the corner some young, jealous kids started to sing the theme from "Popeye the sailor man." He had wanted to hit them, but before he might have done anything, one of the regulars went over to them and whispered something, and they had left. He had been bought a lot of drink, and it had been a better night than he had expected. The only thing to spoil it was that his stepfather had been there; patting him on the back; mucking about. Bastard.
It lasted a week or so. He had been a hero. Then someone made the usual remark; in the Navy, is he? Backs to the wall, boys! Then it was back again. They had never been sure about him. There were always the sly digs. It was the same in the mob, in the messdeck. Somehow, they could tell. Sailors were tolerant people; they didn't mind, they didn't care; but they didn't agree either.

He was not a homosexual, never had been. He had just been attractive towards them. It had started with the old man, he must have worn that experience like a badge. Teachers, some sailors, some strangers...he did not want it, though. It happened. He never wanted it to happen. He liked women, he wanted kids.
He was a married man, damn it. He rallied cars and enjoyed radio-controlled aircraft. He liked to shoot, and to fish. He was not his beer-swilling, slack-mouthed drunken bastard father who liked to get pissed and come home and make everyone in the family know he was back; he was a different person from his father. He was a man, a proper man, with a lovely wife and a good job, and an expensive house and the two cars. She was happy, he was happy, her two children were great kids and they were a good family and they loved him to bits, even though he was their stepfather.

His mind went away from the reality of the home. It dwelt on the car, the guns, the crimes, the murder that was no murder and the thefts that had never happened. He pushed away the reality and elaborated on the details of the crime for which he was in prison. That damned flail mower. The mower, with his best friend and the man who was married to his mistress, he wouldn't have to tell the whole story, just hint at the details. The cons would spend all their time discussing whether he had actually killed the bloke or if it had been an accident...that was fine. As long as they had the story, they wouldn't think up any others. If they knew...if they knew. He could not wait any longer, and he burst from his room with his arms swinging and his chin down and he didn't look directly at anyone as he went to the recess and then came back again later, making sure he showed his full expression to anyone, because somehow there was always someone who would see it there; he was not proud to be gay. He did not want to be a homosexual, it had been forced on him, he didn't want it to be there at all; but it was.

The Ops Room had been ideal. Close, quiet. People were friendly there, cooperative; you were on one side and the Argies on the other; people were polite, helpful. The uniforms all looked the same, the gauze masks hid the mouths and only the eyes showed in the dim, orange light from the screens or green from the radars. He spent more time there than he had to, and it showed up in his reports. He had done very well in the Falklands; then, as soon as he had returned to UK, he had slapped in his notice and left as soon afterwards as the Navy had let him.

She had listened to him with open admiration. He had never seen anyone as lovely; she was quiet as she packed the car and controlled her two sons, neither of them old enough for school, trailing around her as she packed away their blanket and lunch basket after the day on the common. Her car had a flat tyre, and the ground was too soft to take the jack. He had shuffled over embarrassed, and found some flat stones for a base. That had been that, really. A drink, a meal, another, another. The kids had loved him; radio-controlled planes, radio controlled cars. He had a small dory, and they motored out to bays when the weather was right, and as the boys grew bigger he towed them in an inner tube at the end of a water-ski rope, and they loved it.

He worked for the telephones as a line engineer; plenty of money. No probs.
She had a house, and she sold it. He bought a bigger one after they married, and the kids enjoyed the garden, never saw their real father after a while, although he came once or twice, out of curiosity. They had bought the Granada by then. Williams had polished it when he knew her ex was coming, and he left the car on the newly-raked gravel drive outside the Georgian door, let him see that and wonder. The man had come and muttered embarrassed words to the boys and the ex-wife, and then shuffled off. Williams had felt like a king.
The boys really liked him.

Williams stopped his walking, took down a magazine from the small shelf above his head, sat on the bed and tried to immerse himself in the study of sound chips for radio sets. He read steadily, his eyes on the page but his mind in the Ops Room. It had seemed so safe. It had been as easy to forget about the sea on the other side of those few millimetres of steel, a world wide and miles deep. There had been tempests, force twelve winds, hundred-foot waves; he went to the bridge once, and had to crane his neck and twist his head upwards to see the crest of the great wave into which the ship appeared to be butting. It was a granite wall, above a bridge roof so high that it could only be glimpsed by looking straight up in the air, under the overhang of the bridge roof...and the bridge was over a hundred feet from the waterline. Then the ship rose, and climbed; and the crest was underneath them, and the next trough was hundreds of feet below them and they rushed down the slope of water like a lift. He had been pleased to leave the bridge, and to return to the gloom. It was unsteady, but after a while nobody noticed. Rock and roll a little, but not unless it was an enormous wave. The fact that the sea could burst in, or a bullet, or a bomb, or a missile only occurred to him when he had nothing to concentrate on. Like now. He stared at the door, secure, closed, flat wood, safe. The orderly's door must have seemed safe. His old bedroom door...his kids' bedroom door...yet at any minute it could burst open and they would run in, burst in, flames and destruction and beer on his breath and screaming exploding burning steel and metal and bristles and grabbing hands like they did to him, and he did to them, and they might do to him if they ever found out.

Williams remembered the aerials, and Thatcher. They were going to find out; the aerials first, and then him. He needed to do something. He needed to get out. They were going to find out about him, and kill him. He tried to think and saw the boy and the shutter chopped away the thought immediately. He heard the thin, desperate cry and then felt the heat and his weight push the boy down into the bed so carefully designed and bought for him by his mother, the soft cloth and the car pictures, the fresh smell of the washed bedclothes and beneath him the frightened boy, and the shutter cleared the thought again, gone as quickly as it came. He had been in the Navy. He had stolen metal from the rigs. He had been found guilty of the death of his friend's wife. He had done anything except frighten and sexually molest a small boy, grinding down into the clean smelling duvets, ejaculating against the blue flowers and the pictures of cars, doing to the boy what his own father had done to him, tearing away the good work done by the boy's mother and condemning future generations yet unborn to the same life and fear as he now felt. He heard the scream of the boy and the outrage of the mother, just for a second, before the shutter dropped again and head down, arms stiff by his side, legs propelled by fear spearing upwards through his body, he walked fast from his room and down the stairs, and out across the prison yard.

Ron looked at the fish finder. The light was on the starboard beam, and the trawl was running well. He checked the position of the race, glanced astern, and his instinct and local knowledge made him as aware of the margins and safety of his position as any navigation system could have done. He would need to recover in half an hour; it would be time to pack in, then. They had been out two days, and had enough. He yawned.
"Sea Trout, Sea Trout, this is Chipset over."
The VHF was set into a shelf to the right of the wheel. Ron hoisted his thick thigh onto the shelf, and pulled the handset towards him.
"Chipset, this is Sea Trout."
"Chop sixteen, Ron. If you've time for a chat, over."
Ron grinned and stubbed the buttons.
"Chipset, Sea Trout; hear me, do you?"
"This is Chipset, hello Ron. Had a good day? Over..."
"You bloody Navy boys, you like your Overs. How come they don't know you're wasting all this government time talking to fishermen, then?"
"This is Chipset; test transmissions, Ron. We have to make sure that the system is up. This will go down as a signal strength test. How are conditions? Visibility, sea state? Over"

Ron stared up at the skyline of the island as he replied. Chipset, or whoever he was, had been on most evenings recently, transmitting from one of the naval sites along the island. He looked at the radars and radio arrays; no shortage of them, he thought. He wondered which aerial was sending this message. The evening was darkening and the air obstruction lights on the radio masts were beginning to stand out from the orange and purple haze over the rock. He chatted with Chipset, easily rolling jokes and gossip, and listening to the stilted official format of the replies. He asked about the aerial.

"This is Chipset: not sure of your exact position, but you might be able to see our mast. What do you bear from the prison, over?"

Ron laughed. "What do I bear from the prison? Bloody funny sailor you must be...what part of the prison, then?"

"Chipset, sorry Sea Trout, I wasn't thinking. Can you see the Church cross, over?"

Ron could see a cross, just above the edge of the wall around the old fort. He gave a bearing from there. Chipset said that he was too far around the point to see the radio masts, and Ron assumed that it must be part of the old naval air station array. They continued to talk.

"This is Chipset; I must be as far North West of the Prison as you are South West. How is reception over?"

Ron told him, and listened to the Navy lad make some confusing remarks about signal propagation patterns.
"Don't understand all that, Chipset. Takes me all my time to work out how to make my beer money last all night. Speaking of which, I have to get her ready to come in, now. Beer's a-calling..."
"Where do you drink, over?"
Ron told him the name of the pub. He talked about his work, how long he stayed out, how often he was away. The navy man asked about fishing grounds, and how often he spent a night abroad. They talked about duty-free beer, and the price of a pint in the local; how much cheaper it was to drop in to some small port in France and load up, and come back. They discussed the rules, and the customs, and port checks on duty-free beer.
"Personal use, that's what you have to prove. Nothing to it, see."
"You going over again soon?"
Ron wondered what had happened to the radio procedure for a moment, but answered,
"You wouldn't like it. Not all grey paint and Olympus turbines, just an old smelly diesel and a lot of water green over the bow."
"I'd really enjoy it. I mean, it would make a change, from frigates, I mean. Over,"
They talked on. Dates, times.

"This is Chipset, where do you usually drink, over?"

It would be interesting to see this Chipset. They could take him over as an extra, no problem. Ron often took the locals for a cruise, as long as they worked their share and presented no risk to the others. He gave him directions to get to the pub, and Chipset seemed very interested in local short-cuts. He asked so many questions that Ron realised he had stood further out into the race than he had intended. No harm done; he listened to Chipset going on about the prison. Did the paths cut across the front of the prison, or were they near to the wall?

"No need to worry about that place, Chipset. They're all locked away. They could get out easy enough if they knew, of course; but they don't." Chipset wanted to know what he meant.

"Just the wall. We kids knew the fort long before it was a prison. It's not much of a wall, once you get past the moss. The blocks are so big, you can climb up them no trouble. Those deep moats they go on about...nothing to them. If the lads inside knew, they'd be out in a minute, I expect. Well, must sign off, Chipset; have to haul trawl. What's your name, if you make it to the pub?"

"This is Chipset; it's Terry, Terry Williams. Don't mention that to anyone, Ron; security, over."

"Roger that, Terry. Bye now; out."

Ron crammed the handset into the slot, and heaved himself and the boat around to a better course for recovering the trawl. By the time the winch started he had forgotten the conversation. Williams sat in the micro electronics workshop, and later in his cell, staring at the wall as he pictured the layout of the fort that Ron had described to him. He could see its moat, the footpaths and the village in which, soon, Ron would be drinking. That night, Williams listened to the noises of the prison and stared at the blank wooden door, still fearing that it would suddenly open, hoping that it would remain closed and keep his previous life and memories at bay. He needed to get away.

He would see Higgins the next day and get up on to the roof. Those aerials; he had to get access to the roof and he would tell Higgins that the aerials needed to be removed. They were too long; they would cause trouble if the governor knew about them. He would take them down and nobody would be any wiser. Higgins would have to get the works people to lift him up there. He had to get out of the prison.

He knew, he was absolutely certain, that they would soon find out all about him; they probably knew already. Something had made the piano player shout confession all over the block, and Williams thought he knew what it had been. It was bursting out of him, despite the fact that to admit it would earn at least a beating, and possibly worse. If he did not get out of prison, his secret would get out of him. It had managed to break through the fronts he had set up; the stories about his offence, the walk, the head-down stiff-armed ex-sailor personality, the teaching and skills and the favours for the screws; the truth was worming its way through tunnels and over walls and it was going to get out; he had to escape before it did. He had to go now.

Chapter 5.

"He's a prat." Thatcher threw the sheet of paper onto the desk of his driver. It was designed on a word processor package, and carried a banner title "Memorandum." Below it came the title of the education officer complete with retired rank, MBE, all his degrees and memberships and the full address and communication numbers for the department. The message seemed irrelevant; the cherry-picker would be needed at 1130 for half-an-hour, for the purpose of servicing electrical gear.

"We service electrical gear. What's the man on about?"

The driver grinned. "Aerials. He let some con rig aerials on the roof. He wants to get them down before anyone notices."

Thatcher's eyebrows gently ascended. "Higgins has made a mistake, has he?"

"Seems that way," said the driver. "He knows how to remove them, but he says it's a specialist job and that his inmate tutor needs to be present when they're disassembled."

"Can't you just wrap the cherry picker around them and rip them out?"

The driver tutted, and looked hurt at the suggestion.

"On the other hand, we could just tell the Governor and get the pompous little fart shifted...oh, go on then. Get him out of the mire. We'll have a favour off him in the future..."

Brian left the office and strode across the compound, squinting up at the two offending rods, high on the wall. He saw Williams walking across the yard, and called him.

"You'll be the aerial expert?"

The man looked up hesitantly, and grinned. He shrugged, and looked down again.

Thatcher said, "You a volunteer to go up there?"

"Makes a break, Guv."

"Mind you don't break your bloody neck,"

"Used to height work, Guv. I was on the steel for a while."

Thatcher nodded wisely, still staring at the aerials. "Of course, of course." He knew the man was lying. Cons do that. If you have to go to a funeral, their father has just died as well. If you are ill, they are worse. If you ask a question about any area of expertise, they have to convince you that they are far more highly qualified than most people in that field. It was a continuous and habitual need to impress, to dominate. "Just be careful, right? How long will it take you to get them off my wall?"

"Hour should see them stowed, Guv."

"I don't know. Time I retired; not only lifting prisoners over the wall, but providing the ladder as well. Right then."

Thatcher walked on to the gatehouse. The con trailed beside him, for no apparent reason. They came to the yellow line, painted on the ground by the gate and across which cons were not allowed. Williams stood and watched as Thatcher went to the slide door, pressed, and was allowed in. He nodded at Williams as the door closed. Williams stood there, looking through to the next door and beyond it, the open road.

The wall was ridged like he said. I knew it would be.
The top of the wall is the roof of the old embrasures. It is covered in grass and old concrete bases, and the grass slopes gently towards the edge, sprouts up at the edge of the roof. It is quite dangerous; you have to walk carefully to the corner, and then suddenly there is a bit of gravel, and nothing. You're looking down the outside wall, and under it is a moat which is a dry ditch, then the ground slopes away across moorland and gorse and there is the village, about a mile away.

Never been very good at heights. It is like looking at the end of the world. The wall makes it worse, just falling away like that, but the wall is made of granite blocks and there are plenty of corner stones and gutter channels, all carved into the stone. At the foot of the wall, about as high outside as the prison yard wall, the moat slopes gently and under the grass I could still see the outline of the stonework, covered in turf in places but still there. I could make out one of the footpaths, too; quarrymen from the village used the path to get to the quarry behind the fort. Ron told me. His father had been one of the quarrymen.

I heard the driver mutter something, but I did not hear clearly. His head is below the level of the roof. I heard the motor of the picker increase its rate, and slid back from the edge so that as the man's head came level with the grass, I was well into the centre of the roof, pulling at the co-axial cable with both hands. It came away.

"Sorry, guv. Couldn't get this away."

"Just hurry up, will you?"

Surly bastard. I had no problem taking the aerials out of the u-hoops holding them, and I lowered them into the yard on their own cables. I looped the top of the co-ax carefully around the concrete posts that the U-hoops had been bolted around, twice and then into a figure-of eight. Then I walked carefully to the rim of the picker basket, and stepped across the razor wire.

"What about that?" The driver pointed at the two cables running down the wall, pinned and clipped against the gutter channel for all of its length.
"It was there before. I thought I'd better leave it."
"Where does it run to?"
I told him that the bottom lines went into the classroom in the micro-electronics class and the top leads were fixed to junction boxes on the roof. He knew no better. He wouldn't have known a junction box. He nodded and we came down. I think he was cold, up there, but I felt fine. When I had stood on the edge over the moat, my fear of heights had suddenly gone. I stood there with the wind from the sea lifting gently at me, until I just suddenly knew that there was not going to be a problem. The basket came to ground level, passing the three layers of strands of razor wire between the ground and the gutter. Not a problem. I went to report to Higgins, and give him another feed of crap about aerials, and radios, and the electronics course I wanted to set up.

They need ideas. The job they do demands administration, and it takes them all their time to keep on top of the forms. I have seen Higgins, from my room; he stays there until the night security patrol throws him out. We are going to bed, and he is still in his office, lights on, and working. He is really working hard, I've watched him; columns of figures, computer sheets, checking and rewriting. They have no time for ideas of their own.

We have time for nothing else. Cons dream ideas, talk ideas, they write and make up and paint ideas. It is so easy that most of us cannot be bothered, but if we want a change, a break, a music afternoon or a drama night or a fun run for charity we just sort out the plan and suggest it to a screw or better still, a governor; then we sit back. Some screws know the score, but the younger ones cannot be told. The older ones know we are working it; they say so, and the younger ones accuse them of being dinosaurs. Young ones see it as a chance to get notice. Governors tell the Home Office as proof of how progressive and constructive their prison has become. They take it and run. There will soon be an assistant governor in top charge and under him a Senior Officer; there will be a committee of prisoners and a probation officer or a teacher. They will have meetings and take minutes, and the demands you can make from them! If it's a play, you demand scripts and costumes. Extra rehearsals mean special meals, tea brought to the rehearsal room, more time off the block. If it's a sporting event we can ask for sports teams to be brought in from the out, to give us better opposition. We had medals made up, last time, extra time in the pottery room and more hours for the kiln. It is so easy; the kiln turned out pottery which was sold for phone cards, the sporting teams coming in brought dope and fags, messages were passed to the out, business was done. The Music Day was excellent; two of the lads had it off with some of the musicians who thought it was a turn-on to have sex in a prison, and addresses were exchanged for when the lads got out. There was special food, cakes, biscuits; the television was there...just have an idea and suggest it to the staff, and watch them go. Wind them up; and watch them go.

They do not need to have ideas of their own. We do all that for them. I hope that Higgins wants to listen. I've planned a course, and all I have to do is mention NVQ accreditation, he'll be there like a pointer. I could even write some draft Instructional Specs, if I can remember how we used to do them. He'll think of nothing else for at least a week. It might stop him snooping about the micro shop, and wondering why we still need those two co-axial cables.

I hope they stay behind the gutter. They should do; the party stringing the razor wire had more to worry about than two aerial leads; instead of asking what they were for, they just made sure they would not chafe on the wire. I watched them. They tucked them into the downpipe culvert, about a foot deep and made of carved rock. They were so busy not damaging the cables and not cutting their hands off, they never thought to ask what the cables were for.

Behind the wire; shame it was not in front. Going to take some thinking out, that wire.

Chapter 6

The Governor stifled a yawn. Higgins seemed a reasonable enough chap, but he was such a bore. He tried to drag his mind back to the previous twenty minutes' worth of accreditation plans, Instructional Specifications, lead bodies and costs.

"Arthur, just one question; how many inmates will be able to benefit from the course?" Higgins beamed, and produced a reasonable figure. "And the total cost of the course each year?" The Governor despaired as Higgins frothed long-term costings, examination and accreditation fees, installation and equipment costs, financial sources and so on, but from the cloud of numbers he picked one and divided it by the number of inmates that could do the course in a year. Right; it looked reasonable. A large number of inmates could complete a cheap course and gain a nationally recognised qualification. He did not care about the course, or the content, or the value of the qualification. This course seemed to be all plusses as regards the home office returns, and the government was keen to flog NVQ's in prisons; presumably because nobody else wanted them. The Governor stood;

"Thank you Arthur; that seems fine. Crack on, liase with the industrial side for any commercial applications, and let me know, would you? I'll tell the college about our side. You have done a good job on this one."

Higgins hesitated. There was a lot more he needed to tell the Governor; but he could see his time was up. He stood, and left the file on the desk. "There is the pack, Sir, if you would like to read through it when you have more time..."

"Exactly. Thanks, Arthur." As the teacher left, the Governor threw the pack onto a side table, where it remained until, a few days later, something stirred in the Governor's memory and he began to read through it, flicking through pages at first, but then stopping, and re-reading slowly, and with infinite care.

The bar was full. Ron was pushed into a corner with Brian, who gazed easily over the heads of the crowd, enjoying the night.

"Bloody crowd, bugger them," Ron muttered. His beer surged against the far side of the glass and then poured down his shirt, as a young and dust-covered student from the training quarry, tired after a day of sculpture and instruction, pushed to the bar.

Brian laughed. "Couple of years ago, you'd have been on your way to the nick by now...and he'd have been in hospital." They looked at the earnest, thirsty, rude young man.

"Spilling my beer?" Ron asked. He looked up at Brian, and grinned. "I was a naughty boy then, wasn't I, Mister Thatcher?"

They smiled. Ron had spent a few months for the odd car theft or assault, once when Brian had been on the staff. They rarely mentioned it. They had known each other all their lives, and their families had lived on the Island for generations. It was as natural that some of the lads stole cars and fought as it was that they should dive off Sermon Rock, or catch Bass, or (on an Island with a small population, little work and four prisons) join the Prison Service.

"How many up there now?"

"About six hundred, six fifty. Bursting at the seams."

"They're not bad, are they?"

Brian shrugged. "Mixture. None of them are bad, really; not inside. Let them out and away they go."

"What, home? Or committing crime again?"

"Both, I suppose. These courses are meant to be very good. Stop them re-offending."

The landlady heard this and snorted with derision as she struggled to pour a pint of draught stout. "Courses!" she said. "They didn't need courses when my father was up there, Brian Thatcher. They broke stone. They were too tired to get into any mischief, and the island had plenty of rock. That's what they need. It did you no harm, Ron Freeman."

Ron laughed as the landlady shouted across the bar what most men on the island would have thought twice about whispering. He nodded, and his local accent thickened. "Aye, you'm right Mrs.Gibbs, you'm right.."
"I know I'm bloody right, you little bastard. You stopped trying to steal my bloody car."
Brian 's head had tipped back an inch, making him look even taller; the angle of his head was a good indicator of the level of enjoyment he was feeling.
"Hard work wouldn't help some of them," he said. The landlady snorted. "Like psychiatric cases."
"Oh those. They shouldn't be in a prison in the first place. If they are mad, treat them; but these buggers who pretend to be mad just to get off their punishment, I'd have that lot."
She served the stout to the young student, who tapped on the bar impatiently as the conversation went on above his head. "One eighty, thank you, and let me tell you young man that I don't care how tired you are, that's a bar, not a drum set and if you barge in here again, spilling the beer of my regular customers and tapping on the bar at me in my own house, I'll set that man in the corner on you; and he'll eat you."
The boy turned and saw Ron for the first time. He stared around for help and met the eyes of Brian, bigger than Ron.

"Eventually," said Ron. The boy excused himself and took his pint to a group of his friends across the room, where after he joined them, the noise level dropped considerably. Mrs. Gibbs almost smiled, and nodded grimly.

"They use excuses but they commit the same old crimes, don't they?" Brian just nodded. "Well, don't they? All this nonsense about treatment. Thieves steal, rapists rape, murderers kill. They're not ill, they just wicked. Lock them up; or shoot them, I don't care which."

She inspected a glass and saw a minute chip in the rim.

Ron winked. "And what about sex offenders, Mrs. Gibbs?"

The glass broke against the corner of the bin under the bar. She picked up the base, still spiked with ragged remains of the pint pot. "Sex offenders? Sex goes wrong, Ron, as well you know, and there are a lot of men in prison accused by silly women, and they shouldn't be there. I know that, and so do you.."

She looked at Brian, who nodded.

"But those who have done it, and especially to kids...I'd use this on them. I would. I would straight."

"Cock and all?" said Ron, and ducked as she leant across the bar and swung at him.

"That's enough of that. You should take it seriously, Ron, it's a growing curse. These bloody people make excuses for everything. It is becoming fashionable to use children for sex, and you have to stop it. It's no matter for joking, and it's no matter for filth."

"Sorry, Mrs. Gibbs," Ron said. He meant it, but she had already turned to serve another customer. It was Higgins, who seemed put out by the noise of the busy pub and once served, he joined them in the corner of the bar.

"A lady of some spirit! Nonsense, of course."

"What was?" Ron's shoulders, Brian decided, looked like those of a Brahmin bull. Higgins seemed oblivious of the body language.

"Mutilating sex offenders. Most primitive societies would, of course."

"Even those who attack children?"

"Every crime has a victim, Mr Freeman...old ladies, children, what difference does it make? If a man is driven to offend in that way, cutting him up will cure nothing. And which if us has never been attracted by a pretty child."

Brian said, "Attracted? You mean sexually attracted?"

"Lolita, the old story, it's a male fantasy to have sex with a female child with the body of a woman. Surely you have seen young girls that have excited you?"

Ron said, "Only if they looked like women. I didn't fancy young girls because they were young girls. If I find out they're young, I don't want anything to do with them. Jail bait."
Brian noticed Higgins' colour. The man was excited, almost aggressive. He argued with Ron about what it was that made a woman attractive, talking loudly about availability and the coquette, and the fact that even young girls flirt. Ron's easy laughter about young teenagers that he had chatted up slowly gave way as he became aware of Higgins' vehemence.
"So you like young girls, too!" Higgins exclaimed.
"No I bloody don't. I keep telling you..." Ron stared around the pub, and pointed at the group of students in the corner. One of the girls was pulling her work smock up over her head, and underneath was wearing a black vest that had pulled up with the smock, and until she pulled free she stood in the crowded bar showing an attractive midriff, bare to the world. "Look, that's what I mean by a young girl. She's pretty, anyone would fancy a kid like her...but say I chatted her up and she went off with me, and then she told me she was fourteen...what then."
"Well, what?" said Higgins. "She's willing, and sexually mature, and you're interested. In some societies you can marry at much younger than fourteen."

"I don't know about that," said Ron. He was usually aggressively sexual, and had been banned on more than one occasion when Mrs Gibbs had seen him pester complete strangers who had attracted him; but telling a pretty girl she was beautiful and demanding a kiss came from booze and a sense of fun, and a lack of experience with women. This discussion with Higgins contained an energy and an urgency that was foreign to Ron. He wanted to mock it, or turn it into something more coarse and funny, laugh it away, forget it.

Higgins said, "So you admit it. You could end up in bed with a child, even if you did not realise she was under age."

Ron shrugged. "I expect so. Some young kids today..." he tried to leer in a meaningful but jocose way at Brian and Higgins, but Brian was steadily studying the ceiling and Higgins was intent on his next point, looking at his fingers as he counted off each word.

"So you are excited, you have been intimate, you are in bed, she is willing and probably trying to excite you...and you find she is under age. What would you do?"

"You'd stop." Higgins stepped back as if he had been hit. Ron went on, " Most young girls try it on. They want to know they are pretty, I suppose. Some of them are dafter than others...plenty of them around here, sporting their first baby before they leave school...but anyone can have them, take advantage of them. The lads of their own age haven't any money, we have. It's nothing new, this. There have always been silly young girls, and there have always been nasty sods who would have them for the price of a few drinks. Doesn't make it right, does it? Say it was your daughter, or Brian's... sorry, Brian.... Children have to flirt a bit, they learn what they can do and what they shouldn't when they're flirting...but it's a dangerous old game. It's up to adults to keep them safe. If a young girl tries to flirt with a grown man it's up to the adult to protect her by doing nothing about it."

Mrs. Gibbs was surprised to hear Ron speak for so long on any subject. "Quite," she added, nodding. Higgins realised all three were staring at him, waiting for him to say something.

"Oh, don't misunderstand me...they are beyond the pale, beyond the pale. But they will go to ground if they are let out without support. We'll lose sight of them. It is more dangerous to be prejudiced and witch hunt them than it is to help them, keep trace of them, help them.."

"Don't let them out," said Mrs. Gibbs.

"Come, come, Mrs. Gibbs...due process of law, all that. You can't keep a man in prison for longer than his sentence."

"Give them longer sentences, then."

"And the overcrowding as a result? What of that?"

Mrs. Gibbs raised an eyebrow. "So, what you are saying is that they cannot be kept in prison, and our children cannot be kept safe, simply because the state will not build enough prisons?"

She turned to Ron. "In that case, Ron, in answer to your question; yes, cock and all. Now excuse me, I'm in a bad mood and I am going upstairs."

Higgins stuttered "But my order for food! Mrs. Gibbs, I was about to order my evening meal..."

"The kitchen is closed, Mr. Higgins. Goodnight. Jeannie, mind the bar. There is a pint in for Ron when he wants it." She stared at Ron. "That's for speaking good sense, and may I say it's the first time I have been able to say that about you, Ron Freeman." She left the bar, and as she opened the door marked "Private" she paused and said to the barmaid, "And if Mr. Higgins offers you sweets and a ride in his car, I suggest you say no."

Brian looked at the ceiling, laughed short and sharp, finished his pint and slapped Ron on the shoulder. Ron waved, and continued to be harangued by Higgins, and Brian walked back to the stonecutter cottage that had been his family's home for two centuries.

Nine-year old Peter and his daughter waited. Peter seemed to enjoy his childhood on the island as much as had Brian. The boy ran the same paths and climbed the same rocks. His daughter thought it odd that when the boy needed to be found, his grandfather seemed to know exactly where Peter would be. Ella fed him, grinned and insulted the pub and all who drank there; and Brian laughed, sharp and short, a bark of laughter that echoed for ever. His meal was well cooked, the boy was washed and about to go to bed, and later Brian smoked a pipe and walked the dog, up the path and past the pub, heading down to the small beach and back along the cliff edge to the cottage.

He looked in at the pub windows, still uncurtained because Mrs. Gibbs had gone up early and the staff had forgotten the windows. He could see the bar was busy; the students were singing across a table loaded with empty glasses and bottles. Higgins sat near the window, alone, eating a packet of crisps with angry, tight movements that semaphored the fact he had not eaten properly. Ron lurched across the room, and threw an arm around the pretty student in the black vest, who smiled and willingly gave him a kiss. Ron blushed, and walked back to his place at the bar, the student smiling and laughing at him, sitting facing him, wide open for more requests. Ron saw Brian, and pointed at the girl with his thumb, then nodded and tapped the side of his nose. Brian walked on, as the girl stood up and walked over to join Ron at the bar. It was a deep blue night, cold, clear but with hammerhead clouds building up to the south. Brian remembered the conversation that had spoiled his second pint. He considered a man in bed with young girls who might be women, the difference between a sexually willing fourteen year old and one of sixteen; he thought of some of the cases he had heard of, some of the perpetrators he had known. He thought of their victims; the babies, the two-year olds, the girls, the boys. The animals. He saw a series of faces, men of all descriptions and backgrounds; some of them were stupid, some were professionals;

some were innocent, accused because the victim wanted a payout from Victims' Support as the salvage from a relationship that was over. Some were stitched up by angry wives. Some were just innocent. Some were inadequates, small in stature and cowardly, frightened, damaged men; and women, he reminded himself. Others had been extremely capable; big, physical people who took what they wanted and always wanted more. They were the rapists, the humiliators, the child molesters who either took fulfilment from a body, or if it was unsatisfactory, had no further use for that body and destroyed it. There were those who planned and killed, and those who killed almost as an afterthought. They all talked freely and made demands, and called him Guv or Mr. Thatcher, and he would speak to them about their service career, their surgical practice, their unfaithful wives or their fears and hopes and plans, always neutral, usually friendly, they had been punished when they left the court and his job was to keep them safe and keep society free until the day came when they had earned the right to be released. That was enough; the right and wrongs of it were another problem, but he only had time to do his job, and to trust that those in charge used his hard work well. Higgins was obsessed with borderline cases and with marginal age differences; they were the least of the problem.

As always, when he sank into such thoughts, he made a mental heave and emerged from them again, a slight shake of his head clearing the last of them away. His head went back and he studied the horizon, still dimly visible. He barked, half laugh, half sob, and the short noise resonated in his own mind, while the dog pulled at the lead, and then, released, corkscrewed joyously along the narrow track that dropped steeply down to the sea.

Chapter 7

The segregation unit was a small L-shaped corridor with six cells, proper cells with borstal doors and observation ports. There was no furniture, a raised bed made of brick, a blanket and steel lavatory basin concreted in to the wall and floor. There were no external pipes or protuberances from which a ligature could be tied, and there was a small room set aside for the hearing of adjudications, furnished with chairs and table made from compressed paper. Very light, they would cause no injury if thrown and their components would not make a particularly lethal weapon. The musician was throwing himself from wall to wall of the cell, and had managed to bruise and cut himself fairly seriously, but he would not die and did not appear to want to kill himself. The two prison officers were injured. One, a small, young man who prided himself on being fit and an expert in self-defence, thought his arm was broken; the other, an older man, was an ex-Royal marine called Wrench. He had been kicked twice on the inside of the knee, and then as he fell, the con had stamped on the knee joint.

"Bastard must have done some unarmed combat training." The officer had been taught the kick and had used it himself in the past, and to a lot better effect; it was a vicious move, and even the Marines would only use it for real if life was in danger, in Northern Ireland or real warfare...the con had probably read the technique in a combat comic or some wannabee book about the special forces; it had hurt but had been clumsy, and whoever taught the con the kick had not warned him how serious it could be, and had not taught him the counter. As soon as the officer saw the foot coming towards him he had straight-armed into the con's groin. His hand still hurt; must be out of practice. He was more concerned about washing his hand after its contact with a con's groin than he was about the evident discomfort that his prisoner had displayed for some time after the blow.

His knee was painful but seemed to be improving. Luckily, the prisoner had been wearing training shoes and not boots; but he was a tall lad, and well built. The other officer, cock-sure and too confident of the power of his uniform, needed to go to hospital; and then, back to basic training if he could still use the arm. Stupid sod. Calling the con "Inmate Preston." Might as well have gone up to him and poked him with a stick.

The con had been in Seg for a couple of days, after losing his temper in the music room. Bloody guitarist. Wrench thought musicians were gentle souls. Harry, the old bloke who was education block officer had thought so too, he had angled for months for the cushy job looking after the sort of cons who book on to education. Most of them were wasters, some were gentle types who were frightened of the machine shops or the woodmill. People get hurt in workshops; there are too many sharp edges and heavy weights. The teacher had refused to let Preston practise his guitar, and Preston had lost it. By the time Harry had got there the teacher had locked herself into the music cupboard and was screaming like an air-raid siren, an inmate had lost some teeth and a piano some keys. Harry, calm and professional, moved with the speed of an elephant and was well over fifty, but he decided there was no other way and he had decked the guitarist, released the girl and then brought the idiot to the segregation unit. They had left him there to calm down, and he had been coming on well; then matey had decided to go into the cell with him and try out a bit of psychology. Shame it was just his arm.

Wrench limped to the door and quietly opened the port. The con was sitting on the floor, rubbing a cut he had opened in his forehead above the eye, and smearing the blood across his face and down the side of the neck. He was probably trying to make it look more serious than it was, going for the sympathy vote when the governor arrived. It would not work; he was going to be shipped out now, and the sooner the better.

The other officer said, "Shouldn't we get in there?"

Wrench sighed, and limped back to the paper chair. He said, "You've done enough, mate. Just sit still until the C and R boys arrive." He watched as the younger man decided this was a compliment. Typical. They used to know what was expected of them. He had noticed more and more, recruits had an idea of what their work entailed that they took from the press, not from the training manual. It was not just prison officers. Policemen went out on patrol wearing side-sticks, anti-stab vests, beltloads of CS and restraint equipment, and they were obviously convinced it was necessary. The press told them they were doing a dangerous job and that was good enough for them. The fact that all the kit pushed them further away from the community they were trying to police was ignored, as was that no policeman in their particular region had ever been stabbed, or ever been assaulted by maniacs baying for blood and deserving a face full of CS gas. The need had been identified, the equipment salesmen had visited police headquarters, funds had been found and now they were all tooled up with pounds of unnecessary equipment that was acting as an effective barrier between the public and its protectors.

It was the same in prisons. In the forces, wannabees were weeded out and sent away. People who tried to join the Marines because they loved guns and enjoyed the idea of killing people, were usually untrainable and had to go. Police recruits who wanted to drive on blue light and siren needed to be sent away, back to their television sets and adventure comics. And prison officers, he decided, who saw their role as representatives of society paid to punish its transgressors, did a lot more damage to their colleagues than they did good for the common wealth of mankind.

"Yeah, you've done quite enough," he repeated, and then heard the iron outer gate open, then the wooden inner door. The duty governor and a four-man Control and Restraint squad, booted and spurred, arrived.

"At last. Lose the locker key, did you?"

"Sorry, Wrenchie," one of the squad said. "Number four. He's quiet now."

The team formed up outside the cell, and released the lock. They ran in, but Preston was already down, arms and legs out ready for them to take a hold.

Around the prison the inmates were locked into the blocks, although free to move around the landings. Roll-call in this prison did not mean a full bang-up, as it was a training unit and regarded as low-risk. The men gathered in groups at the windows, the older and more experienced of them speaking quietly about what had happened and the probable outcome, while the younger men shouted excitedly and indulged in pantomime of what they thought might have happened, what should have happened. They all watched the C and R men go to the block, and waited to see the number of bodies removed, and whether they walked or were carried.

Williams did not stand on the corridor. He sat in his room with the door shut. He stared at the door, and waited. It was the same as when his parents argued, when he sat upstairs and waited for the screams and shouting below to stop. The waited, sometimes all night, staring at the door and the light under the door.` Sometimes the light went out, and he would release his breath and go to sleep. At other times, though, the door would open... he went to the door, looked out. They were still waiting by the windows, and the prats were still running up and down the landings laughing and making jokes about dead screws and dead cons. They speculated about what would happen to him.

"Shipped out, mate...probably done one of them. Look at the number going in...they're still in there...must be serious. You watch, I bet we all get a spin out of this. Concealed weapons, they tear the place apart."

"He had a weapon?"

"Hear that? Preston had a shiv. How the fuck did he get a shiv into the seg unit?"

"He shivved a screw? Fucking hell, Preston plunged one of the screws on the seg unit..."

Williams shut the door, and sat on the bed, thinking about the coaxial cables, and the boat and the fact that Ron of the Sea Trout was going to France at the end of that week.

Somewhere a window went. A group had been standing by the large window at the end of the corridor, looking out over the yard. There was a ripple of movement and the window exploded outwards, the PP9 battery sailing into the night. The group melted away, and the screw ran from the front office to the landing to be met by an empty corridor and a fresh sea breeze from the empty frame. The block officer sighed; every other week, this was happening. He went back to the office and called the works section. Then he phoned the duty governor. Someone was calling from the cell, howling, not to anyone in particular nor about anything coherent, just calling. Across the yard in a different block, the call was taken up.

Williams heard the noises and the glass as he sat in the stark room and watched shadows under the door. He had heard the glass and waited for any further noise but there had been no cries or calls for help, so he assumed it had just been a battery. He leaned back against the wall, staring at the door. Then the light under the door was blocked out, and whoever it was did not go away. His head jerked up as the door was thrown open.

The duty governor and Brian looked down on the nervous face. The jaw worked but made no noise, and Williams' eyes were wide and staring, The man was hunched on the bed, hugging a blanket to his chest.
"Williams?" The man sat on the bed and made no reply, made no movement. "Williams, you all right? What's wrong with you, man?"
The governor moved forward but Brian stepped in front of him, and gently took hold of the con's shoulder. "Had a fright, have you?" Brian asked. The deep local vowels rolled warmly around the room. "It's all finished now. Come and give us a hand, there's a good lad."
Williams seemed to recover. He moved suddenly, swinging around on the bed and putting both feet on the floor at the same time. He rose to his feet, and bounced, like a gymnast. He stared angrily at Brian, but still said nothing.

"The glass has cut through the TV aerial cables on the outside of the frame. You look after the TV in the rec. space don't you? I want to know if it still works. You understand, Williams?"
Williams nodded, and walked off, head down, shoulders hunched. He walked out of the room and shuffled stiff-armed and head down towards the stairwell and the recreation space below. The governor raised an eyebrow at Brian, who shrugged.
"Must be going through a bad patch, Sir. He had a fright."
"We had better keep an eye on him, Brian. One episode like today's is quite enough, for this month's returns at any rate."

Williams heard what they said. They knew! That bloody works governor, TV aerials…he knew. Terry had to get out, and it had to be now. He faltered as he walked along the corridor, when the thought struck him. It had to be now! His stomach seemed to fill with ice water. He was calm, though, and the panic had gone. He smiled, it was a relief to know he was sure of what he had to do. It had to be now.
"Where you going, Williams?" The screw in the office leaned against the doorway. He knew Terry often did work on videos and the transmission system, and was not concerned.

"Going to the TV room, guv. The works governor sent me. He wants the TV aerial checked out. In case that daft bastard cut it when he broke the window."
"Which daft bastard, Williams? You see him throw it, did you? Give me a name, then..."
"I didn't see anything, guv. I was in the room."
"Yeah, yeah..." but they both knew that the screw had been joking. Nobody gives names inside a prison. "On your way, then. If you need to get outside at all..."
"Please, guv."
It was as sudden as that. The chain came out of the officer's pocket and he unlocked the door. "Knock when you've finished. Knock hard, I might be on the upper landing."
"Right, Guv."

He was outside and the rest of the nick was locked in. He was in tracksuit bottoms and a T-shirt and it was a cold wind. He moved quickly to the corner of the block, and then across the concrete road to the edge of the training block. It loomed above him, the old fort, huge blocks of stone and a border of decorated stonework that stretched above him like a ladder. He was out of sight of the block office, and the training units had been closed since five that afternoon, and now they would not re-open for evening instruction, not after the window. He climbed. He reached behind the downspout and found the two co-axial leads, which he pulled free, popping them from behind the polythene clips that held them in place. He used them as top ropes and he swarmed up the wall, quickly reaching the razor wire. Leaning back on the cables, he rested his feet on the rock, and then on the outer strand of wire, but was caught where the razor wire formed loops and coils around the horizontal strands. He kicked his right foot free, feeling the clean painless slice of the blades through his skin; he hardly noticed. He leaned upwards, taking a firm hold of the cables, and then kicked hard away from the wall, curling his body upwards to miss the wire before he crashed back into the wall. That was worse...he had been an inch too low, and the side of his right leg had rested heavily on top of the razor wire coil before he had pulled up enough on the wires to take his weight off. His left foot found a toe-hold, and soon afterwards, so did his right. He was perpendicular from the wall, holding on to cables that he could feel were beginning to stretch, and where they looped around his hands and wrists were cutting into the skin. He fought to free the coils of wire, and then hand-over-hand he rapidly pulled his body upright until he was over the wire and back climbing the decorated edge of the stonework. He breasted the top, and mantle-shelved onto the grass roof of the fort, into the full force of the freshening wind, now very cold, cutting through the T shirt, chilling the growing dampness of his right leg.

The top was about thirty feet wide, and he had climbed eighty. He threw the cables over the edge, and used them to climb down the outside of the unbroken wall. There was no decoration; these were blocks, fitted roughly together, each about three feet high, some with significant cracks between them but others with the mortar smooth and intact. Apart from the quarrying marks on the outside of them, they offered hardly any hand or foothold, and the wall was vertical. He descended quickly using the cables, but looped them as he neared the end, and looked down. They were thirty feet or so short of the bottom of the wall, where there seemed to be a narrow path between the rock and the beginning of the edge of the first moat. Finding a foothold and the edge of the block with both hands, he let the cables go.

The first three blocks were manageable. Nine feet. If he fell now he would not kill himself, just break something. Another block; twelve feet. He had a grip, and searched with his left foot for the next toehold. Nothing; he reached further down, and suddenly his fingers slid ..one hand...both hands...he pushed away, brought his feet together and bent his knees, rounded his shoulder and tucked. He had a half-thought about rolling but the ground hit him, a terrible dreadful shocking blow that drove the breath from his body and the sense from his mind. It was not a fall; the rock and stones reared up and slapped him and the ground seemed to continue to hit him, again and again. He lay still, his head over the edge of the moat, and it was dark in the shadow of the wall and in the falling night. He still had enough senses left to see that the fisherman had been right; the moat was made of stones, edged to create a slope. Moss and grass grew in the reveals of the stones' edges, but they were still hard, firm steps; and after lying very still for a long time, he began to slowly make his way into the depth of the ditch.

In the prison, Brian called in carpenters to block the broken window with plywood. The wind was very strong, and he checked that the battens were strong enough to prevent the plywood being blown in. By the time he checked in his keys and radio at the gatehouse, it was difficult to hear anything but the wind, and the thick glass doors hammered against their rubber cushions and vibrated alarmingly when the doorkeeper pushed the button and the door hissed back into its mounting. Brian hunched into his coat, and was glad he had decided to come up to the prison by car; it would have been a rough night for walking. He drove down the long road that passed through the outer wall of the fort. It ran along the bottom of the moat just before the outer gate, the rim of the moat high above the road and even higher after that, the 100-foot walls of the fort itself. The sea could be seen on the far side of the island, wracked and foaming as it surged across the outer harbour and with breaking waves inside the harbour itself. On the far side of the island there would be towering waves and great clouds of foam, being blasted across the cliff faces, the houses and the paths leading up to the village. A good night, he decided, to stay at home; but he still made for the pub, for a pipe and two pints.

He had to drive to the foot of the hill, and then through the bottom town, out the far side and then follow the long, curving new road past the hotels and holiday parks and out the old village at the far end of the island. By car it was three or four miles, yet when he walked it he could be home in a quarter of an hour: there was one short cut between the sides of the island, and that was the prison itself. At the foot of the hill he watched a coastguard helicopter making low passes along the pebble beach, a searchlight quartering the beach, probably a training flight taking advantage of flying in storm conditions. The great white and red Sea King passed over his car as he turned into bottom town, and he noticed that the red flag was flying denoting danger on the causeway between the island and the mainland. The road through the town was streaming, and the long new road ran with the rain now lashing across the island. He leaned forward and drove carefully until he parked outside the front of the pub, in the lee. He knew that if he used the car park, which was in the full of the weather, he would have been wet to the skin and shivering by the time he reached the bar.

Williams walked away from the fort, south into the wind. He had lost blood from the deep gashes to his legs but the cold and the shock of the fall, combined with adrenaline that drove him further away from the prison, had reduced the bleeding. He had found a polythene sack and torn a hole in its base for his head. His arms were inside the sack, folded across himself for warmth, until he nearly fell. Then, he pushed his hands through the polythene and stumbled on across the gorse and pits of an old quarry edge, the wind cannoning into the sack, the rain hitting against it like pellets. At the edge of the gorse, there was an old road which ran along the edge of the southern cliffs of the island, dropping almost to beach level in places and rising to three or four hundred feet in others. The sea, solid and grey with tearing foam contorting and writhing along the backs and rims of the waves, occasionally threw out a tongue of water at the land which reared high into the air and added itself to the rain. The run of the sea was parallel to the beach, though, as it tried to turn against the point of land at the end of the island. There, wind over tide broke the surface of the sea into blocks, and one of the worst tide races on the coast of England. In a southerly wind, in the dark, it was a hellish environment.

His lips were salt, and he could feel it in his eyes. He limped and trotted through the night towards a shape that he had hoped would be a building. The road fell away and as he approached its end he saw it was the remains of a jetty, and the shape was an iron davit with a hand winch at the base. The jetty was empty, without a shed or even a boat, and the breaking sea periodically swept across it. In the lee of the stone jetty three small fishing boats heaved and danced madly at their moorings, one of them so low that it was obviously shipping too much water, and would soon settle. Williams looked at the jetty, but saw nothing for him, and turned back to the gorse line. If he kept low, at least there was some windbreak; he was growing tired and cold, and his leg was starting to congeal and stab darts of pain that made him gasp. Yet it worked still, and he seemed to be uninjured. He stared into the night, a sandwich-board man, streaming with water and abused by man and nature alike, and laughed at the freedom to suffer that he was enjoying.

Chapter 8

Terry woke underneath the sheet of corrugated iron he had found when he had crawled deep into the gorse bushes that edged the path. He had wanted to get away from the wind, but the iron had been the roof of a shed, long-collapsed, and there was still some of the old roof timbers and side posts attached. The roof stood a foot off the ground and was anchored by the overgrown bushes. He had slept, eventually, and now he felt warm.

The sack tore and he wriggled out from the iron, but gasped at the pain as the cuts in his leg and arms cracked open. It was a bright morning, the sea still churned but less than in the night, and the boats in the lee of the jetty rocked at their moorings but less than they had. One had settled, its wheelhouse awash. There was nobody looking for him. He could see the prison, solid, quiet; the top of the cliff seemed deserted. He would not be missed until after the rosters were taken at places of work; possibly not even after then. The block officer must have gone off shift without remembering he had let him out; and the relief would not have known that he was not in the room. He looked at his watch; he had an hour to get as far from the prison as he could, before he was missed.

They would go for the road, and to the station at the end of the causeway. They always picked up escapers at the station. Poor imagination, Terry thought, wanting to laugh. There had been one who had managed to lift the truck cab of a wagon and hide under it; he had almost fried on top of the engine before the driver heard him and stopped and phoned the nick. The screws had let him out: the driver waited for them, not wanting to get involved. The con had been medium rare by then. There had been another who had hidden on the chassis of the trailer of an articulated lorry, but he had fallen off and its axle had caught his head. Terry made his way out of the bushes and down to the jetty. It had to be the same place. The axle must have killed him, there is no way that he could have survived, or else the road would have done: run over more likely. He ran onto the jetty, as best he could, his leg was stiff and painful, but he had to see if the boat was the right one. He stopped by the davit, breathing heavily.
"Sea Trout," he said.

"That's my Uncle Ron's boat." Williams lurched at the voice, and turned to see a small boy, curious but not afraid, looking at him. The sight of a bleeding man in soaking tracksuit and polythene bag did not seem to be so unusual to him. Williams leaned against the davit. The boy seemed disappointed, and said, "We were going to France soon, but she'll not sail out today. We might do an engine test, though, for a few hours. The other one's called Kingfisher. And look at Petrel!"

The boy pointed to the smaller vessel.

"Swamped," said Terry.

"A bit," said the boy. "You could say that, couldn't you?" He laughed. "Totally swamped."

The boy stood up, looked around and then suddenly called, "Charlie!"

Williams found himself standing upright, away from the davit, looking around. Looking at the boy. The boy said,

"My dog. Seen him? There he is..." and an old black Labrador appeared, very wet. "Watch him, he'll shake in a minute, you'll get soaked, he always does that, your leg's bleeding."

"Fell onto some corrugated iron in the bushes, it was in the gorse bushes, I fell on it..."

"My den? You found my den? It's not sharp, is it?"

"There's one piece on the side. I cut my leg, nothing much."

"You could come back if you like. My mum would give you a plaster. If you like."

"No, thanks."

"I'm going now," said the boy, with the relaxed confidence of an islander, "my Granpa will be out to find me for breakfast. He always finds me. 'Bye."

Williams said, "Wait…"

The boy stopped and turned to see what he wanted.

"It's good, here, isn't it." Williams heard himself repeating the old Navy joke, but it was all he could think of to say. The boy nodded enthusiastically.

"Yes, said Peter. "It's my favourite place."

"What do you do here?"

"Oh, you know. Just fish. And my den, but you've seen that now. It probably doesn't look very good."

"I think it looks great. I had one like it, when I was your age."

"Where? Near here?"

"Just along a bit, yes. Nearer to the top track, where the lorries used to load off the hopper."

"It's all fallen over now," said Peter.

"It was a long time ago."

The boy and the man stood in silence for a while. Then Peter made to move off, but politely. Williams said,

"Do you like rocks?"

Peter looked around him. They were surrounded by great slabs and outcrops of rock. "Like rocks?" he said, grinning.

Williams laughed. "You'd better, living here."

"Not much choice about it," Peter agreed.

"I meant, do you like what you find in rocks. Shapes. Old shells, and stuff."

"I've got a collection of fossils," said Peter, dropping his voice. "Do you mean fossils?"

The man nodded his head.

"I go looking for them, and sometimes dig them out, but you're not allowed to so I don't tell everybody. Did you?"

"I had a set of drawers, full of them."

"Really? So have I. Collectors drawers? Just like mine. My Grandad gave them to me, and a hammer, but you have to have a permit to dig for fossils, and the rock can collapse. It's dangerous. I find them in the rock that has already fallen away."

"If you're digging in a rock fall, what if the rest of the rock comes after it?"

"Well, that's right. That's why you should never do it."

"Quite right."

The boy nodded. Then the man and the Peter both grinned, and Williams said, "But you do."

"All the time."

They laughed.

"I'd better go."

"Don't mention that you saw me, will you?" The boy looked puzzled. "I might decide to find some fossils myself. I don't want to be disturbed."

"I won't tell anyone, no. Try down the far corner, just off the path. That's where I found loads of mine, and the rock breaks away really easily. Mind your leg, though."

"Goodbye." Williams waved, smiling and suddenly feeling ridiculously happy. Then he remembered where he was, and why, and panic seized his chest and suddenly

Williams was almost panting for breath as he watched the boy and the dog walk away. About eight or nine years old; maybe younger. He turned and looked at the boat, snubbing hard at the mooring, and then he waited for the sea to rush into the cove, and then as it withdrew he went with it. Behind him he heard the boy laugh and call to the dog, and he thought he heard a man's voice shouting "Peter!" but then the side wave from the jetty hit him and he struck sea bed hard, then shook free, then went down again, deep and being twisted hard by the cross wave. When he surfaced, he saw he was near to the stern of the boat but that such was its freeboard, he would find it difficult to take a hold; it was also rising and falling violently, and he jerked hard to one side to pass astern of its rudder, like a blade, rusted and hard against his arm as he brushed against it. There was a line trailing from the boat's port quarter. He took it, feeling the wave lift him, letting the rope slide through his hands and then grabbing tight as the wave beneath him dropped away. His feet scrabbled for the water door set into the scupper, and found the lip of the devil. He hauled, but seemed stuck. His backside and thighs were under water and he moved, then the wave fell away again, and he rolled forward onto the rail which dropped with him across it, and then bucked hard into his ribs as the wave bounced up underneath the keel. Williams groaned, and

rolled onto the deck.
The hatch was padlocked, as was the wheelhouse door. He kicked the hasp and it parted, and he was out of the wind, out of his clothes, freezing, rubbing at his skin with a donkey jacket he found hanging in the wheelhouse. It was filthy, and he was covering his skin with oil. He found a Samson bar and used it to break to hasp on the hatch coaming, and let himself below into what looked like a small, very dark galley and bunkspace. There were curtains for the bunks and he pulled one out and wrapped it around himself. He twisted as much water out of the clothes as he could and put them back on, wet and tight against his skin, pulling against the cuts. Over them he pulled foul-weather trousers and the jacket, and shivered as he waited for some warmth to come. He rolled the curtain around him, and shuddered as he lay curled on the bunk, as the boat bucked beneath him as if trying to rid itself of its sudden and unwelcome master. He lay, shaking and smiling and waiting because he knew that there were provisions on board for a trip to France, and as soon as he could, he would find them. It stank of fish and he was in great pain, but he grinned as he lay on the bunk.

Brian inhaled, pulled a wry face and spat into the gorse. The pipe tasted foul. It was his own fault for smoking first thing in the morning.

"You must have been out early."
The boy nodded.
"I wanted to see Petrel. I knew it would sink."
"It looked pretty full."
"Swamped," agreed the boy. Brian smiled.
"Swamped, yes. We'd better go and tell Ron that he's about to lose a third of his fleet."
"What's for breakfast?" peter asked.
"Mushrooms and bacon. For me. Cornflakes, for you."
"Can I have some of your breakfast, Granpa?"
"Will you leave some for me, more like. Hurry up, now," said Brian. He looked back at the jetty, and could see the tops of the boats, still pitching but much steadier now. Ron would be able to sail that evening, he reckoned. No point before.

The Governor said, "What aerials?"
Brian looked across at Higgins, and sighed. He considered helping, but in the end decided it was quicker to let the man carry on. The search was already well in hand and the more Higgins said now, the more clearly Brian would know how much trouble his department was in for.
"Is this true, Brian? You let Williams onto the roof?" Higgins turned and stared at him, daring him to deny it.
Brian nodded. So did the Governor, and turned back to Higgins.
"Carry on, please. What part of the course did you think they were for?"

Higgins blustered on. The weather had improved that day, and even behind the thick walls of the governor's office the warmth could be felt. Where the hell would he have gone? Lucky not to have broken his neck on the wall, of course, but after that he would have made for the road. They could see it from the wall, and the causeway. Brian thought it was most likely he would have made for the mainland, same as usual. He heard the Governor's question.

"Badly cut, Sir. There was blood on the wall below the wire, and quite a lot above it. I think he was probably cut about the hands, maybe the head; the wire was flat, too, and I think he's fallen on top of it. I'd say his leg had been caught."

"Right." The Governor was very calm. Brian seemed imperturbable. Higgins was frightened and blustering. "We will leave it there for now, gentlemen. Brian, a word if I may." Higgins seemed to want to stay, but left eventually, after stuttering some further justification for his trust in the man. The door closed.

"Bad one, Brian," said the Governor.

"Sorry, Sir.. Stupid of me, not to check more carefully."

The Governor nodded. "Still; this is the man we saw in his cell yesterday. I am right, am I? The one who seemed in some state of shock?"

Brian nodded. Frightened stiff, of course. "That's how he got out then. We sent him to check the TV cable. They must have let him out, and in the fuss of the repairs forgotten all about him. Bugger..."

"And the shock of the incident has sent Williams over the top. Literally, in fact. The police seem to think he made off across the moor, towards the village in fact. Does that make any sense?"

"From where he was...no, not really. Unless he was lost in the dark, or shaken up. He must have had one hell of a fall. The cables were too short for the wall, and it's sheer for the last forty feet or so."

"I just hope he's not out there, in the gorse somewhere, dead. Or dying. Oh, hell. What time is it?"

"Ten forty, Sir."

The Governor nodded. "Right. Let them out, get them back to work. They will be able to get something done before lunch. Let's hope the police can tell us some more, after the dog teams have done their bit."

Ron groaned, and opened an eye. The girl lay asleep beside him.

His head hurt; he hurt all over. He thought of the night, and once again felt the surprise at the antics the girl had performed, and made him perform. She looked such a quiet maid, too...he groaned, and suddenly she was awake, startled, and then immediately relaxed.

"Ah, my fisherman."

"What's left of him," groaned Ron, falling back onto the pillow.

"I thought you were marvellous."

Ron groaned. "Thank you very much. You've been badly brought up, I can tell..."

"For such an old bugger..."

"Old?" He sat up and was in time to glimpse her naked back and legs as she flitted through the bathroom door. He could hear her laughing.

"I'll show you who's an old bugger, when you come out o' there."

"Will you be able to? I mean, no beer, stone cold sober...all that?" He heard the toilet flush, and then the door opened a crack, and she was standing there. He could see a very brown leg, one deep brown nipple and a beautiful eye.

"Just let me be for a minute, and I'll see what I can do." She laughed and stood back, then watched him as he urinated.

"Camel...I thought you were sailing today," she added as he finished. He washed his face and hands, and then looked opened the bathroom window and leaned out. She wrapped her arms around his back, and he felt her breasts hard against him.

The clouds, small and white, were racing across the tide race, seagulls looking like small shreds ripped from them, being fired towards the mainland. He looked down at the sea, and imagined how difficult it would be for the next few hours. The chance of a better catch would be higher, but he looked down at the long leg that was wrapping itself around his; this girl was bloody gorgeous, and she'd be going home in a couple of days.

He turned, with some difficulty, and watched her eyes widen.

"Think I'll give fishing a miss for a day or two. All that bobbing up and down..."

"Yes," said the girl, holding him extremely tightly and pulling him back towards the bedroom. She said, "You don't want to miss all that, now do you?" Later, as he began to concentrate, she murmured into his ear, "By the way, do you know that your ears shine in the dark?" and the two of them fell apart in a splutter of laughter and spoiled effort.

Williams woke up suddenly. The boat was still snubbing against its mooring but the movement was less violent. He was warm, he noticed; he was sore, but if he stayed where he was on the bunk, he stayed warm. Inside the foul-weather kit his tracksuit was damp, but warm. He had stopped shivering.

After a while he rolled carefully onto his back, and stretched. The cuts on his leg pulled as he did so, and he stopped before they opened again. He held his hands up in front of him and in the light from one of the windows he could see the long, thin cuts had sealed. He rolled from the bunk but kept hold of its edge, and made his way aft. He needed to find food, and the galley space was abaft the ladder.

He found some tins. There was no water, and he needed to drink. Four tins of lager were in a box under the small sink. He found a tin of corned beef and some tea but no matches, and he slammed through the cupboards and drawers trying to find some way of lighting the gas. He had worked out how to turn on the supply, and suddenly wanted hot tea more than he wanted food. He looked at the beer. For years, he would have given a great deal for beer. Williams shrugged, and opened one of the tins before climbing up to the wheelhouse.

It was a clear, fine day. He looked at the controls; a key starter would be no trouble, and there was a single Morse lever which would mean there was local control of the gearbox from the bridge. He checked the cliff top path for as far as he could see, and the jetty; and then went onto the fo'cs'le to look at the mooring. And gave up any idea of stealing the boat. The anchor cable was doubled and was locked, a padlock as thick as the cable links and one which would need a power cutter to split. Williams stared at the lock. He had expected some clip or wire mousing, but not a lock...even the Navy did not use locks. Why a lock? Who the hell did he think was going to steal a fishing boat? Williams caught the thought, and almost laughed aloud. "Ron, you suspicious bastard," he said.

He looked at the winch, toying with the idea of breaking the cable, or letting the drum run until the cable ran out. It would be shackled in the cable locker, though, and he would probably not be able to undo the shackle. He walked back to the wheelhouse, flicking through the lockers and drawers. He flicked the radio on, but it was dead. The GPS had some life, probably with battery back-up. He found some old fixed-focus binos, and sat for a while looking at the prison, trying to see any signs of extra activity although he knew they would be searching on the road to town by now; there was nothing.

"Show me your boat."

Ron looked at her as she leaned against the sill of the window. Her arms were close together as she leaned forward, and her outline against the window was magnificent. Ron stretched, then slowly scratched under his arm as he lay back on the pillow. She certainly looked as if butter would not melt, but he was knackered. It might be a good idea at that...

"What do you want to see the boat for? Smelly old scow. Stinks of fish and diesel..."

"You stink of fish and diesel."

"Well, maybe so." She laughed, and so did he. Strange, Ron thought. He liked this kid. Usually, afterwards, they could not wait to leave and he could not wait for them to go. He sighed and rolled off the bed.

"Poor old fisherman...are we going?"

"Pint first. Then we'll go. I should check her, after last night's weather. Get your drawers on, Annie; we're going to the pub."

They drove to the pub, along a the rain-washed street of stone houses, the air gin-clear and the street washed clean by the night's storm. It was a bright day, the wind had dropped although the sea still surged at the memory of the storm, and over the tops of the houses at the bottom of the street the sea was a deep blue streaked with green and torn by foam. It was a beautiful day. The girl would laugh, for no apparent reason, and look across at Ron, who found himself laughing with her. The barmaid looked up in surprise as the two of them walked in from the porch.

"Won the pools, Ron? Laughing at this time of the day? Usually you don't make a sound until evening, and then it's to complain..." The barmaid looked closely at the laughing girl who came in after Ron. "Oh," she added, with more than a trace of jealousy.

Ron ordered, and turned to Annie. She looked lifted an eyebrow and nodded towards the barmaid.

"Mind your own business," Ron whispered. Annie spluttered as she drank, and they laughed together again to the fury of the girl behind the bar.

"Food?" Ron asked. The girl nodded, and they ate ham sandwiches thick with mustard and drank another pint, then he climbed into the old Volvo estate while she slipped into the passenger seat and curled her legs underneath her as she rested back into the seat lithe and shapely as a cat. Ron shook his head gently as he turned on the ignition, and checked the rear mirror as he pulled out. The car pulled a trailer which carried a dinghy; he had meant to paint out some scrapes on the keel, but had not found time.

"There's a surprise," he murmured. She asked what he was talking about, but he shook his head and she let it go, relaxed, unworried. They turned off the road and drove slowly across the old quarry track and down the slip road that led to the jetty. She was sitting up, alert and interested. The tops of two boats were bobbing in and out of view over the top of the jetty.

"They look lovely, don't they?"

Ron nodded. "Two of them do; the third looks sunk..." He stopped the car and got out. He stood on the slip, swearing under his breath. She had enough sense not to make light over the swamped boat. She stood beside him, her arms wrapped around her against the wind. After he had thought for a while she said, "What can you do?"

"Ah, don't know.. pump her out. Pump her, I suppose, and drain out the engine compartment. The engine and the electrics will be stuffed. Well, the engine will be all right, but you know...you can't afford to take chances. The stuff in the wheelhouse will be ruined...charts, fishfinder, radio..."

She asked, very carefully, "Will it mean a lot of money?" He noticed the care she took, and he realised she did not want to spoil what had been a happy day. Usually, this would have made no difference. Ron had managed to stay in a rage for days over matters far less serious than a sunken boat. This time, he realised, he felt the same way. He carefully smiled, turned to her and put his arm around her. He said, "I've got insurance, you see. So it is a nuisance, but it's business. See?"

She nodded. Then, they unclipped the straps around the dinghy, and Ron backed the trailer to the slip and ran the dinghy into the sea.

"Swim?" She nodded, but he leaned into the Volvo and found a filthy lifejacket. He threw it to her and she put it on. He put on half-boots and pushed off, swinging easily into the dinghy and figure-of-eighting the short oar across to the Sea Trout. He tied on, and as Annie stood and leant against the trawler, as he knew she would, making the dinghy swing away from the hull and leaving her stretched beautifully over a widening stretch of water, he pulled the dinghy in on the painter and with one arm took her around the waist and swung her up until he felt her grab the rail and pull her weight up. She stood on the deck, and found he was there before her.

"Acrobat," she said, staggering for balance as the boat bucked. She shucked off the lifejacket, and looked around. Ron suddenly wanted her to like the boat as much as he did. He looked critically about him, seeing how much cleaner it could have been. He saw the broken hasp on the hatch coaming, and the wheelhouse door hanging open, and with a curse he ran forward and pushed the door open. He saw the binos sliding across the chart counter, but also that there was no damage. Then he left the wheelhouse and went aft to the coaming. He opened the door, slid back the cover and took two steps down before he leant forward to peer into the accommodation space. He heard the scream from out of the darkness, then a screech of

"Leave me alone!"
and then something heavy hit him in the face, and he fell. He rolled onto his back and looked up at the man who seemed to be towering over him, his fist raised, holding something...a tin? He sat up, started to speak, but then his head was hit again, and again.

Chapter 9

Bastard. The perverted bastard. But I had him. I saw the shadow under the door and I knew that this time it was not going to happen. It was different, too. I listened to him for a while, grunting and snuffling as he crawled around the floor. Not very tough now, was he? I hit him again, on the back of his head, and the again. He went down for good then. Bastard. Then I was up the stairs and away.

I never saw the other one until she started screaming. Not screaming out of fear, she was screaming at me, running at me the cow, blue black trousers and jumper, one of those bloody bitches of the duty blocks, women in prison, taking the piss out of men. She was calling me filthy names and trying to hit me. They can't get away with that. One of these days, we used to say, that stroppy bitch in the office, one of these days...and the thoughts of catching her on her own in the recess and giving her a sorting out, they talked about it for hours, some of them had really done that to women, we would end up listening to them, some of us would. If a hard man came in, they wouldn't talk about it then, not if they wanted to keep out of trouble. But there were groups of men that would listen. They talked about it, and went off to their rooms and fantasised, and there was a lot to be said for the idea of teaching one of those bitches that we were still men, and it was all fine for them to show us they could treat us as if we were ordinary sorts, but we weren't. We were bloody dangerous, and she would find out why. They couldn't treat us like that. She came running on at me, screaming and shouting, as if she was invincible, and I got her right across the side of her face with the tin. I could see her jaw had gone, her face seemed to fall in half. Her eyes went dull and she sat on her fat arse on the deck, looking like a stuffed doll, all eyes and big fat mouth, but a good body on her. She was out of it. I rolled her over and threw her onto the deck, and she just lay there moaning, her jacket up over her arse and her legs splayed out. In those thick tights like the probation officer wears, might as well wear nothing. I pulled them down around her knees and her arse was white and stupid, but good legs. I dropped the tin, and managed to push between her legs but the tights were round her knees and I couldn't get her legs apart, and she was trying to say some thing and rubbing her face across the deck, smearing blood and spit on the wood. Hell, I was hard. I hadn't had a woman for years. I really tried to do her, but her legs were jammed, I pushed with my knees and I could hear the cloth of the tights tearing but not enough, and I couldn't get in, but I could feel her on the end of it, just warm and wet, and that set me off. Oh, I thought it would never stop, just kept coming on and on, it was all over her arse and her back and she was pushing from side to side and screaming as best she could, but I rolled off her leg and couldn't be bothered then, I just lay against the hull and finished off. Her legs had red lines in the skin where the cloth had dug into her skin. Stupid bitch, trying to speak and shout, her mouth hanging open and covered in blood and spittle, and her arse and back dripping. I had to laugh. She lay there, pawing at her trousers, trying to pull them over her backside. I laughed my

fucking head off. When I got up, I could hardly walk. I'd come but it was still as hard as a rock; no interest in her, though. Later on, perhaps. The man was still out, and she had crawled over to him and was lying across his chest. What a state those two were, he was out of it, I'd got him good and proper; and she looked as bad as he was, crying and pulling at her clothes, slobbering on him. People are disgusting.
"Be quiet," I said. "Stop it, now. Stop making so much fuss…it's all right now." But she kept screaming, crying. I went over to her and she screamed more, I was trying to cheer her up. Bloody stupid woman. "I'll get you something..what? You want anything? You want a drink?" She was nodding, wide eyes, nodding and saying yes, yes, yes please, leave us alone, please…people are disgusting when they get like that. They don't mean a word they say. They just want you to go away.

"You just want me to go a fucking way. Don't you? Don't you?" I was shouting and hitting her, hitting her on the head, and she was screaming again, huge open mouth, sloppy jaw, winding me right up. I had dropped the tin, and couldn't reach it or I'd have put her out, but she was pathetic with her hands over her head and her pants round her knees, bawling and puking. I pushed the bloke off the ladder into the cabin, and she went scrabbling after him, spitting and dribbling and calling his name. Ron? Not the same...? Bastard, filthy bastard. I got him, good and proper. I locked them in, shut the door and pulled the coaming up, and stuffed a spanner through the hasp.
I went off. Went into the wheelhouse. They do it to you, they make me sick. People are disgusting.

I picked up the binos and watched the prison. It was strange looking at the outside of the place. The stone was well worked, and I could see the star design; it would have been a difficult place to take. The British understood military matters in those days. The experience of generations of soldiers had gone into the design of the fort, and while it was not too difficult to leave, it would have been impossible to take, especially it had been well defended. A group of determined men would hold it for ever. If the state knew how dangerous it was, to imprison six hundred men in a fort at the top of a hill like that...if we had wanted to, we could have taken over that prison and they would never have got us out; especially if we had taken hostages.

I leant against the wheel, and rode the wave as it lifted the bows until they snubbed against the mooring.

I had hostages.

The man probably owned the boat. He could get us away. And the woman...well, they wouldn't do anything to hurt a woman, would they? I left the wheelhouse and ran to where the painter to the dinghy was tied to the rail...they were still there. She was moaning and lying across his chest. She groaned as I reached over her, but I wanted the bloke, not her. He was moaning too. I told him to wake up, and shook him about, but there was nothing there. I looked in his jacket pockets and found the keys. The mooring chain was doubled up onto a padlock on the bow, and it opened with the second key, but I made the loose end fast to a staghorn on the foredeck, and went back to the wheelhouse.

It had heater plugs. I let them burn until the lights went out, and then started her up. There was a burst of thick blue smoke from the stack, and it revved on the starters for so long I thought the batteries would flatten out, but it started. Slow revving diesel, donking away; a Perkins six point three. It revved, and settled, and after a while I set the Morse levers to idle and let it tick.

I picked up the binos. Nothing. But it would take more than one man to get her out of the harbour wall, because as soon as I let go, the bows would fall off to port the way she was riding, and I'd never turn her in time to clear the wall before she grounded on the slip. The man was out of it, and she would be useless. Shit...I picked up the binos and focused on the base of the wall. All the small blue blobs jumped out of the lens. They were men; and they had dogs.

That was when I heard the boy, with his "Uncle Ron! Uncle Ron, you said I could come!"

It was the kid.

The dinghy scraped along the wall, and the boy jumped lightly in.

"Hello. You're coming too? Not to France, though. Will you be coming to France?"

Williams hesitated.

"How's your leg?" the boy added, polite but looking at the boat, keen to be off.

"He sent me to get you. He's staying by the engines. Hurry now, or we'll...er..."

"Miss the tide," said Peter, steadying himself in the bucking dinghy. "I know. You've only got half an hour. I saw the smoke and knew he must be going, Mum sent this, I don't think there is enough for you, it's only sandwiches and a thermos. Is Uncle Ron's new girlfriend with us? There's some for her. You'll have to share.." the boy had taken an oar and was eighting the dinghy to the boat. "Where is he? I can't see him..."

"He's down below."

"I bet he's doing the gas alarm, it's always going off. Have you got your ticket?"

"I'm taking us out. He'll come up later."

Peter nodded. "I'll let go, then." He jumped for the rail, swarmed over it and made the painter fast astern. "Now?"

"Yes."

"Right." The boy was wearing a fleece jacket, old jeans and training shoes. He ran to the foredeck, and unwrapped the chain from the staghorn, then took one strand and wrapped it around the cleat. "Singled up forward."

The man set the Morse to slow astern. "Let go."

"Let go for'ard," shouted Peter. He pulled on the chain and the end came up through the fairlead..

"All clear for'ard. Oh, your trousers..."

"What?"

"Your trousers are undone. You've forgotten to do up your zip."

The man nodded, and zipped up the trousers, as he eased the Morse ahead and turned to port. The revs built up, and Peter stared over the port bow.

"Now!" shouted Peter, and the man swung the wheel to starboard, and the boat sheered across the incoming waves. It came perilously close to the harbour wall but the Perkins revved high and with a plume of diesel smoke the boat surged into the tideway, and rolled to starboard as the tide caught the hull and ran it beam-on, the rudder losing purchase. The bows tried to turn to port, but the revs increased and it finally, clumsily, throbbed to starboard, wallowing in the tide race, and in danger of being swamped as it surfed southwest along the coast.

"Bring her round," shouted Peter. The man tried the wheel to port, and Peter ran aft and joined him in the wheelhouse. "There's the break," the boy shouted, and ahead he saw the change in the wave tops as a back-eddy from the next inlet caught the tide. He pushed the Morse lever as far forward as it would travel. The boat could manage ten knots best, and the tide was running at eight, but slowly the bows cut to port and the relative bearing of the point light drew astern. He kept the boy taking bearings, but the lad kept looking aft to the wheelhouse.

Finally, he said,

"I'll go and help Uncle Ron. He can never get the alarm sorted out."

Peter walked towards the door, sure as children are when there is something wrong. Williams managed to bundle him into the hatchway, and jam the door by sticking a bolt through the broken door hatch. He heard the boy saying to the woman, "Your trousers are undone too," and then, "Uncle Ron, you've cut your head." Williams heard the pump over the sink working as he went to the wheelhouse again, and looked aft at the prison, already distant. There were people on the headland above the harbour, but nobody on the harbour wall. Williams found a tide atlas and a chart in a drawer beneath the table. His watch still worked, and with a stub of pencil from an ashtray under the window he roughed out a track, and began six-minute fixing. As he worked, he whistled tunelessly, as the old skills came back and he once again found himself charting a course through a difficult sea. The basket the boy had brought was on the side bench, and he opened the sandwiches, and poured some tea from the thermos. Then, he turned back to the chart. He ate steadily, and drank; he concentrated on the chartwork, and as he was warmed and fed, his body finally relaxed.

He had hostages.

Chapter 10

It had been a poor day. The pub had been empty, Ron apparently having taken his new love to sea with him. Higgins was in the bar; desperate to tell anyone who would listen that the "break out" as he called it, had been no fault of his. The landlady had been preoccupied with the skittles night they were about to have, and Brian liked skittles: but he suddenly could not find any interest in it, and walked back to his daughter's cottage feeling uncharacteristically gloomy. He walked in and called a greeting, but the cottage was empty.

He had watched an hour of TV, and was about to go to bed, when his daughter came in.

"What is it?" Brian realised without being told it was Peter. His daughter was silent, worried, at a loss.

"Where is he, Dad? They were only out for the engine test."

Brian looked down at the table, frowned and tried to make some sense. He felt panic. He loved his daughter, and he loved his grandson. His stomach was tight.

"He's gone with Ron. He'll be all right with Ron. Ron said they were going out today. He's been working on the engine and they were going to take it out for an hour. The weather was bad, and he met that young lass last night so I thought he wouldn't go. He's with Ron."

"But where's Ron?"

Brian looked at the window. It was fully dark. Ron would never have stayed out so late, not for an engine test.
"Have you been to the cove?"
"Sea Trout's out. She's gone. She's still out, Dad, and it's so late."
Brian put his arm around his daughter's shoulders, and hugged her.
"Well, that's where he is, love. Go and make some tea, now, there's a good girl." He picked up the telephone and called the coastguard. After a short conversation, he called the prison.

The governor met Brian and Wade, the Chief Inspector; They stood on the harbour wall. Ella had stayed at the cottage. A white van was parked near the slipway. A uniformed officer left it as they arrived, blowing on his hands in the cool of the night.
"This is where they lost him, Sir," he said.
The Chief Inspector nodded. "You local?"
"Regional, Sir. The Prison dogs have been sent back, now. They're not much good for this anyway. Mine's good, and if he'd been around Ben would have found him. He stayed under a bush for a while...you can see it up there, there's a bit of a shelter in it, and some blood. Then he came down here. He has not come out, and there's a boat gone."
"Sea Trout," said Brian. "Ron Freeman."
Wade asked him, "How do you rate Freeman?"

"Good as gold. He'd not help a con. He's with a new girlfriend. If this lad's on the boat, he's gone through Ron; and that would not be easy, Ron's a tough lad. "

"What's this Williams' form?"

The governor said, "Murdered a kid. Violence against children, not adults. He's desperate of course; and Freeman would not have been expecting anything. I suppose it's possible..."

Brian said, "Ron has not made any contact with the coastguard since he sailed, and that's unheard of. He hasn't filed a course, and he was going out for a test run to check his engine. I think he's with a woman he met last night..."

"Romantic evening beneath the stars?" said the Chief Inspector.

"I doubt it. I'm pretty sure my grandson's on board as well. Rough as hell, getting through the tide race; the boy was due to go out for the ride but Ron would never take him if it was risky. Only going for an hour or so, see? No, it looks as if Williams is on it, all right..."

The police officer said, "How old is your grandson, Mr Thatcher?"

"Nine," said Brian. "Handy, but small for his age."

"Oh, dear," said the dog handler, and stared out over the harbour wall, into the dark night.

A Sea King Helicopter was scrambled from the nearby Naval base, and its pilots swore softly as they tried to pick up a surface contact on their radar. The SAR helicopter was well fitted for the role, but there was a great deal of water to search and no shortage of surface contacts. Fishing vessels dotted the sea from the time they took off, and each one needed to be overflown and visually identified. The separation schemes to the south of the tide race were busy, full of contacts, some merging into each other as they overflew; and with a carelessness about light that would have appalled the Royal or Merchant service, once the pilot overflew a foreign vessel, lights ablaze on the upper deck, his night vision took minutes to return.

Williams listened to the calls on the VHF, until he grew tired of hearing "Sea Trout, Sea Trout, Hail Ford Coastguard, over," and switched off the set. He watched the Sea King for a while, about three miles off his starboard quarter, as it dipped, then turned and banked away and then settled near its next surface contact. It was like a night time bee, sipping at flower after invisible flower; and after each contact the pilot's vision grew worse, and Williams slipped away to the South, hoping that having lowered the radar reflector from the mast, the helicopter might not notice the small contact disappearing away from the bottom of the screen. He reached for the handset, then changed his mind. He talked gently to himself, about hostages and the plans he would make, and rehearsed the conversation he would have when eventually the Sea King left the area and he could make the call. He made an imaginary call, again and again, speaking aloud in the dark of the wheelhouse, arguing with the bastards who replied to his message and setting out no-nonsense terms that would get him away free as air.

Annie listened to him rambling, the drone of his voice rising and falling over the sound of the engine and the water against the hull. The motion of the boat had steadied since they had stood out into the Channel. Her head ached, but worse was the pain as the boat recovered from a roll, and swung the opposite way. The broken bone in her jaw moved slightly each time, until her head seemed to float in pain. The boy was in the corner of the cabin, murmuring to himself as he played with some control panel; she could see small, square red lights blinking from it, and occasionally an alarm seemed to begin, but it was quickly shut off. She had managed to cover herself, to both her and the boy's relief, but he was confused and frightened and had decided, it seemed, to concentrate on something that was familiar. He looked down at Ron occasionally; and Annie moved carefully over to where the man still lay, but she felt he was asleep rather than unconscious. He was breathing noisily through what seemed a badly damaged nose, and there was a wound on the side of the forehead which seemed depressed. It was impossible to see in the cabin. Peter had opened a deadlight and some light entered through a scuttle, but very little. Annie found an old towel, and with infinite care, tore it into three strips and tied them under her chin, and up around the back of her head. She slowly tightened the knot, squealing with pain as she did so, panting to try and cope as she tied two strips, one behind the break and one in front of it, so that her mouth was almost closed and the jaw was not free to move sideways with the motion of the ship. When she finished, the floor of her stomach seemed to fall away and she lay back against the deck, rolling onto her back slightly to favour her broken face. Beside her, she felt Ron move nearer against her. Incredulously, she realised Ron thought he was in bed. She closed her eyes, and waited to steady up.

Annie was not particularly tough, and was in shock; but she had a sense of right and wrong, and the actions of the man in the wheelhouse did not fit with her idea of what was tolerable. She had only been vaguely conscious of the assault against her. Sexual assault was something she had always dreaded; and yet there was no feeling of shame or weakness. She felt strong; stronger than the man, the weakling who had attempted to pleasure himself with her, and failed. She despised him, and more, felt a deep and steady fury that such an inadequate man had assumed the right to attempt to be intimate with her. She longed for a bath. She longed for a weapon.

She had no particular morality; conventional ideas wearied her, and politically correct fashions seemed trite. Instead she believed in a sort of tolerance, and spent most of her energy in doing rather than thinking, hoping that experience of situations would teach her what she liked and disliked in life, what was right and what was wrong. She had disliked the study centre on the island, she had liked the pub. She had liked Ron, and his body, and their sex; she had disliked the man in the wheelhouse. She had thought about the problems faced by women in modern society, discussed it, read about it hundreds of times. She knew she was attractive, and had heard and managed to cope with the jibes and the eyes for years; rape was a constant threat but not one she worried about. If it happened, it happened; she had always been determined that it would never happen to her, though, and if it did, the man would not walk away. And yet, the thought of her laying helpless on the deck while he pushed and prodded at her with his filthy body infuriated her. She knew from her reading that she should feel guilt, shame, a feeling that she should have done more. There was none of that. He had beaten her, used her, had tried to rape her and had failed. He had started, finished, walked away and she had not been able to do a thing to stop him, just laid there like a stupid cow, with her backside up in the air and her clothes around her, like all those helpless pathetic cows she had always despised. He hadn't raped her, but no thanks to her.

The boy moved away from the panel, and slid uncertainly to the end of the bench.

"Can you..are you awake?"

Annie could not speak, she did not want to nod. She reached out, and patted him on the knee; then she left her hand on his knee, and gently squeezed his leg. The boy sounded infinitely sad.

"Is Uncle Ron...is he ..."

It hurt to speak. It served her right for being a stupid, pathetic cow and letting the man walk away. "Asleep. He's asleep."

Bloody stupid...he's asleep...can't fight, can't talk; but the boy seemed to understand. "Wake him up. Go on, wake him up."

The boy knelt beside Ron, pulling and pushing his shoulder, with little result.

"What's your name?" After a couple of attempts, he understood and said,

"Peter."

"M' Annie."

The boy nodded, solemnly. "And you have hurt your mouth." Annie forgot, and nodded. The pain was instant. She lay back, fainting almost, but then felt a straw being pushed with great care into the corner of her mouth, and cool sweet liquid in her mouth. She took hold of it. Peter had found a paper carton of fruit juice, one that came complete with a small drinking tube. He sat back, drinking one he had found for himself. Annie tried, but could not manage to say "Thanks." She raised the carton instead, toasted the boy, and he solemnly toasted her in return. Then, he moved to the counter, pumped at a handle and returned with a wet cloth which he used to wipe Ron's head and face. Annie patted him on the back, she could not nod or speak again. The boy wetted the cloth some more, and continued to bathe the man's face. What a kid...

The man was going to kill them, Annie decided. The man in the wheelhouse must be ready to kill, maybe even if he did not intend to. The way he had attacked them, it had been detached and vicious. If she could have talked she might have been able to argue with him, but it was impossible. She wouldn't talk anyway. She did not want to talk. She wanted to rage, or to cry. He would come back and see their injuries, and start in again. They would have to be ready. She managed to sit up, and to take hold of Ron's shoulders, and to raise his head and shoulders until he was half across her lap. She pinched the lobe of his ear, hard, but he muttered and laughed, and did not fully wake up, but said something about his head, half-laughed, and slept. Ron was used to headaches. He would go on three or four-day binges, and not be able to see straight for a week at the end of them. He had often taken his boat out to sea and then hove-to and slept until the worst of the headache had gone away, and this was just another time for him. There was no point in trying to wake up when it was still hammering away. He dropped into a deep, comfortable sleep.
The boy looked at Annie. "What do I do?"
She patted him on the shoulder. "Have a rest, Peter. Well done..." she patted him again, and he leant back against the hull, staring sadly at the two adults, and occasionally at the hatchway. He was going to kill them.

Ron grew heavy, and she pushed him off. He was breathing more easily, she thought. She carefully attempted to straighten up, and then felt her way across the panel that the boy had been playing with. He saw her looking at it, and slid across. By now he had realised she could not talk without hurting herself.

"It's a gas alarm panel," he said "It makes an alarm if there is a gas leak. You have to set it. If you turn it on, the hooter sounds after a few seconds but you have to switch this on, here, and push this button and keep it pushed...and then it I set and won't go off all the time. Look..." He switched off the alarm, and then turned it on again. It alarmed, and he quickly pushed the button which was labelled "background Level." The alarm stopped. He kept his finger on the button, and a red light showed. After a few seconds, a green light came on, and he released the button. The red light went out. "It's set now. It stops the gas bottles from setting on fire. Sometimes they leak, and the gas is heavier than air. The gas would sink into the bottom of the boat. Then, if it got a spark, it would blow up. Uncle Ron can't do the alarm, he makes me do it."

Annie looked out of the small scuttle. What would trigger off the next attack? A radio call, a boat coming too near them? The sea was in a long, smooth swell, and far off she could glimpse lights of other small boats, probably fishing. It was dark, but a hint of light hung over the sea and she thought she could make out land as a darker line on the horizon, and then a light flashed, and went out, and flashed long, and went out. They were off the coast, then, and heading ...she thought for a while. She was on the right side of the boat; the light must be the East, the land must be the South Coast. They must have come around the headland on which the prison stood, and were heading across the next stretch of water towards the South West...or had they crossed the Channel, were they heading north along he French coast? Had they been gone long enough? How fast did the boat go, she wondered.

Another light moved between the boats she could see, far off. It was shining on the water between them, shining then going out, then coming on again. It seemed to be moving quite quickly. Peter looked out of the scuttle, and said,

"It's a helicopter. It came over us when you were asleep, but not right over. It was near. I saw its light going on and off. It shone down on another boat but it didn't look at us."

That must be it. The man was watching the helicopter. Soon, it would give up and leave the area. That might be enough to set him off. She rested her shoulder against the bulkhead. It was warm; wood, not steel.

Wood. That bastard would know it was a wooden boat. He would have to be frightened of a gas alarm in a wooden boat…any boat.

"Wake up Ron. Wake him up." The boy pushed and pulled and Annie half rolled him from side to side, lifting his shoulders and dropping him down, again and again. The man groaned, and slowly came to. It seemed to take hours.

He pushed he boy away, and then turned in surprise when Annie shook him, his voice ready to curse, until he saw it was a woman.

"Who's that, then? Peter, who's here, eh?" His voice was thick, slurred. His mouth seemed to drag down at one side.

"Annie, Uncle Ron."

"Ah…" he tried to paw her, he thought he was drunk, and like a semi-conscious affectionate bear he put out an arm and missed, then tried again.

"Ooh, too much to drink, too much. Poor old head, splitting headache. Best get a bit more sleep, eh? Don't you worry, I'll be as good as new in the morning…"

"Tell him..he's not drunk."

Peter looked puzzled. "Tell him!"

"Uncle Ron, a man stole your boat. He's got your boat."

"What boat?"

"Sea Trout. He's locked us in, and you're in the cabin and he's in the wheelhouse. He hit me, too. You're not drunk, he's taken your boat and he's locked us in.."

Ron patted the boy and hushed him.

"Better in the morning. Get some sleep…" Annie pulled at him again and he said louder, "No, leave me alone. I'll have a few more minutes, so leave me be!"

She closed her eyes; it was hopeless. Anything she planned, she'd have to do alone.

She'd get him first, though. Her head ached, the pain in her face had been helped by the bandages but her nose, mouth and forehead all felt as if they had been smashed, burned, pulverised. She couldn't let him touch her again. With a shock, Annie realised she would rather die than let him hurt her again. She looked around the cabin, at the small boy and the battered hulk of a man; it was the anger, the outrage that he had done these things; and the hatred, caused by the knowledge that he had enjoyed doing them. Annie wanted to kill him. The boy was happier now that he had heard Ron speak, and he settled down on the bench again. Annie thought that the cabin was growing lighter; she could make out the edges of the counter, the shape of the lockers; she moved carefully over to them, opened them, and began to search through their contents, mainly by feel, and occasionally holding an object she could not identify into the green light coming from the gas alarm panel.

Five miles to the south, the Sea King called in to its base, gave pigeons and warned it was returning for fuel. Annie saw the light blink out, and it did not come on again.

Chapter 11

"We've got him, Sir!"

The police constable passed a headset to the Chief Inspector. It was patched through to the local Coastguard HQ, and monitored VHF traffic. The man's voice was almost shrill.

"..if you want them unharmed. They're safe now and if you want them to stay that way you will do as I say. You keep that bloody dipper away from me, you hear? You keep it away, and any other boat you've got, if anything comes near me I'll kill them, I'll kill them straight away. You understand, Sea Trout, over..."

The police officer frowned. Mad. All the rage and nonsense, followed by the oddly formal, official call sign. He looked up at his sergeant.

"Tom, was Williams in the Forces?"

"Dunno, Sir. Only got details as far back as his offence."

"Find out. Get onto the governor of the nick. It sounds like he might have been, and if so, we're in trouble. Find out if he was in the Navy."

"Right."

"Any combat service, Tom. Check it out."

The man was still talking. The Chief Inspector called through to the Coastguard on a mobile.

"Ops room? Keep him going as long as you can, would you? Where was the last position of the Sea King?"

"I'll have to check with the Navy."

"Quick as you can. He's been watching it."

"Oh...right." Quick on the uptake, anyway, the policeman thought. God bless the sailors.

He listened to Williams. The man was raving. Snatches of the conversation caught his attention as he described light under doors, perverts, bitches, people being set on fire. He hoped that they would be able to save the people on the boat but all his experience warned him that the woman and the child had no chance. The owner...Freeman?...they said he was a tough nut. Williams must have already done him, to get the boat away. What kit did they have? He put a call through to the police marine section, thirty miles down the coast; and soon afterwards, to the local Royal Marines HQ. After a rapid conversation with someone who seemed to be extremely sure of himself, the Chief arranged a meeting, then went back to listening to the headset. The coastguard had managed to get Williams to talk about the marine safety of the vessel. Brilliant. Williams was a pompous little sod, and was making speeches about the law on safety at sea. "Keep going, son," muttered the policeman. "Keep him talking." To the east the sky was growing steadily brighter, and the last thing they needed at the moment was any more light.

His sergeant threw a file on the desk, made up of sheets of foolscap. They were notes he had taken over the phone, from talking to the prison. The Chief Inspector read quickly.

"What's an RP?"

" Radar plotter. He would have served in the operations room, and be used to seeing a sea plot. Navigation, force deployments, helicopters, surface screen, all that sort of thing. He'd know about tides, he'd have some idea about surface operations. He served in the Falklands."

"Did he? Oh aye...any medical?"

"Still checking, but nothing obvious, no breakdowns or injuries."

"Doesn't matter. Anyone who's done that is bloody mad, it just takes longer to come out. Is he still talking to the Coastguard?"

"Yes Sir."

"Get them to find someone who was in the same campaign, and talk about it. Quickly, now; before he gets bored. Tell him he's a hero and it shouldn't happen to a dog, let alone him. Build the little bastard up, keep him happy. We've got to get him on side, and keep him there."

"How long for, Sir?"

The Chief Inspector shrugged. "Until we can get him off the boat, or his prisoners...or, get close enough to shoot him, I suppose."

Annie listened to snatches of the conversation. The boat had turned, and the engine not changed as it increased revs. Out of the scuttle, she could only sea the horizon, now, and the lights had disappeared. He must have reversed course. They would be heading out to the Channel again, if she had been right first time and the land had been then English coast. That meant they would find it more and more difficult to get away from him, as time went by. If only the engine would pack up, or run out of diesel...but it sounded as steady as ever, and the boat started to lift and then thump regularly into the tops of the slow, long waves as the speed of the boat built up. There was another alteration of course, about at right angles to the original. The speed dropped. She heard the man shouting, for a moment, then nothing over the engine noise as he increased revs. What was he doing? Clearing his view astern, frightened something was creeping up behind, perhaps. Her hands close over a rubber torch, and she tried it. It glowed, but only faintly. It shone on Ron's forehead, and the girl moaned and quickly moved the light away from the damage. His temple must have been broken, it dipped like a saucer and the skin around it was black with bruise. She felt a surge of pity for her fisherman; he was so proud of what he had done, building up his little fleet. It seemed terrible to have done these things to him here of all places. In a pub car park, perhaps, or

in a street fight, but not on his own boat. There were matches. She had already seen the gas range on the cooker, and the ring would light the cabin and warm them up. She finally managed to light the ring. The boy came over and sat near to the stove, watching her and the light, and casting frightened glances at the Ron. She must look terrifying enough, Annie realised, tied up in towelling and her mouth and face bruised and swollen. She pointed at the cupboard, and said to Peter, "Eat...eat.."
and the boy found some biscuits, and pretended to eat them.

Annie had some tools, wire and rope, a hammer and the matches. There was nothing she could use. By the time she had got near enough to use the hammer he would have overpowered her. He would only have to touch her face, let alone hit her, and she would not be able to do anything. She stared around the cabin. The gas bottles were bolted into a locker, and were too big to throw. They would be enormously heavy. The hose that joined them to the gas main was quite long but was held to the main manifold by a spring clip that needed to be unscrewed and she did not have the tools to do it. There was nothing else. She thought of garrotting the man with the string, but again it could not work. She looked around the cabin; there was a small locker above the hatchway. She opened it and it glowed orange, but there was nothing in it except a fluorescent aerosol Ron used to mark pots and gear...there was the shelf...she looked at the boy, and the flame, and suddenly felt a rush of hope. It might be possible, as a last resort...she sat next to Peter and slowly, very painfully, began to tell the boy what she had in mind.

Wade and Bottrell, the Marine officer, set up a control centre at the Naval airfield, and then went with their sergeants to the harbour. The small boat was still swamped, and had been examined by the local police at low water. It had been thoroughly searched for signs of deliberate damage or any connection to the man on Sea Trout, and been ruled out. It had been a waste of considerable time, but necessary; and Ron's two helpers, Klaxon and Digger, had come to the harbour to pump the boat out and get it afloat before the next tide. Later they joined the group on the wall, where they were asked a few technical questions about the Sea Trout, and they remained there after giving their answers because nobody remembered to tell them to go away. Thatcher was with the police, and this gave the two crewmen confidence enough to stay. Neither of them had much time for the police, and although Digger was more charitable towards the Marines, they barely disguised their disbelief of the boat handling abilities of the trim, well spoken officer who sounded, as he was, very Eton and Staff College; that the tall, brooding Warrant Officer treated him with great respect puzzled Klaxon, who did not know much about the details of the work of the SBS.

"They're not much bloody good," was his verdict as he and Digger walked back to the pub. The group on the wall had discussed the situation and then decided to return to the HQ. Brian had walked home with the two fishermen. "Farting about with tides and arcs of visibility, what bloody good's that? Radio the bastard and tell him what will happen to him if he hurts them, do that first, then go and get him. None of this negotiation. They've been talking to him non-stop, they say, for the past twelve bloody hours..."

Digger frowned, and shook his head. "He's not normal, he can't be. If he stops talking to them, he'll probably start in on the girl."

"With this one, it will more likely be Peter." It was so rare to hear Thatcher give details of the workings of the prison, his two friends took a while to realise what he had just said. then Digger just muttered,

"Oh hell, Brian, mate..."

and Klaxon rubbed hard at the back of his head. He had long, greying, tangled hair and a weather-beaten face that was even more lined than usual, as he thought about his friend.

"How the hell did he do this to Ron? I know he's daft when he's been on the drink but he'd never let any bugger take his boat...I reckon the chap has killed him."

"Surely not.."

"Near as, Digger. Must have done. Say what you like, there's a girl out there, and a kid, and a con, and seems to me they must be on their own. The police aren't doing anything, they've called off the chopper, and those soldiers are bugger all use." He turned and looked back at the harbour. The cars and a Land Rover were being driven away. Below them, the Kingfisher tugged at her mooring and the small boat rode easily enough on the reduced swell. Klaxon knew the waters around the point as well as the bar in the pub. He had feel for the tides, though he would not have been able to plot one on a chart. If floating gear went overboard he often as not would find it; and he was a fisherman. Hunting fish came down to technology, and skill, and luck; and in that one respect, Klaxon was a valued crewman, because he knew how to find fish.
"This bugger's got nowhere to go, Digger. What's he got?"
Thatcher looked steadily at Klaxon, waiting for the next thought.
"He's important here, and frightened to go anywhere else. He's got the boat and people frightened of him, and he thinks he's in control. That means nothing anywhere else; and the further he gets away fro these waters the more frightened he'll be. He thinks he knows where he is, here."
Thatcher said, "I thought he might make a try for abroad...France, perhaps..."

"Easy to think about, not to do. He'd start off but then he would begin to wonder how much water under the keel, or where were the rocks as he got nearer to the shore…mark my words, he'll suddenly feel scared, and he'll turn, and try to go over the same water where he's been. He won't even be able to get that right, mind. No, I know what he'll be like. I've seen them. All brave and adventurous one minute, scared to turn or alter course the next…"

Thatcher nodded. Klaxon had crewed for amateur motor launch owners, on and off, and had been famous for his scathing assessments of their abilities.

"He's been in the Navy, mind."

"What Navy?"

"The RN. He was an RP..radar plotter, do you call it?"

Klaxon nodded. "Not much good in small boats, but he'd have some idea…not much for him on the Sea Trout. Tide tables and some old charts, it's not exactly a warship. He'd like the radio and the GPS, that sort of stuff... probably why he spends so much time on it." Klaxon took a deep breath, and sighed. It was darts night, and he hated going to sea when it did not result in fish or money, but this was different.

"Get your kit, Digger."

Thatcher said, "What are you up to?"

"You coming too?"

"Coming where, Klaxon?"

"We're going to find Ron."

The Kingfisher had a Volvo diesel and could motor at fourteen knots but Klaxon kept it at half power, both for comfort and the boat, but also because the speed of the boat did not matter very much. People do not travel, at sea; not as motorists travel, at least. They leave one port and arrive at another, but in the mean time, they live. Digger and Klaxon were like farm labourers, working their place of employment but living there, too. They made tea, they ate, if there was nothing immediate needed doing they rested but if there was work to be done there was no point in wishing for any other situation, and they just got on with it. The man in the Sea Trout would be trying to find a way off the sea; the two fishermen lived on it, with it.

Brian Thatcher sipped the tea, and stared out of the scratched windows of the wheelhouse. The swell was deep, so that they gained some view if they crested a wave but for most of the time were surrounded at least on three sides by blue-black mottled sea walls, while behind trailed a foaming apology for a wake. Klaxon shifted the wheel, slightly, enough to stop the corkscrew kick at the top of the wave rhythm but occasionally missing it, leaving the three of them suddenly wrenched from the support they were using and staggering for a balance.

He took them south, because everybody goes south leaving the harbour; then he kept them south through the tide race to the point that he judged their man would have been too frightened to alter course, and he stood on through the worst of the tide race. Where it flattened out, he went against years of training, and instead of taking the inshore passage past the rocks and light, he altered to port and stood well out into the smooth but fast waters of the bay. Astern, they watched the afternoon light on the headland as it dropped astern with the combined speed of the boat and the water in which it floated, which was travelling South West at between nine and eleven knots. Their course made good was west, and the stern of the boat slowly passed through south as she swept through the outer waters of the great sweep of bay that had been such a hard training ground for generations of sailors, and she ended up pointing towards the loom of land and rock, seven miles ahead, on top of which Brian could just make out the outline of the prison walls. He peered through the battered Zeiss binos, at the few craft and the merchantmen anchored in the lee of the rock. He was looking for a small fishing vessel.

Klaxon put on some revs and steered for a point two or three miles off the headland.

"He'll decide to round the head, see? He'll want safe water and he's been here before. He won't trust the shallows, and he won't know where the rocks are. He'll point here out, and increase speed because the daft bugger will want to think he's going somewhere."

The evening sun was highlighting the land ahead as they steamed towards the point. The bows were digging deeper into seas and occasionally strimmed the top few inches of the wave which hissed across he deck and the windows, causing Digger to curse and to jam himself further into the shelter of the wheelhouse. He took the wheel, while Klaxon went below and made some tea. Staring down at the kettle, he shouted up, "Come right a bit, Digger," and later, for no apparent reason, "Hold her at that. Where's the spoon? Aye, steady on that, Digger."

They crossed the headland at a range of four miles, and stood out into the separation scheme, where Klaxon put the wheel to port. "He won't like merchantmen, won't know how to deal with them. Rule of the road's all right when you've got a boss to check with, and he'll have been used to bosses, in the Navy. Different when you're on your own, staring at the bows of eighty thousand tons of car ferry, wondering which way's the safe way to go...he'll go back in. Anyway, the sea feels different out here." And it did. At the bottom of each trough inshore, there was a feeling that there was an end to the motion, a turning point. Here the boat moved down, then surged upwards, but in a way that seemed controlled by the sea, not the engines or the floatation of the hull. In shallow water it seemed you were safe because man made you safe, by skill and design; out here, you were allowed to be safe only by permission of the sea. "He'll not like this. He'll go back in."

Not too close to the rocks; back over where he'd been; and ahead, black against the final glare of the setting sun, the land stood like a backcloth. Against it, they found the Sea Trout, five miles ahead. It was motoring slowly, making odd and occasional alterations of course, and Klaxon nodded when he saw it.

"Right. Well, Brian, you and Digger had better get busy. Might be we make a few bob from this trip after all."

They hoisted shapes, rigged lights, and began to fish.

Chapter 12

I like the guy on the other end of this radio. He knows what it was like. Spending seven months in the dark, making paper flowers and building a garden, and hoping that there would not be a sudden noise, a flash, and then people running around like candles, burning, falling, trying to crawl with the flesh hanging off their arms and falling onto the deck from their hands. I saw the skin, when the Turk set fire to the poor old bugger. I saw his bones, white and then black. The island is almost out of sight, and the prison on top. There are three merchantmen in the lee of it, and a small fisherman to port, trawling. I can see them, working the winch, one man in the wheelhouse drinking tea. Lucky to have it. There would be tea back aft.

"Make some tea, you bitch! Make some tea, you hear me?"

It is too dark to see what was in the trough of the waves. They could all be there, canoes, swimmers, marine bastards...they will come from the south, black clothes, black canoes...they'd be armed to the teeth and they will kill me, kill me and not even notice...his head jerked upright and he listened. It was an alarm, steady, quite loud, coming from the cabin. Williams ran out of the wheelhouse, tore the spanner from the door hasp and found the door of the cabin was being held from inside. The alarm was louder now, and as he pulled the doors they parted then closed again, and when they parted the noise was huge, a blaring klaxon of an alarm, what was it? Gas alarm! They'd opened a gas bottle, the boat could blow. That was what she was trying to do, blow the boat, bring the marines, get him back inside....he pulled at the doors, again and again...

...the boat swung slowly around, nearly reversed course, then swung again. Brian and Digger watched it from the deck. The sky was lighter in the East, and the shape of the convict's head was clear through the wheelhouse. With a good rifle, thought Brian, but then the deck heaved, while the other boat fell off the crest of a wave, and Brian raised his eyebrows and muttered to himself,

"Maybe not, then."

Klaxon and Digger looked around, and nodded, and looked back to the winch. They had baited and laid pots for a while, and then the dan buoy was set to the line and the two men heaved the buoy up and over the transom, and they watched it drift slowly astern, bobbing and rocking in the water.
"Something's up," said Brian.
Across on the bigger boat a rectangle of light grew then closed, and the dark shape moving along the port side of the deck was almost indistinguishable, unless you were familiar with the Sea Trout, or you had a night light. Williams ducked and scuttled from the wheelhouse to the after cabin, trying to keep below the level of the gunwale, staring into the dark waves for a sign of the canoes or the soldiers. Annie heard the rush of his footsteps coming across the deck as she pushed at the alarm button on the gas panel, and she nodded to the boy, then ran over and lifted him and as he pulled, she heaved from below and he was half in, half out of the locker over the ladder. The doors were pulled, nearly opened, then fell back again, tied together across their handles with cod line. She heaved again, while he managed to turn, and then she nodded as he settled, facing outwards, into the deep locker. She closed the door, and heard the door of the cabin creak and rattle as Williams pushed and then kicked against it.

"You bastards, let me in..."the voice cracked, screamed, and Annie recoiled a step or two at the fear she could hear. For a moment, she hoped that they might have been boarded, by the police perhaps, but there was no-one there except Williams, sawing at the cords and the door crashed backwards again, straining against the few pieces of line that had not been cut, and that she had managed to jam in the lock. They unravelled, fell off, and the door suddenly flew backwards, hitting the hull next to the ladder. He crouched at the entrance, staring wildly into the cabin, not seeing her immediately and then recognising her as she stood, in front of Ron, at the foot of the ladder.

"You locked me out. This is my boat and you locked me out ." He came into the cabin, and she walked back a step. It seemed to decide him. He raised his hand, and moved forwards down the ladder step, ready to strike. Behind him, he heard the locker door creak as it opened, He turned and looked out of the door, but there was nobody in sight. Puzzled, he looked up to the locker, now above and behind him, over the door to the cabin. He frowned. He saw the boy in the locker, and then he noticed the can of paint. It was glowing. He noticed that it must have fluorescent paint in it. The boy's hand was glowing where it touched the tin. The paint suddenly hissed from the can, making a small pool that spread on the boy's fingers, glowing in the dark of the locker, then in the cabin as a jet of paint sprang from the tin, the boy moved his hand, and it was free to cut through the air in a fine mist. Williams felt it on his face. He jerked his head to save his eyes from the paint, irritated by the nuisance of the paint and the boy, and he felt the girl push past him. Immediately, he struck with his raised hand, hard, at her head and again at her shoulder, good hard blows that made her hurt and cry out. He raised his hand again, looking for a point on her head to strike, but better still saw she had turned and had her open face, bandage and slack mouth, all towards him, and her stupid hand in front of her face, holding something...he pulled back his fist to hit her injured jaw, and the lighter flamed, and lit the spray of paint.

On the Kingfisher they saw the light and heard the man scream. Then a ragged flame danced up out of the cabin and seemed to flutter up and down the deck until eventually moving aft, very quickly, and the screams came from the flame, and the hands were on fire and there were three flames, two waving and dancing and jerking around the third, the biggest of the three, which moved towards the stern of the boat and took the other two flames with it. There was a final scream as the three flames became one, and just as the first streak of sunlight lit the eastern sky, the flames fell from the boat and into the leaden sea.

Chapter 13

The island was warm, dry and suddenly dusty. Rock dust settled everywhere on the Ford, and quickly dried with a little sun and a fresh breeze. Then, it left a light grey coat on any leading edge or surface. The landlady sang under her breath as she watered the hanging baskets over the door of the bar. She had a clothes prop with a hose pipe tied to the end, and she stretched up and soaked the baskets, then ducked away as the water cascaded onto the pavement, and the baskets dripped steadily for a minute or two. "You'll be soaked," she said, gently. Annie smiled back, as she pushed the wheelchair down the street, bringing Ron for his morning pint.

"Hello Mrs. Gibbs. Stand aside, we're coming in…" the woman held open the door and Annie rushed through the water, Ron laughing as best he could, making a crooning, rolling noise like the distillate of the local accent, but with no words. Annie stroked his head, and copied him gently. "Ohdledohdle durr, indeed…you know when it's time for your beer well enough." Ron blew a raspberry, and reached for the pint. His thumb was clawed across the palm, and the fingers of the hand suddenly clamped against each other, the wrist turned inwards, and the forearm shook violently, juddering the wheelchair and had it not been for Annie, the beer would have sprayed the bar. She held the glass to Ron's mouth, and wiped his face when he smiled, and finished. She smiled back, a lop sided, sweet, twisted happiness.

Ron said,"Gardurdlarr," softly, contentedly. Mrs. Gibbs went into the kitchen behind the bar, busily setting napkins into small baskets and measuring chips into them. The girl who helped looked up, and Mrs. Gibbs brusquely wiped her own face.

"Water from those flowers. It gets everywhere."
"Ron and Annie in?"
"Just in. How that girl looks after him, it's a real pleasure to watch them."
"So sad for her."

"Sad? Rubbish. She loves him, and she's stayed with him despite what happened to the poor lad. It's not sad. Not ideal, but she's not being forced into it."

The girl wisely left the topic and put chicken portions into the baskets.

"Just as his fleet was getting going, poor lad," murmured Mrs. Gibbs. "Still, he'll do well with those two skippering for him, and it's been the making of Klaxon."

"Brian runs the other boat?"

"Since he retired from the prison it is all he wanted to do, he said. I can't blame him. All those years locked in with those people, you'd want to get some fresh air into your lungs."

Mrs Gibbs took the tray of food into the bar and set it in front of Ron and Annie.

"Try not to throw it all over the bar, young Ron. Otherwise I'll make you clean it up."

"Rugardlargard," and Ron leaned forward and shook his head on one side at Mrs Gibbs, and at Annie, and they laughed and Annie began to feed him. Mrs Gibbs picked up an anorak from the hallstand and called the pub's old dog.

"I'm off, Jeannie," she shouted to the girl in the kitchen. "The dog needs a run. Look after the bar. It's quiet, and I'll be back directly."

She ducked under the hanging baskets, and walked briskly along the wide pavement until the point where it petered out, where she walked on the roadway, and turned off towards the cliff and the old rock workings, the dog dragging along behind her as she strode towards the clifftop.

Ron and Annie sat together, as the girl steadied his pint and helped him drink. She had liked him before, but had loved him as he grew weaker, yet tried so hard to keep his mind in one peace. The operation had worked well, and he had come back to the cottage and they had lived and made love and been happy for a fortnight. The weather had brightened and the Ford now sparkled under the sun and warm winds of early Spring; Ron could walk, slowly, and then one morning, she had found him flat on his back on the concrete path in the yard, just as if he was sunbathing; and he had tried to say,

"I can't remember getting here," and then, "I can't get up," and he had twisted to the left, and his face had turned into a mask, the mouth drawn back and his left arm and hand twisted and tense, trapping her hand in his and making her cry out as the thumb nail had driven deep into the skin on the back of her fingers.

He had lost his speech, gradually over the next week, and his left side was weak and unreliable. Scar tissue on the brain, they said, and inflammation. It might improve, she was told, and she fed him Epilin and held his beer, but they lived a relaxed and happy life, one hour at a time.

Higgins walked into the bar. It was his lunch hour, and he had taken to leaving the office and having a sandwich and a pint in the pub. It was better than the mess canteen, where he imagined they still blamed him for the mistake that had led to the prisoner escaping and doing so much damage. Ridiculous; if he had been a Home Office teacher, and not working for the College as a contract manager, they would never have blamed him as they did...and there had been no great harm done...except for Freeman of course.

"How is he, Annie?"

She hated him calling her Annie. The girl looked up at his fat, self-satisfied face, its jaws working busily at the sandwich. Some grated cheese fell onto his coat, and Higgins licked the end of his finger and stabbed each piece of cheese, and licked it off.

"Who?"

"Ron, poor old Ron. How's he getting on? Still having problems, is he?"

"Ask him. You may have missed it, but he is sitting beside me."

"What? Ah. Of course, yes." Higgins raised the volume of his voice, and slowly said to Ron, "No more fits, then? No? Well done, old chap," and he looked up, and around the bar, smiling and proud to be seen to talk to a cripple.
"No news of Williams, then."
Annie shrugged.
"No, no. Best thing, in many ways, but a dreadful way to die. First being burned, and then drowning. Filthy tides, around here, of course. What a sad end to a life."
Annie said, "It doesn't bother me either way."
Higgins smiled. "I quite understand that you feel that way, my dear. Especially after what he did to …er…what he put you through."
The girl flushed, and her eyes filled at the memory. Higgins said, "Quite, quite. Most upsetting. I am sure you would cheerfully have killed him with your own..er.." but then he realised that was exactly what she had done, and he said, "quite. Well, you all did very well. Who would have thought it? Terry Williams."
"Chipset." Ron threw his head back and the word came from the back of his throat, but Annie spilled the drink and then put the glass on the table, and used both hands to cup Ron's face.
"What did you say?"
"Chipset." Ron smiled, and looked towards the pint. "Garrardle."
"Here," said Annie.
Ron said, "Annie."

She put the beer down again, and put her hand to her face, turning aside to stare out of the window.

"Jolly good!" said Higgins. "Very good indeed! That is a distinct improvement, isn't it Annie? Excellent. What is a chipset, anyway?"

He leant towards Ron. "What is chipset?"

Ron frowned, and growled. His left arm twitched and began to shudder, and he held it against his chest.

"What is chipset, eh? Funny, he came out with it just after I mentioned Terry Williams."

Ron raised his right hand and took hold of Higgins' by the front of the tie. He tightened his grip, and the teacher's face darkened as he opened his mouth to protest but found he had very little air in his lungs. Higgins choked, and Annie looked up, her expression of happiness changing to one of alarm. Ron had lifted his arm as high as he could reach, and Higgins shoes were only just in contact with the floor. Ron began to shake him slowly back and forth, muttering as he did so,

"Chipset, chipset, chipset..."

later, when Higgins had left and Jeannie had returned to the kitchen, Annie sat facing Ron again.

"You are a wicked bugger," she said, feeding him some beer. He tried to nod, and laugh, making his chin a mess of spit and beer, but Annie wiped it clean, suddenly full of hope.

Higgins was furious as he drove back to the prison. More glances from the gatestaff reminded him that he was out of favour, and he was glad to close his office door once he had run the gauntlet of prisoners waiting in the corridor, more as an excuse to get out of workshops than as a means of satisfying their educational needs and requirements. They all asked about Williams, as if he were some favourite son who was late home. "No, no sign of him at all. Of course, drowned, what did you expect?" What did they expect? It had been six weeks; people do not survive going into the Hail Ford Race in late February. Yet, every time, the prisoners would seem to show sorrow and spend a while discussing the man, remembering him. A grubby little sex offender, a child molester, a killer and yet they seemed to mourn for him. Higgins shook his head; he would never understand prisoners. Sentimental people, he decided, were capable of great evil.

There was a department head meeting that afternoon in the Governor's study. Higgins arrived late, although the room was quiet. He noticed that the other HOD's looked at him in the same way as had the gate officers. Really, it was time he said something to them. He took his seat and then forgot everything else as the governor repeated,

"The Home Secretary is particularly annoyed, as is the Minister for Prisons. They will be here this afternoon, and we will meet again when they arrive. I need not tell you that she is going to be looking for scalps, if only as an offering to the press. The pressure groups are up in arms, and the press is whipping it up the best that it can. With all this nonsense about publishing the names of offenders, these thugs seem to think they are crusaders, and the tabloids imply they have every right to kill released sex offenders, as if they are doing the public a service. It's the rule of the mob, the age of the thug. So-called children protection societies are springing up on the mainland...thank God our locals don't like London anymore than they like us."

"The prison is part of the local community, Sir."

"What?"

The new works manager was embarrassed, but persevered.

"They have men who work here, some have sons who have been here as inmates, they come to the shows and to the garden parties at the Young Offenders' Unit...the prison has been here a long time. During the war a lot of the older ones were stationed here. We're part of the local scene, Sir. If the press try to stir the locals up against us, they'll back us, you watch."

The governor stared at the works manager for a while, in silence.

"I hope you're right, John," he said, eventually.

Higgins wanted to contradict, but the manager came from the Island and he did not, and he realised it would be stupid to say anything. Instead, he focused on the plastic-wrapped package which seemed to be the centre of attention. It seemed to contain clothing, the inside of the wrapper was very wet, and in the dark office it glowed faintly.

"You were late, Mr Higgins, and so I had better explain. This was found yesterday, and it would seem to be a prison issue tracksuit top. It seems reasonable to assume it was Williams'."

"Washed up, eh?" said Higgins.

"Would that were true," said the governor. "It was found under a hedge, near to the Flete housing scheme. Some children saw it last night. It glowed, you see...their parents called the police."

"What is the glow?" asked the works manager. "Is it marker paint?"

"As used for marking fishing floats, yes; and deterring attackers, if you have a lighter handy. You can see the charred cloth around the neck." Higgins leaned forward and saw the burn marks. "But the housing estate..."

"Is a very long way from the coast, exactly. Now, does this mean that a passer-by found the jacket on the coast and threw it away on the estate, or did its owner wear it and throw it away himself? How long ago? It seems to be in a fairly poor state, but has it been there for six weeks? In other words, has our man survived, gentlemen? And if so, what do we tell the residents of the estate, loyal though they may be; what do we tell the investigation team, and more important than anything, how does the present beleaguered political administration get out of yet another embarrassing prison story? And this one has got the lot. Sex offender, child killer, hostage taker, beautiful woman victim, tragic cripple who was once a rugged fisherman..."
"Well, he was..."
"Yes, sorry Tom. I know he's local, and you know him. I was trying to see it from the Press point of view. No offence."
"He is not the only local, Sir."
The governor nodded. "That's right, of course. The prisoner had links, too, didn't he?"

"Brought up here until he was ten, Sir. The father was an incomer, lived in a dump near the old station and treated the boy badly. The mother ran off, his father tried to bring him up but then he had enough and disappeared, the lad was brought up by one of the locals and then taken back by his mother who was living away by then. There no local relatives, none anywhere as far as I know; ended up on a care order to a place in Wales, and left there and joined the Navy, and then we got him."

Higgins said, "No family links to the island, then. He must be long gone by now."

"Must he, though? I think to be sure of anything we have to assume that there is a chance he made it ashore, don't you? I mean, simply for form's sake? He was a very dangerous prisoner, as shown by his subsequent behaviour. I am afraid we need to refer this upwards, gentlemen. We also need to give every assistance to the police. I need not tell you that we will have to search the region thoroughly, very thoroughly indeed. I had hoped…"

He had hoped that the man was dead; the governor wondered why. He wished that Williams were dead, he supposed, both for his sake and that of Williams. It was a great relief when a lifer died; just as it was when a man was released. It was the end of an unsatisfactory and awkward situation, at least for that one person.

"He is probably dead; I cannot see how he could have survived. However, if there is the slightest chance he has survived we had better make sure he is put into the safest place as possible both for him and for the public, and we need to find him. We also need to find how he has managed to survive for the last six weeks of one of the coldest winters this area has seen for years. Now; let's get on to other matters. Mr Higgins, the Education Budget, I believe..." and a muted groan from the works manager did not stop Higgins from launching into Item Two on the governor's agenda.

At the end of the meeting, the governor closed the file and nodded to his secretary who closed her notebook and went to begin typing the minutes. He then smiled at the others; the senior probation officer, the padre, head of works, head of workshops, head of education, the other governors that ran the blocks-head of inmate activities, head of security. They were an ill-assorted lot. Higgins would not have lasted ten minutes under the old Home Office system. The others were old in service, like himself. They were glad to be at a C-cat, a training prison as they had once called it. The Ford; you could have left the gate open, in the old days. They never even though of absconding from here. It was what they had been aiming for all their prison sentence.

Not now. An influx of prisoners had over-crowded the prison, and the Home Office had begun to give C-cat clearance to some prisoners who had no right to be in a soft prison like this one. They had razor wire on the inside wall, but also along the outer edge, and the moat was patrolled regularly, as well as having a new fence along its outer edge. English Heritage had played hell about altering the external appearance of the fort, as they called it; but a hasty look at the newspapers must have shown them they were on a loser, there. The public was screaming for security to be increased, and the press was full of stories about electronic balls-and-chains, the inference being that her, the governor, should be wearing one for letting such a dangerous man out onto the streets.

"I wondered, if you wouldn't mind…please, smoke if you want to." Higgins coughed fussily, but the governor silenced him with a frown. "I am sure that nobody will object. Gentlemen I've got a problem. We all have. It's obviously about Williams.

You all know what he is in for. "Higgins tutted and looked seriously disapproving. The others tolerated this display with the stoicism that came from twenty years or more of dealing with prisoners. "The press is going to have a field day, and we need to plan out how to manage the publicity.

Williams is dead. I know that he is. He was last seen on fire from the waist up, he had been alight for at least a minute, he must have inhaled flame, then he hit the water and we know from the marines who were out shadowing the boat, the water temperature that night was about three degrees. The shock would have been enough, probably. He went in at the tail of the race, so he'd have gone out to sea before he went back in. The man is dead.

So, how did his jersey end up a mile from the coast in the middle of town? Washed ashore, I'd say, and then carried up by someone who saw it glowing in the dark on the beach. They got to the street lighting, saw the burns and the state of the thing, and threw it away.

So now what? Well, look at some of the stories in the news. Two parties, one trying to keep power and the other to gain it, are banging the same drum on crime and the causes of crime. They know it's untrue, but they dare not say anything to countermand the papers' opinion that these places are rest camps, lax, and that the threat posed by our worst prisoners is compounded by the fact that we do nothing to correct their behaviour and, even worse, we occasionally let them escape."

"They have a point, there," said Higgins. Head of inmate activities sighed loudly.

"Relax, please, Mr. Higgins. I am not about to apportion blame." The others grinned, and Higgins looked uncomfortable. "To do so would be a negative exercise. We have seen the weakness in our security, we have rectified it, now we need to look out for the next one. Because if it's there, these men will find it. Prisoners include some of the cleverest men in the country."

"Some of the most wicked," said Higgins.

"The two are often linked," said the governor. "Talking of clever, wicked people, let's consider the gentlemen of the press. Their wickedness is of a different sort. They want their story, and they must realise that the panic on the mainland…and I stress, there is no local panic on the Ford…is hysteria. But the press loves hysteria. They are going to play this one up for all it is worth, and they will find many self-important people who need to see their names in print and are therefore willing to go along with the press circus, using any claim they might have to authoritative opinion as a justification. Well, I don't want any of those people to include us. Is that clear? Gentlemen, I will not tolerate any unauthorised interview between any person in this room, and the press. Unless you give a clear 'No comment' to any press inquiry, I will have you prosecuted under the terms of the official Secrets Act if there is nothing else I can have you on. You, Mr. Higgins, are not directly employed by the prison, but you are a contractor, and the contract is issued under certain well-defined terms, which I invite you to review. I would also remind you that the Secrets Act applies to you as well.

The Probation Service needs to be particularly careful." He nodded towards the Head of Probation." Tell your people not to discuss it with anyone, and especially not with their colleagues in courts or with members of the social services. We know there are leaks from those departments all the time. Someone in there has got a tip-off account, and if I ever find out who it is, they'll find out a lot more about prisons than they ever wanted to know. Is that understood?"

"Yes, but what will we do, if the press ask us for an opinion or a statement? We can't field it to the Home Office." The Head of Inmate activities leant forward as he spoke. "They have no idea about truth, let alone reality. I think it's important that we make sure that this paedophile nonsense is not directed at this prison. We're not a sex-offender's prison. I don't want to see the local vigilante brigade meeting all of our released inmates at the gate, like they do on the Isle of Wight. Ask the Home Office about sex offenders in Hail Ford and they'll use it as an opportunity to regurgitate government policy on the sex offenders' register."

"You're quite right. That is why I have decided that we need our own spokesman."

"Brave man, whoever he is."

"I have decided that the best person to speak for us would be Mr. Higgins."

The meeting was stunned. Smiling, the governor explained.

"He works, not for the Home Office but for the College of Education in Camford. That is where the protestors are likely to come from. That is where the press will whip up fear and loathing, and mark my words, when they do, the protestors will come to the Ford and they'll attack the whole community, not just the prisons. That is one source of dispute that runs very deep indeed.

Mr. Higgins is used to discussion on matters connected to prison policy but cannot be held to be an official representative of either the prison or the Home Office; just of the education department and the College. It might be that the college does not want him to accept this role; but then, we might plead, you owe us a favour, Mr. Higgins?"

Higgins nodded, not happy that the responsibility for the escape should be directed at him even in such a polite manner, and not altogether displeased at the thought of the exposure the press interviews would give him.

"We will offer various guidelines and expect you to keep within them, but I think you will find you have quite a reasonable amount of leeway in interviews. But there is one thing I have to make very clear; and that is, nothing, I repeat nothing, is to be allowed to further disrupt the stability of this prison. It is on that stability that the welfare of very person in here depends, and I mean by that inmates and staff. The inmates watch the television as well. Remember that.

Paedophiles are not society's problem. Neither are murderers or rapists; not once they have been caught and convicted, and sentenced. They're our problem, gentlemen, and it is up to us to ensure that we treat them as they deserve and have a right to be treated. Don't join in this clamour against any group of prisoners. There are no nonces in this prison. There are no nonsense prisoners at the Ford. They are all prisoners, all inmates, all under a plan of programmed development and all equally deserving of our best efforts. This government may have seen fit to use public fear of certain categories of crime to whip up support for some of its more stupid policies; double jeopardy, getting rid of jury trials and restricting the right to select trial at Crown Court. The government may see fit to countermand Magna Charta, but we do not. If society's set of values has hit the skids, so be it; we need to operate to a higher level of behaviour, and we will. If we let any category of prisoner become the lowest in the pecking order, the scapegoat for all the other ills of society, then we are no better than those thugs, some inside but mostly outside the prison, who want to lynch sex offenders without any reference to the justice system whatsoever.

I trust we all think as one on this? We have all come up through the same tradition of public service, after all…" he looked around. The professionals all nodded. Higgins sat, thunderstruck. It was as if several new ideas had been presented to him in a short time, and had robbed him of the power of speech, but it was quite clear he wanted to argue several points.
"Thank you. Mr. Higgins, will you give me some more of your time? We need to discuss how we are going to conduct ourselves on this. Thank you, gentlemen."
And as the HIA walked down the stairs of the admin block, and stood at the front door while the head of works fitted a key to the door to let them out, he murmured,
"And from the way the Governor shut the door after us, I would not like to be in Higgins' shoes for the next hour or so."
"What a spokesman!"
"Oh, I don't know," said the HIA. "I somehow feel he might turn out to be a very good one."

"Still alive?" Brian stared hard at the little man. Higgins was the centre of attention in the pub for once. He revelled in the attention his announcement had received, and after the initial stunned silence the questions had come thick and fast.

"There is that possibility. The enquiry will begin in earnest tomorrow, and the Minister for Prisons and the local Chief Superintendent will be joining us at the prison tomorrow when we will form the steering group."

Brian seldom felt violence towards anybody but was suddenly gripped by the desire to boot Higgins. The little man was so pleased, so fulfilled. Brian more than anyone knew, better than anyone, that Higgins was probably not connected to the enquiry at all, except for being the cause of the initial problem...

"I suppose they will want to see us all again...oh, damn it."

The prospect of going through the whole thing again...Brian looked fondly at the two figures in the corner of the bar, Annie leaning over Ron, wiping his face, gently stroking his head. Ron rested the damaged part of his skull against Annie's breast, and closed his eyes, smiling.

"Indeed. Very regrettable, of course, especially for..er...well, really!"

Higgins looked hurt as Brian finished his pint and turned, and left. Outside the bar he saw Peter, waiting, sitting astride his mountain bike. The boy looked up at his grandfather, and said nothing but lifted an eyebrow.

"Yes, go on," said Brian, and the boy looked relieved and cycled away, towards the footpath heading over the cliff top, where Mrs Gibbs walked her dog. Brian hurried across to his daughter's cottage, hoping that she had not seen the news.

She had. As he entered the front door, she said, "Where's Peter?"

"I've just seen him. He's gone on his bike, and Ethel Gibbs was about three minutes in front of him. He'll be all right."

"It's all over the news. That bastard; if only he had drowned."

"They think he probably did. Anybody could have found that top. It could have been washed up, and kids could have taken it home not seeing it was damaged. As soon as they saw it was burnt, they might have thrown it away. He might very well have drowned."

"They had that Chief Inspector on from the mainland. He said he is going to take the island apart, just in case. They're searching outhouses, disused quarry huts, everywhere. "

"All for show. The government's having a bad time at the moment, over prisons. This one has already made the news, now they're going to milk it all over again to show how efficient they are at searching."

Ella served the tea. She was red faced and upset. "Stir it all up. They were filth, those journalists; hanging around all hours, ringing the doorbell early in the morning and then printing photographs of me and Peter in our night things...filth. That pig who caught Peter and started asking him those disgusting questions..."
"Never mind, now, Ella."
"He couldn't sleep for days, Dad. They'll do it again."
"Aye, perhaps they will. And Ron and Annie, they'll have no peace."
"Why can't they leave us alone? Nobody needs to be interested in it, except us. Where is the boy..." she walked over to the kitchen window and looked out along the top path. "Oh no..." Her father's chair fell backwards as he left the house and ran to the end of the path. Pete looked towards him his eyes very wide in his face as he sat astride the bike; its handlebars were held firmly by a middle-sized man, hatless and bald, glasses and suit, and a modern Gore-Tex rainproof. He was speaking to the boy, smiling, and as Peter pulled back on the bike he held it effortlessly in place. He was speaking as Brian gripped the collar of the expensive coat, and the hood ripped away just before the journalist's fingers were forced open and he let the handlebars go; Peter immediately backed the bike away and rode home.

"Now look here," said the man, in tones of outrage that Brian realised were not even slightly assumed. This man was not justifying himself, but instead reeked of righteous annoyance at having been prevented from doing his job. From the little Brian had heard, it consisted of describing to a small boy various acts of sexual violence, and then asking Peter if such things had been inflicted upon him. The man's mouth opened again, and then changed shape as Brian hit him in the stomach.

"You'll leave my family alone." He hit him, again, hard and very low in the stomach. "Get away from here now, and stay away." He heard Ella running towards him, shouting. He shook the journalist, wanting to hit him again.

"Do you understand me, you bastard? I see you near here again and I'll break your bloody neck..."

"Dad, leave him. Let him go..."

Ella pulled at his sleeve. The man's face turned against the tight cloth of the collar, and he glared at the newcomer.

"You must be Peter's mother, eh? I just want to have a little chat..."

Brian let him go, and used both hands to push his daughter away. She tore the air in front of the man's face, nails like spears, aiming for his glasses, his face and eyes.

"Look, we don't expect you to do it for nothing..."

Brian walked away, his daughter in the crook of his left arm, and his right fist back-handing the journalist as an afterthought. He took Ella into the house, while two other men joined the reporter, who was now sitting on the cliff path, holding his face. Ella went upstairs to the boy, and the meal cooled on the table. Brian closed the door, and picked up the overturned chair.

Later, he poured another cup of tea for Gary, the local police constable, and nodded as
he was given a caution and warned he could be reported for common assault.
"Yes, yes. Keep them away from the lad, though, can't you?"
"Not really, now, can we?"
"Gary, that fat-faced bastard was describing anal sex to a ten-year-old boy who had never met him before in his life. The reporter might believe he was carrying out investigative journalism, but I think he was enjoying it too much. What effect do you think that will have on the boy? You've got a son, haven't you?"
"Come on, Maggie..."
"What if it had been your lad?"

"They phoned the Superintendent, Brian. Use your head, can't you? You're bloody lucky I haven't arrested you and taken you in to Central; they'd keep you in for the night. Just help me out and stop buggering about, you'll have half the world back here now. Go away for a bit."

"Stuff them. This is my home..."

The policeman shrugged. Brian nodded, and sighed. "I'll send Ella and the lad away, I suppose."

"Where to?"

"Relatives. Probably be best.."

"Get them packed, then. I'll take them with me now, if you like. The press will think twice of pestering a police car. If any of them follow, I'll make them drive too fast and then book them. Come on, I'll wait for you to get them ready." Gary grinned. "We'll make a show of taking them to the railway station, and then when I'm sure there's no press about, I'll nip around to my place. Plenty of room there since the daughter went to college. They can stay with Heather and me."

Brian nodded. "You going to book me?"

The policeman had a mobile face. The sides of his mouth reached down almost to his chin, his eyebrows lifted, he shrugged. "Not much future in nicking retired prison governors, I suppose."

"Probably best if they don't know that, Gary. Imagine the headlines."

"Oh, they'll have plenty of good headlines out of this, don't you worry. Go and get them ready, eh?"

The police car surged away from the group of five men and one woman, all of them rigged out in the best outdoor clothing that London could provide. "Must plan to be here for a while," Brian thought, hoping that the weather might turn bad. The visitors obviously thought it already had. Brian decided not to wear a coat, and ignoring the young man who had entered the garden and was standing on the flower bed by the sitting room window, staring into the house, Brian walked steadily through the group, pipe clamped between his teeth, on his way to the pub.

"Your wife gone away for a bit, eh, Mr Thatcher is it? Upset is she? How's the little boy..."
he felt the heat from the back of his neck spreading through his upper chest and down the backs of his arms. His hands clenched, and he pushed them deep into his pockets as he strode steadily through the group and strode out along the path. It was a fine evening and the sun back-lit the evening sky, pushing long shadows across the top of the cliff and painting the gorse a deep green. The journalists, running beside him, trampled the path and the gorse flowers at its edge, then when the path narrowed, shouted inane questions as if they really cared, and the questions really mattered.

Annie sat next to Ron in Mrs. Gibbs' front bar, her face white. They had run a gauntlet of reporters when they left their cottage. Was Ron angry? Were they married? Had his injuries damaged their sex life? Had she been married before she met Ron? How did she feel about their attacker? Was she sorry that the man had not died?

"I'm sorry they haven't died. Bastards. Filthy minded bastards. Who reads their stuff anyway? Nobody wants to know about this place, about us; they're disgusting." She reached across with a tissue to dab at Ron's mouth, but he jerked his head away, angrily turning his head. His mouth was working, muttering, agitated. "They even tried to question Ron, and to photograph him. One of them took hold of the wheelchair and wouldn't let go, shouting questions at Ron, about me. He was shouting about me and Ron...could we still make love, did he still love me...what has that got to do with finding a killer?"

Mrs. Gibbs handed a drink to the girl. "That's enough, now. There are no surprises in all this, now are there? We knew what they were like from last time. It's just a shame we have to go through it all again, that's all. Now, let's just calm down. They'll be in here later and I don't want to give them the satisfaction of seeing they have upset us. Give Ron a drink, Annie; he'll soon forget all this business when they go away."

The night was tiresome. When they had driven away the regulars, the journalists found a willing source in Higgins; and when they tired of him, they turned to the bar. They spoke loudly, competing for attention, throwing out possible ideas and implications of the facts they had been able to garner, surprisingly ready to share information with each other. Mrs. Gibbs listened to interpretations of the local character, society, of her customers and the community in which she lived, the personality of the fugitive and the reasons for his crime. The babble was immediately familiar, as if she was sitting at peace in her private room, watching a television discussion that she could not be bothered to switch off. It needed an effort of will to remind herself that they were discussing her friends, her town...her.

They discussed other news items, but not in the way she and her customers talked about the same issues. Terse summaries of the facts of the story were followed by a theme statement. A famous model had left her young husband to live with a seventy-year-old press magnate; they looked at the bar copy of a tabloid, then dissected the story.

"Great pictures of her; she'll be in the top ten again."

"Not bad for the News Group. Watch the old goat now; there'll be some charitable trust for the education of mannequins next, to match all the other funds he's set up."

"Shame about the husband..."

"Dope. As if she'd have stayed with him. It was fashionable then, rich woman, poor struggling artist husband. He'll do all right..."

"Great story."

"Run for months, yeah..."

The political stories were torn apart, the underlying messages quickly identified and re-modelled, the simple story-line patina of the issue stripped away as if it had never been there. The reporters all spoke the same language and did so in the same way. They looked alike, came from the same middle-class background, had gone to the same universities and new the same friends. Tabloids or broadsheet, radio or TV, the only difference between them was the way they took the same facts and amended them to suit the advertising profile of their own particular paper. They saw the locals as a resource to be exploited, but they did so in a neutral, generally pleasant but determined manner that was chilling as the professional detachment employed by medical personnel; if the patient is going to live or takes bad news well and makes little fuss, then the work is pleasant. If not, the work still is completed, but the strain increases and perhaps an extra drink will be needed that evening.

Mrs. Gibbs shrugged and worked methodically, taking money, pouring drinks, reaping profit from them as best and as quickly as she could, but chilled by the gulf between their news and hers. Her customers started their lunchtime sessions with the papers these people wrote. It was important, the morning news. The reports would start the early conversations, and the rest of the day would be given over to reflection on the stories, followed through the news programmes on TV and radio. Even in her pub, the level of conversation dropped when the news came on the TV, and if a local event was featured, the pub was silent. This story had filled the news programme, and the reporters watched keenly when the programme came on; as it did now, the short ten-minute summary before the start of the late film. She called time, and the opening shot of the newsreader filled the screen. The escaped prisoner was the third story, after a civil war in Africa (arms sales, said the journalists, and the foreign office desire to stabilise the central trading routes so that western investment in sugar production could be rebuilt. The press stories had focused on war crimes, atrocities and children soldiers...nothing to do with the real reasons for the conflict, the journalists knowledgeably asserted; but it kept the readers...her customers...happy) and an astonishing near miss over London between an airliner and three RAF Jaguar aircraft

(publicising the need for investment in the air traffic control system, and giving the government some chance of saving face over reversing its decision to privatise the system after all; nice side-swipe at the RAF as well, in support of further cuts in the defence budget). The screen filled with a picture of the outside of her pub. The crowd at the bar fell quiet.
"Look after the bar, Jennie," Mrs. Gibbs said, and she locked the till. "I'm going upstairs."

She switched off the TV, and her pub dissolved and faded from the screen. She heard the reporters protesting, but she walked up the stairs to her flat and the noise faded as she closed the door. Blasphemy had been committed; she had ignored the product, and would continue to do so. These people came from a different world; they took facts an modelled them, wrote stories which were accepted by their readers as truth, but in creating that truth they taught, and controlled, and moulded attitudes and beliefs and values. Well, not any more. She knew the people in this story; she had grown up with some of them, known some of them as children. It had not seemed all that important before, but now she could see the scale of the lie, she would take no further part in it, and she wished she never had done. In the bar, the group of angry newsmen continued to clamour for the TV to be switched on, although they had seen the same story broadcast three times that night.

Chapter 14

Mrs. Gibbs stood outside the pub, with some of the locals. The journalists had already left, and there were three or four photographers running backwards, taking photographs, sprinting from one side of the road to the other to manage a shot that showed the reaction of the locals to the group of over a hundred chanting demonstrators, that was marching across the whole width of the road that went past the pub. Some had drums, which they beat in time to the march; others blew whistles, and the rest followed the mantra led by a cheerleader at the front of the procession.

"Who are they?" Klaxon shouted, over the noise..

"Apparently, they are anti-paedophile protestors," said Mrs. Gibbs. "These are the sort of people that recently chased a doctor from her house because they neither knew nor cared about the difference between a paedophile and a paediatrician. They have decided that we are in danger of attack from an escaped paedophile, and will benefit from their support."

"I'll benefit from smacking their bloody heads...look at that little bastard."

"You mind your language, Klaxon...oh, I see what you mean. He's broken the wing mirror off the car outside the post office."

She walked over to one of the demonstrators, who was red-faced and shouting what did they want, safety for kids, when did they want it, then.

"Your colleague over there is smashing mirrors from cars," she said. "What part of your campaign does that belong to?"

"What do we want? Safety for kids, when do we want it? Now!"

The demonstrator was carrying a placard and a well-printed poster was stuck to the board above his head. "If you can't, we will," it read. His face was red, and his eyes were glazed over with the effort of shouting and marching. There were a number of similar posters among the crowd.

"Why are you making this fuss here?" Mrs. Gibbs pointed. "The prison's over there, about a mile."

The man walked on. The youth with the mirror walked past, tight jeans over a pair of combat boots. He had very short hair, the usual face jewellery, a thick-set and aggressive youth who was obviously proud of his membership of the demonstrators' cause, and thoroughly enjoying his right to walk along a public road, barring it from traffic and destroying the peace and the property of those who lived there the year round. Mrs. Gibbs took the mirror from him.

"You old cow," he said. She brought her hand around and hit him hard on the back of his ear. His face set immediately into a snarl, and he ran straight into her, pushing her back against the kerb and making her step backwards wildly, to keep her balance. He jerked as he ran, his pelvis pushing out and then in, his hands palms-up, lifting his forearms then dropping them again, repeating the ugly, jerking dance as he crowded the woman onto the pavement. "You old cow, fucking interbred old cow, you need a good slapping…" The crowd roared its agreement. He followed her, hands raised, eyes blazing. His fist went back, and Klaxon hit him very hard, and he fell backwards into the arms of those demonstrators that had followed him.

The demonstrators eddied and swirled about the fallen man. They chanted, but behind the chant was another sound, and the object of the chanting was not the prison, but the group of people standing outside the pub. "Interbred bastards," sneered another, taking up the fallen man's idea. Suddenly the crowd were shouting against the locals, not against the prison. The cameras flashed, and more photographers ran to the front of the pub. The men in the group pushed Mrs. Gibbs into her own pub, and then remained outside the door facing the demonstration, much to the consternation of a group of youths, similar to the one Klaxon had hit, who had made similar shuttling runs at the locals, expecting them to back away. One approached Klaxon, and spat at him; Klaxon hit him, and the group backed away again, resorting to chanting. A journalist pushed a microphone into Klaxon's face, and the fisherman pushed it away.

"What is your opinion of your local prison's efficiency?" shouted the reporter.

"Get that thing out of my face."

"Are you worried that this child molester might be on the loose, outside your house?" The reporter shouted over the noise of the crowd, and one of the demonstrators shouted,

"That's right, fucking child molester."

Those around him doubled their chanting, directing their venom at Klaxon. To them, he might have represented the community that had let the offender go, or he might have been an offender himself. It did not seem to matter. They wanted to demonstrate their feelings against paedophiles, and this man had hit their colleague. One of the demonstrators began hitting his placard against the double windows of the pub, behind which Mrs. Gibbs shouted and waved him away. The press photographers took rolls of film of the incident, and when the widow finally cracked and then fell inwards, they photographed Mrs. Gibbs and Jeannie running behind the bar, and one of the demonstrators trying to climb over the sill. Klaxon shrugged, and hit him until the placard and its bearer fell backwards, off the pub's sill and onto the pavement. The crowd roared. "Thank you for your support," said Klaxon, and hit another man who was trying to break the other window. The other men in the group of customers now moved towards the window and the door, and the crowd turned so that it was no longer facing along the road, but was fronting the pub. An upstairs window smashed, then another.

"They're all the same," a woman shouted. "Perverts, perverts."

"Who the hell are they," muttered Klaxon, pushing a table hard up against the inside of the window and then dragging a bench behind it. The locals leaned against the bench, and for a while the demonstrators could not get in, and they fell back, and withdrew further when a van-load of town police arrived, forming a well-protected cordon along the front of the pub. Their inspector appeared in the bar. He was supporting the man who had stolen the car mirror, now huddled into his overcoat, mouth bleeding and apparently in tears.

"You assaulted this man?" The Inspector stared at the group.

"That man committed criminal damage to my neighbour's car, officer." Mrs.Gibbs gave the policeman the mirror. "I saw it, we all did. We will all give a statement if you need one. He assaulted me, made me fall backwards over the pavement and tried to punch me in the face. I want him charged with assault." The youth turned and ran through the door, into the centre of the crowd. He could be heard shouting, "They're trying to fucking arrest me," and the Inspector left and reformed the cordon, pushing the group away from the pub, breaking it into smaller groups and pushing them on along the road.

"Sheepshaggers," someone in the crowd shouted.

"Interbred bastards, sheep shagging bastards."

"What do we want? Safety for kids. When do we want it? Now!"

Another window broke, and policemen ducked as the glass rained down onto their riot helmets. The chanting grew, and the drumming was a solid barrage of noise that only stopped when two police cars and a van went past the pub, blue lights blazing, and pulled up at the entrance to the lane leading to Brian's cottage. The crowd followed them, and the bar emptied as the locals and protestors, differences forgotten for the moment, surged forward. The riot police forced them into a group at one side of the lane, and prevented anyone further from approaching the cottage, and they stood in cordon, round helmets and shields in ranks, the side-sticks forming a fence hemming the crowd in.

Two police officers left each car, and three more came out of the van. The reporters began their litany of questions, crowding around the vehicles and the officers until they were firmly forced aside. The cars parted and the van reversed to the door of the cottage. Then, a sergeant and two constables went into the cottage, and soon afterwards led out Brian, handcuffed and obviously under arrest.

The crowd bayed. The cheerleader, highly excited, began shouting,

"That's him! String him up!"

and his colleagues picked up and added to the refrain.

"Leave him to us, the bastard," one woman was crying as she screamed. "The filthy bastard, leave him to me."

"What are you talking about?" Mrs. Gibbs shook the woman's shoulder. "He's not a criminal. He's a retired prison governor. Listen to yourself."

The woman shrugged her aside, and pushed against the line of police, her hands reaching out towards the van, through the lines of shields, the fingers clawed and scratching at the air, trying to reach Brian.

A camera had been produced and the blue lights reflecting from the front of the cottage were supplemented by the flat, hard white glare from the TV lights. A policeman tried to push his shoulder between the camera and Brian's face, but shrugged and gave up the attempt. The questions rose to a crescendo as Brian mounted the rear step and was pushed into the van; then the two police constables climbed in and pulled the door closed behind them. The first car pulled away, slowly. It was followed by the van, and then the second car. The flashing camera bulbs lit up the impassive faces of the two officers in the front of the car, and journalists remembered the bruised face and torn coat of one of their colleagues, who even as he was driven to the station to make his complaint was composing the feature he would write as soon as rules of court procedure allowed, on the innate violence he had discovered in this isolated community, unused to the sophistication and respect for others that was so essential for cosmopolitan social harmony. Could be something on the effect of misbehaviour on Prison Service pensions...could he find out how much Thatcher was being paid? Interesting..

You needed to be strong.

Rocks feel like seals, I can imagine just what they look like, blue slate white veined rocks, wet and cold and hard. There is nothing about the place to like, and the clothes and blankets are damp no matter how often they change them. There's the old steel shed, the one we called the torpedo shed, and the old rails down to the water. The shed was built inside the cave, and the rails were for recovering test fired torpedoes years before; before the First World War. It was derelict for years, the roof open and full of slabs of rock from the roof of the cave. They cleared them all out, and made it dry and warm; but not lately. No fire, they say, not for a while although there used to be a fire; no fire, no heat. No hot food. They bring hot food, hot drinks, no fire though. The beach is softer than the rocks, and in the hut at the end of the rails there is an air bed that is waterproof and covered in damp warm blankets, so there is comfort here, as long as the blankets are pulled up high and do not fall off, because there's nothing to pull them back on; a thumb, no fingers on one hand, and what is left of three fingers on the other. It is hard to get hold of the heavy blankets. Teeth help, but it is no use trying to grip the wool between your chin and your neck if the skin is raw and rubs away; It is dark without the fire, except for the entrance, which is very low and usually dry, except for Spring tides when it only has about a couple of feet of water there, and not for very long. Most of the damp comes from the rock, draining down into the sea. There is no way to shut the light out, thankfully. Footsteps just mean food and hot drinks. Someone pulls up the blankets and tucks them in, or changes them for dry ones; not so often lately, though, not since there has been no fire. Typical. No fire, no change of blankets. No fingers, no skin. There is light from the entrance, though, and the shapes of rocks at the edge of the shale beach, long round coils of slate blue rock, rolling on to the water's edge, veined with white, wet and cold like seals. Remember them. Feel them. Somehow, I can see the light, I know when it's there.

Footsteps. She's coming, then. No feeling of panic down here; no door, no fear of what is behind the door. The light dims as she comes in then it gets brighter, and she is next to the airbed, pumping it up, pulling up the blankets, tucking them in. It is hot soup, and there's another thermos being poured into the bottle, and then the bottle is pushed under the blankets, next to the foot of the bed. It is warm against the toes, and the soup is very warm, and hardly hurts at all, where the lips used to be. It must smell of something, but there is no smell, no taste, just heat and smoothness and comfort. It would be better to smell, and to taste. It would be better to be able to spoon the soup, to grip the blankets. It would be better to be able to use the vocal chords and the lips and tongue, if just to thank her for making it all so warm; but they were all burned away. The last thing they did was scream, and then the intake of breath sucked fire deep into my larynx and burned them away. I know she does not care. I just wish I could thank her.

She did not care; an islander, looking after one of her own. She did not care about him, what he had done, who had hurt him; she just fed him and kept him warm, listening to his ruined nose and open mouth and gaping, lid-less eyes, watching the clawed hands jerk and flutter, listening to the fluid in the lungs and the grunting slurping noises as he absorbed the heat from the soup. He knew that she had no feelings for him; but if only he could thank her.

Higgins had become the media's specialist on the relationship between the prison and the local community. He was regularly quoted in the newspaper stories, and had twice travelled to London to take part as a panel member, in discussions about the situation, once on the evening news and once on a news discussion programme. The infamous interviewer had rattled quick-fire questions at him, and he had regretfully refused to answer some in order to protect the sensibilities of the prison, to which he owed his first loyalty as he told the interviewer; or to the local community, of which he felt so fond, so accepted, almost a local. The locals watched such performances without comment. Mrs Gibbs cleaned furiously while he spoke to camera, and the drinkers frowned at the surface of their beer, and drank deeply. Higgins sat nervously on the edge of the group he loved so well, and which had embraced him so effectively.

His pre-recorded interview had been closely followed by the footage of the riotous demonstration and the details of the damage to the pub. A picture of Brian being taken out of the house and into the van had been shown, with the details of Brian's face distorted in a sham effort to preserve the anonymity of a man whose house was shown in great detail. Almost everyone who lived on the Ford was watching the programme. So were the police in the regional headquarters over on the mainland, and the local M.P, and the Chief Constable of the region, Sir Stewart Parnell. He had served in the police for thirty-two years and was well aware of the nature of local communities. They watched as a presenter in London set out the situation in line with agenda decided upon by the editor of the programme. They had tired of the alarmist story line and of the laxity of the prison system for allowing the man to escape. Now they were concentrating on the unsophisticated nature of the Islanders, and the apparent hostility between them and the demonstrators. The programme presenter suggested that the demonstrators had been protesting in support of the rights of the islanders. This was put to Klaxon, in an interview recorded on the pavement outside the pub, the damage to the building clearly visible. "Protecting us?"

"You are most at risk from escaping convicts. Doesn't this worry you?"

"Convicts out of the prison don't hang around here. They make for the cities, up-country. No, it doesn't bother me."

"So you think it is acceptable to have sex offenders on the loose around communities such as this one. Isolated communities? What about the children in areas such as these? Are these demonstrators not right when they ask for greater protection for you on the Ford?"

Klaxon jerked a thumb at the broken windows of the pub.

"You must have been watching a different demonstration to the one I saw. Those evil bastards were trying to loot the pub. How does that protect us from sex offenders?"

The interviewer then smirked at the camera while Klaxon went out of shot, and the rest of the commentary was given in a slightly apologetic manner that apologised for the crudity of the Islander, an attitude that was taken up by the studio presenter later.

"Simple people, simple truths. If only modern life was as uncomplicated for most of us as it is for the Islanders of Hail Ford. There, life is simply a matter of fishing or quarrying, or for an increasing number of them, the task of keeping the prisoners of the Island's three prisons safely locked away. This is a task, as we have seen, which is apparently too much for them."

A spokesman for the prison officers' association protested. "One prisoner escaping from a low security prison hardly gives justification for that. Hail Ford has an excellent record, and the Offenders' Institution up the road from it has never had anyone abscond. As for the security hospital, their record could not be better…"

"I am sure that this is all true, but we have also seen a complete lack of understanding from the Islanders to the wishes of the demonstration. Whose side, so to speak, are they on?"

The prison officer said," Those demonstrators were thugs. It seems very odd to suggest that, just because the islanders did not want their pub smashed up, they were against the idea of safe custody for the inmates. Are you trying to say that the Islanders are on the side of the sex offender?"

"It's certainly not for me to say anything of the sort, but we are lucky to have the Islanders' opinion represented here by Mr. Arthur Higgins, who not only lives on the Ford but is also Head of Education and Training for the prison, and was the employer of the paedophile, Williams, before he escaped. Tell me, Mr. Higgins, is there any support among your fellow-islanders for Williams? He was, after all, a local man, was he not?"

Higgins spoke for a while. He demonstrated that he was as sophisticated and verbose as anyone else in the studio, and that the islanders could not all be written of as simple fishermen or rock drillers. He ridiculed the idea of the local population supporting anyone convicted of paedophile offences, local or otherwise, and stressed how grateful the locals were for the support they were receiving from the rest of the country. He pointed out that counsellors were available at the Island health centre, specially trained to help those worried by the trauma of having such a person possibly on the loose, near their own families. It was true; four bemused counsellors had arrived and worked every day at the health centre, waiting for their services to be called upon. They had been sent by the Prison Service, and had not yet had a single consultation.

The studio conversation ranged along the usual predictable lines. The presenter suggested that the official system of punishment was not strong enough. Offenders such as Williams deserved no sympathy, and had to be under supervision for the rest of their lives, and who could expect a local community to accept such people? Higgins admitted that the system was very soft on sex offenders, and that the national register of sex offenders was not working well. The discussion branched off, discussing how best to ensure cooperation by the offenders, and a new less conciliatory role for the probation service, a new name for it to reflect its role as a post-release enforcement agency. An M.P. from the government party spoke sneeringly about bleeding hearts and those soft on crime, and blithely assumed that society could even attempt to exert control over the tens of thousands of sex offenders. Matters of human rights were ignored or over-ridden. Concepts of freedom, of the efficiency of sex offender programmes in prisons, of the right of a convicted offender to eventually be free of restraints on his personal liberty, were ignored. Yet, wondered Parnell, what hope existed in this new system? What reason would the offender have, to cooperate? It meant in fact, that all sex offenders would be subject to a lifetime of constraints on their behaviour. Nobody knew better than he did, that sex offences were not clear-cut. Many complaints were made for money, for revenge, many convictions were borderline and made against the defendant in order not to weaken the existing law; many alleged rapists were in fact unsuitable boyfriends, arrested after complaints by influential middle-class parents who had found their daughter had been seduced by worldly wise, attractive and opportunist young tearaways. Tragic liaisons, but not rapes. They were often the result on enthusiastic participation by the girl concerned. Jealous wives, neglected girlfriends, it was very difficult to distinguish between the vengeful and the genuine. Such decisions were best left to the courts. Yet, the decision to prosecute was a political decision, made by the Crown Prosecution Service as dictated by stated government policy. At the moment that policy was to come down hard on sex offenders. It was naïve in the extreme to believe that the judicial system could police prisoners post-release. It would need thousands of new recruits to the aftercare services. The television debate had left viewers in no doubt that increased and long-term supervision was necessary. By the end of the programme, with much regret expressed, consensus had been reached between the politician, the presenter and Higgins, by now seen as some type of expert regarding prisons and local opinion, that the government was failing in its duty to oversee sex offenders in community, and to guarantee the safety of the general public from the hordes of released depraved paedophiles who should not have even been released in the first place. The programme switched seamlessly into footage of concerned parents and frightened children at their heels, marching in well-organised rows, doing no damage, respecting the police and the property of those between whom they demonstrated. The programme showed official policy as weak, offenders as unchanged and evil, and demonstrators as orderly and admirable. Higgins was heard, saying that the country could rely on the natural sense of British justice and fair play to ensure that the community would protect its young and control its evildoers, as it always had done.

"Is it democracy, though, or the rule of the mob? That man is dangerous; furthermore, he is a liar," Parnell announced, and his wife and children ignored him completely, used as they were to his outbursts at the television. "He knows nothing. He does not understand the local community. He probably does not like it, and it certainly does not like him. The governor should be stuffed for letting that fool speak for the prison."
"Tell him, why don't you?" said his wife.

The Chief Constable did not reply, but after a few minutes, walked into the hall. His wife heard him phone for the driver, and then the cloakroom door closed and he was obviously dressing for a journey. The doorbell rang, and she heard the voice of her husband's driver, a new and very beautiful police sergeant advanced driving instructor.

"I'm off, dear," he called. His wife shrugged, and opened a magazine. The door closed and the car purred past the drawing room windows, and away along the drive. She wondered how long it would be before the sergeant and her husband would turn off the road and start pawing each other. She stared unseeing at the magazine, running the film of the two bodies in the back of the black unmarked police car, steadily processing the story and its outcome. She was smiling. Soon she would go to bed.

The Chief Constable was using the car phone. "Have you still got that governor in the station? The one who assaulted the journalist? Right. Is he charged, yet? Good… keep him there, I want a word. I need the officer in charge of the search, and the arresting officer for the old Works Governor…what's his name? Thatcher. Right. Better get the local super in as well. I'll give you an hour. I'll be there at eight."

The driver peered through the dark, assessing the severity of the next corner, checking for oncoming headlights, entering the grid, easing off, accelerating. The boss would want to be early, she thought.

"Take me to J Division HQ, Sergeant, if you would," Parnell said, three minutes after she had taken the turning that would save a minute or two on the journey to Hail Ford Point.

The station was calm, but had obviously been recently disturbed. Files were straightened, odd pieces of paper were slowly falling from desks, polishing rags were hidden behind computer screens and the waste bins were overflowing while the desk surfaces seemed strangely clear. The Chief Constable accepted such homage as his due, and beckoned to the three detectives who hovered next to the entrance desk, to follow them as he and the Superintendent swept along the central corridor to the charging unit. He gestured to the Superintendent to catch up with him.

"And why did you arrest Thatcher?"

"The Press, Sir. They were raising Cane about the assault on one of their journalists…"

"The press was? Or that journalist was? Who was this journalist, anyway?"

The Superintendent named a hack.

"So you arrested a man like Thatcher because of a complaint by some hack? "

"Yes Sir. Your policy on press relations, we have set up a liaison office and it is working very well. As your last Admin. Memo recommended, Sir." Idiot.

"Well done, well done; but I'm going to ask you to release this prisoner, Superintendent. Caution him if you like, but I'd rather you did not. The journalist was bothering his grandson, I understand."

How had the boss found that out, wondered Detective Chief Inspector Wade. He watched with interest as the Superintendent's face changed to a deeper shade of red.

"He's a local, you see. We need to keep the locals on side, don't you think?"

"I have had the Home Office on the phone, Sir, and more than once today. They want a rapid re-establishment of good order on Hail Ford, and they have said so. I understand that this comes from very high up in the Home Office, Sir."

"Higher than me, you mean? Probably so. I'm letting him go anyway; or rather, I'd like you to. OK? Right, let's see him. In here?"

Parnell entered the unit without breaking step and even the moaning teenager leanings against the charge room desk stopped his continuous whine as the entourage entered, paused, and then surged on the cell. The door was opened and Thatcher stared at his visitors.

"Mr Thatcher?"

"Sir Stewart."

"We need to talk."

"You need to get those evil bastards off the Island. Stop them pestering women and children, and get them back to where they come from. Then we can talk."

"Sooner than that, unless you want that idiot Higgins to make even more trouble. He's the Island's official spokesman, did you know?"

Thatcher opened his mouth, then closed it again. He sat down. The Chief Constable nodded. "Interview room would be more comfortable. Sergeant, get someone to bring us a drink. Tea all round, I think. Give Mr. Thatcher his shoes, would you? He'll be coming out with me, I think."

"So, what happened Mr. Thatcher? Take your time."

Thatcher looked at the tape recorder. Tom the sergeant had switched it on at the beginning of the interview.

"Habit, that's all." Parnell leaned across the table and turned it off. He opened both cassettes and removed the tapes. "You have not been charged with anything, and you will not be charged with anything. Is that quite clear? Not with assault, and not with any other offence either."

Thatcher nodded.

"So, what happened?" Thatcher did not reply, and the Chief had not expected him to do so. He talked, and Brian listened. The Chief spoke in a monotone, describing the problems that the Ford was experiencing, and would continue to experience. He said that matters would become worse, not better. He spoke of politicians, forthcoming elections, public statements about prison security and effective policing, and the right that the general public had to feel they were safe in their homes. He spoke of local loyalty, of the benefits of a strong local community and of the disastrous effect that exposing such a social system to the full glare of the press would have. Families would not be free to go about their business. Minor indiscretions would be discovered, small crimes, irregularities in any manner of matters from fishing quotas to pub licences. There would be no end to the interference in the lives of local people until the press left the Ford; and they would not leave, until the matter of the escapee was settled. It was a great story. It would never end. Brian stopped listening, consciously at least. He remembered that small boy, always picking through the rocks at the base of one of the training quarries. Always the same clothes, and not many of them; always the same bruises, always in the same places. He remembered the day the child had tried to speak to him, but could hardly breath for harsh intakes of breath, from suppressed sobs. His mother had gone, he tried to say. So lost, so desperate, as the child contemplated life without the only bit of affection it had held.

Yet, once the boy had grown used to him, he had been quick to smile, and shyly proud of what he had found. Brian still had many of them, in his parlour. Ammonites, ferns, shells, all beautifully preserved, white against the pale or dark blue of the surrounding stone. On his rest days he had spent hours with the lad; it had been a pleasure, not a charity, and he remembered the pain in his chest that he had felt when the boy would decide to return home, his thinly shod feet walking bravely through the rock, picking his way over sharp ridges, towards a home that held little comfort and probably another beating. Thatcher had made the usual enquiries.

Social services had visited, but physical abuse was almost the norm among certain families. Sexual abuse had not even been considered, except by those who were specialists in the field, and that included virtually every policeman, social worker, most teachers, all clergymen; sexual abuse of children was under-reported by at least 80 per cent. It still is, Thatcher thought. It was, and is, the great shared secret. Once it is recognised, it releases an uncontrollable problem. Children are abused. They are abused by their parents. If they are taken from their parents and out into care, they are abused by their care workers. They are abused by councillors, by members of committees set over the residential homes, by police officers influential enough to use the children's homes as their own repository of available young bodies, by those councillors on the police committees who have been included in the circle of those who know and can, and by the friends and colleagues and business associates of those councillors who fancy some young flesh. The good council homes will not tolerate such activity, so the bad council homes get it all; they get the worst children, the worst care workers and the greatest numbers of abusers queuing up at the doors. If the children complain they are labelled liars, if they run away they become absconders. Children not on custodial orders are made subject to such orders. Those already on care orders quickly find themselves in secure units or approved schools if they begin to make trouble. The care workers who cooperate are promoted and soon are in greater control of more and more children. There are the great of the country who have visited, and indulged, and then gone on to greater social positions, protecting and being protected in their turn. Honest police officers have been sacked and transferred as a result of attempts to stop this abuse; teachers have been transferred, or bullied into resigning, or sacked. People have been killed, both adults and children. Recent TV publicity did not solve the problem but transferred it from the home to the Home. For many years, official opinion was that as the children were going to be abused anyway, they might as well stay at home where at least everything else they needed for care and stability was in place. Later this became politically unacceptable, and so they were taken into care, and the children's homes were opened which pleased local authorities, created opportunities for employment, reduced the quality of residential care workers, allowed more abusers to approach nearer to their targets. A growing lack of sympathy with the victims led to a reaction in expectations of help on their part, and while a few well-publicised cases made the news and reaped the sympathy of the nation, huge numbers of children continued to be abused and to suffer with no hope of relief or release. Their resentment grew, then faded as they accommodated such treatment into their life, normalised it and inevitably began to act in the same way towards children themselves. Those few arrested for such offences attracted the abuse and detestation of a society full of guilt, not for the behaviour of other people, but for their own behaviour. The 80 per cent of unreported crimes involved perpetrators and victims, and they all banded together in calls for rough justice for paedophiles. They blocked streets, burned houses, attacked innocent people, were interviewed on television and apparently listened to by politicians. The whole witch-hunt was fuelled, as always, by the guilt of the mob, not its sense of outrage.

And that was the background of Terry Williams. The Chief Constable watched Thatcher as he remembered the boy. Terry had grown older, sadder. Thatcher still had seen him in the quarries, but as the boy grew older his interest in fossil hunting had passed. Thatcher had tried to interest the boy in joining in with fishing, or with a youth group that met in the Island centre. The boy had been polite, but never came. He had been too young, barely ten. He had no money, wore the wrong clothes; children are ruthless in imposing standards on those who want to join their groups. Thatcher had noticed that Terry would not join groups of those of his own age, but increasingly was to be seen leading a gaggle of smaller, younger children. He seemed to be caring for them, settling their disputes, guarding them from bullying, ensuring they were safe from traffic and cliff edges; but then parents started to keep their children away from him, and he was increasingly alone. Thatcher eventually went against the social traditions of the Island, and went to see the boy's father in the small, dirty three-room cottage next to the stone yards, next to the railway. The father had been in turns truculent, then spineless. He looked for help; any help that might exist, money or goods, anything. As soon as he realised that Brian was not from the social services and was not a policeman, he lost hope of reward and lost fear of punishment. The Chief

Constable wondered what had really happened; the young Governor, strong, honest, genuinely fond of the boy and appalled by the way the child had been treated; and the father, so manipulative, brutal, self-centred, typical of all the frustrations that must have beset Thatcher in his prison work. Did the father try to attack him, Parnell wondered. Had Thatcher hit the man? Had he planned to adopt the boy?

The man was found dead and the boy was removed to the local children's home. Thatcher had been taken by surprise when a relative was found, who lived in South Wales. The boy had gone, away from the Island, out of their life, and Thatcher missed him for a while, and then hoped he was in a better life, and he continued with his work and life.

Thatcher had not been surprised when Williams appeared at the prison, one Monday. The induction group had trooped out past the prison officers and the duty governor. Some swaggered, some shuffled past. One walked away across the prison yard, stepping carefully, as if his feet hurt and the ground was hot or sharp. Recognition had stabbed Thatcher, and he had drawn that prisoner's file, and found Terry again. He read the record, appalled, and filled in the gaps from his own memories.

Islanders were loyal to their own. They did not live in any special way, they were not tribal, they had many living on the Ford who had moved in and knew nothing about their traditions or common background. The quarries where they had played as children had gone, many of the influences that had bonded them together had gone; fishing had almost disappeared, stone working was now a hobby; yet, when there was a crisis the Island surfaced, and Islanders acted as they had always acted. The Island disliked being different, but they also hated being observed, patronised, subjected to values and behaviour they did not want, could not accommodate, rejected completely. Symbolic of such external values were the prisons on the Island, repositories of people and their opinions and values that they rejected. They liked the fact that the prisoners were enclosed, and that once they were released they left the island, taking their foreign values with them.

With the publicity of the escape and the influx of journalists, the observation and resentment had begun and local hostility to it had increased. It had rejected the incomers, and reinforced the sense of identity of the Islanders. Thatcher was an Islander, even though he worked in the prison. He had been in charge of the building, its security, its walls, safeguarding the prisoners inside and also the Islanders outside. It was the work he wanted to do, and it strengthened the Island and the prison. He was an Islander, as were Ron, Mrs Gibbs, Parker…

"Not Annie?"

"She is now."

"And Williams?"

The small boy with the cuts on his legs. The tattered plimsolls, and the collection of fossils. The courage, and the hope, and the lack of confidence that hope would ever be met. The boy had been so brave, and the memory of it thickened his voice as Thatcher said,

"Born there. He's an Islander, of course he is."

"Was, Mr Thatcher? Or don't you think he is dead?"

Thatcher stared mulishly at the Chief, and then drank his tea. "I'd like to go, now."

Parnell stood, opened the door, bowed slightly and gestured towards the station door. Thatcher nodded and walked out.

Chapter 15

Ethel Gibbs was a tough woman, and the Islanders knew it. She had run the pub single-handed since her husband had gone away, back to the mainland where the weather and women suited him better; and she had struggled to make a living along with most of the people on the Ford, helping out when she had to as they did for her, always done in a brusque, unsentimental way, knowing that altruism and self-interest were too closely tied to be easily distinguished. It was easier to help if the person in need was popular and friendly, but you still helped, no matter what they were like. It was simple sense. She knew most of what went on. Men forgot she was there, or maybe as one of their own group. She was not a person, just an extension of the bar or the beer, the situation that gave them comfort. They went to the pub to escape their cares at home, and she was the alternative to the domestic stress or the problems at work. She found out a lot, and inferred a lot more, and Ethel was no fool. She never passed on what she heard, not directly; but a wise person would do well to take advice from Ethel Gibbs.

She remembered the sad family at the edge of the quarry, along with many other sad facts of life in that area. Given the opportunity she would have done anything to help Ron and Annie, but it was over and done with now. The boy was safe and it was over. The wickedness of it was the stuff of the newspaper reports, but not for her. She knew how complicated life must have been for Williams, and while it made no difference and he was still wicked, the fault went deeper than just one man. He would have to take responsibility for what he had done; but the fault went as far into society, high and wide, as far as you wanted to spread it. The father, the silly weak mother, the Island, the people Williams had worked with, the people in the pub. Brian. Herself.

She had thought this over as she picked her way along the shoreline under the cliff, just past the pub. It was the only place she went on her own. The shops were full of customers, and conversation was best avoided. She had few friends, most of them in licensing and away from the Ford. Customers made poor friends; all they had in common was booze, and it made a bad foundation for a friendship. She enjoyed walking along the beach, hidden from view by the bulk of the cliff, and before the sun crossed over the rim it was warm and peaceful on the rock and stone of the shore, and some of the hollows were sheltered, secluded and quite warm.

That was where she had found him. She had heard him, first. He snorted and crooned as he scrabbled up the stones. They must have been agonisingly sharp on the raw flesh of the ruined hands and arms. The feet and knees worked against the shingle as if he was still swimming, the bony legs and silly long feet. She remembered the feet. As a boy, he'd always seemed to have feet too long for his legs. His neck was a mass of burned flesh and melted cloth, and the hair had been left in tufts that sprouted in small patches from the mass of his sore, scorched head. She had murmured as she bent and took hold of his arms, feeling his quick struggle and then, almost instant surrender, and she pulled him by his upper arms over the shale and to the edge of the smooth concrete of the old slipway. He still crawled, and she had turned him over and hurriedly taken off her old coat, and rolled it up, and set it under him. She pushed him up against the wall of the slip and put the coat behind him. His feet scrabbled a few times, his heels running up and down the concrete, and then he relaxed and lay still. She had stared at his sightless eyes and the ruin of the face, feeling the inside of her heart almost gape with pity, but she saw even then, the boy she had known was resigned to something more that was going to happen to him, yet at that particular moment, was trying to make the best of what he had.

"I'll get help for you. I'll get a doctor. He'll stop the pain. Just stay here."

The wreck had just sat there. He could not speak or nod, agree or disagree, but she knew he had heard her and understood. She had seen it before. He knew she was going to help, and he was hoping that good would come from it. His leg, which had been bent up, relaxed; and his head moved a little against the concrete and he made a noise that might have been a moan, but settled.

Ethel had run for the doctor, and the others, and they had carefully brought blankets and heat, and made him safe while he either lived or died. He had lived, warily, listening out for whatever was going to happen to him next.

The pub went very quiet when Brian entered, stood in his normal corner and ordered a pint. He drank it slowly, lifting his head as he drank, eyes wide open and staring at the people in the pub. Higgins left the bar. Mrs. Gibbs stayed close, but did not make any conversation. The locals gathered at Brian's end of the bar, but read their papers or watched the TV, just showing by their proximity that they were ready to help if it was needed.

A TV journalist walked in. Brian said,

"So, Higgins is our spokesman is he? How's that, then?"

"He's the only one of you who will talk to us, I suppose," said the journalist, paying for his gin. "Got to put someone up, to inform the public."

"Was that the public, out there? The ones who broke the windows, wrecked the cars, wanted to string me up? You tell me, now; how did they get here? Where did they get those posters from?"

"Must have made them."

"Handy, then, weren't they? Excellent joinery on those placards, and they must have a fair old printing press to produce those posters. You're saying they were nothing to do with the press, then? It was not just a group of very stupid and violent people, deliberately whipped up by the press to further pressure a government that is having a bad time on prison policy?"

"It's a hard game, I suppose. But no permanent harm done, I suggest? A couple of windows, a few paint scratches?"

"A story. Anything to pep up a story. It's all based on lies. I wouldn't mind the dishonesty, so much as the cynical laziness of it all. You know that Higgins is not one of us. He knows less about this place than you do. You put him on your programme and you're as big a liar as he is."

"Sorry."

"It doesn't matter, I know. Just a job, filling a slot. You'll all be gone soon, some other news story. But for us, see, it's our life. Our people, our children. You buggers have done enough, now. It's time you went."

"Can't go. The story's still selling papers, still making people turn on their sets at night."

"So what will end the story?"

"I suppose when they arrest the chap, or find him, or his body. Any of those."

"It wouldn't end there, though, would it? If you found him, then you'd want to know where he had been. If you found his body, you'd want to see how he died. There's no end to a story for you people, is there?"

"That's right," said the journalist. "Never kill a good story. They can run for years, decades. They're still getting good copy from Lord Lucan, the Turin Shroud, the Ark of the Covenant…whenever times are bad we can float Myra Hindley or Homosexual Law reform or a cure for cancer…this is a good story, see? The demo was a good story. They were treating you like saboteurs treat huntsmen, you appeared a beleaguered village community, it was great stuff, great images; but I doubt if it'll go on for much longer. People don't lose interest, it's just that something else, something fresher, happens."

Thatcher snorted. "Fresh? Look at the papers today, what are you writing about? Look at what they were writing about thirty years ago. Homosexuality, the Health Service, reform of licensing laws, school organisation, prison policy; they are all the same stories. You don't need fresh stories, you just need further examples of the old ones.

You people set your editorial agendas, and dare not change them. That's the worst of you. It's not that you spoil our way of life, that you pester our children and bring your rotten values and fashions into our community. It's that you're so lazy. The stories you write are so lazy. You have these pro-forma stories, and the only thing you need to do is fill in the gaps left for new names, new details. And do you know why you dislike us so much? Because we don't fit into the patterns of readers that your papers have to have. Your marketing departments need people to live in a certain way, have certain needs, desire certain ways of life. We don't need that way of life around here. We look after ourselves, care for our own. You and your papers cannot tell us what we want; because we know. We know what we need, and we know what we don't need, and we don't need you. So you have to change that. It doesn't fit into your idea of marketing, or news management, or politicians' ideas of a controllable electorate. Marginal self-supporting communities like ours must not be allowed to survive."

The reporter grinned. "You're in good company, though. Miners' villages were self-supporting. Farming communities are. Isolated communities in the Scottish islands were, until they became part of the tourist industry. You're right, of course, and it is inevitable that your way of life will change."

"You agree then? Destruction of any way of life that does not fit the norm, as far as you're concerned, is acceptable?"

"More than acceptable. It's necessary. It's, I suppose, it's my job."

"To spread totalitarianism. To force out individualism. Like Stalin, like Mao Tse Tung. You think that to act in such a way is doing a service to the country?"

The journalist threw back his head in surprise. Thatcher had begun to appear threatening. They had grown used to this big calm man, had been assaulted by him physically which had been a shock, and now were being attacked intellectually.

"Don't pretend that you are any better than us. You read those stories, you buy the same goods and read the same adverts. Your whole community depends on that very society you pretend to despise. If it weren't for the prisons here, this whole area would be destitute."

"The prisons, yes. Full of people who have a different idea of ownership. They like the adverts, and share your opinion of what is desirable, what is valuable. They can't earn the money they need, but they still want the goods. They are well-trained, and they read your papers and they believe what they are told. They do as you tell them. They need and covet and want, and they steal.

You give them the excuses. Papers offer the same old debates; legalise drugs, legalise homosexuality, reduce ages of consent, consider racism or football hooliganism or alcohol. These people read what you write, and try it. They are the people who forge a path for your suggestions, and sometimes they succeed and sometimes they are criminalised, and when they are the papers are the loudest to condemn them, until the next time editors think their news columns are light and it might be fun to rattle society's stability. You are such cowards. You would never dare take on the real evils of society; the profits from organo-phosphates, the sexualisation of children merely for advertising and profit, the manipulation of the political and legal systems by interest groups. You sneer at us running prisons, but we don't just run them for you, we keep in them the people that you inspire to commit the crimes in the first place. It's your idea, your crime, your victims, our problem. Your prisons don't work, but they do best in our stable communities."

"Them and us, eh? So your interbred little kingdom here never produces criminals, just doughty sons of the soil, honest and upright rock diggers and fishermen?"

Thatcher dropped his voice. He sighed, lowered his shoulders, and drank from the pint. Then he turned to the newsman. "Cons accept the messages you put out, and want those things as their right. They want the naked woman who smiles from your paper; then, any woman they want, they want naked and smiling; they insist on it, some of them. They like the stories about the young pop-stars, the girl singers and dancers, they want the social life and the cars and clothes and the sex. You make them feel like that, they learn their desires from you, they can't fulfil them legally so they take what they can by any means they can, and you're right, they end up here. But they're behind a wall. We look after them for you, but that does not make us part of the problem. You are the problem. We clean it up, but you're the filth that causes it. Like anyone who works with filth, we take great care to keep ourselves clean. Not you, though. You know what you are doing, and you are doing it well, so you wallow in it. Wallow in news, in media, manipulating and misinformation, corrupting, spoiling. Those people in the prisons; they're just a symptom; they're not the problem. You are."

Brian looked at Mrs. Gibbs. "There you are, see? Never talk too much. Waste of time. I'm off to the cottage. I'm back for good, now." He turned back to the journalist. "They didn't charge me, and they won't. Tell your mates, would you? I want them to leave me and mine alone, now." The journalist nodded, staring at Thatcher with a new interest. Who did he know, to have the charge dropped? Lodge business, perhaps? Not very likely. The journalist ordered another gin.
Mrs. Gibbs called at the cottage an hour later, where Brian had been expecting her. She sat in the small front room without speaking, and Brian poured tea and in turn, stretched out in his old chair in front of the small fire.
"What did the doctor think?" asked Thatcher.
"Nothing much wrong. Bronchitis. He'll be better in a few days. He's warm, dry, well fed."
"This could go on for ever. I never believed he could be so strong. Half blind, half drowned."
"Totally blind, now. That was one piece of news the doctor did have for us. He'll never be able to see again."
"Ah. But it's a problem, and not one that will ever go away."
"No."
"It can't go on, can it? They watch virtually everything, now. It can't be more than a matter of days before they see what we're doing."
"I don't suppose there is anywhere else we could use?"

"If it's on the Ford, it makes no difference."
"Can we hand him over?" She sounded persuasive, almost pleading.
Thatcher thought for a while, looking down at the floor. Mrs Gibbs nodded.
"No, I see," she said. "When I think about that poor little lad…"
"Best remember the poor little lad he killed."
"You know he did not kill that child on his own, Brian. We all had a part in that. He did it, right enough; but we know how he became what he is. And he's not that person anymore. He's like a child himself, again. You see the way he looks up when he hears the door…and his face. It seems horrible, so little expression left, and all it shows is fear."
" He's frightened? Of you?"
"No, when he knows it's me…"
Thatcher threw a piece of wood on the fire, and stirred the grate.
"They'll never leave us alone, until it's settled. You know that." He sighed. "Best you don't go back, I suppose."
"Just once, Brian? Just to…"
"Best not," he said, quietly.

The woman stared at him, steadily; she was not sobbing, but her eyes streamed tears. She shook her head once, and then sat still, and Brian returned her stare defiantly. "It would be kinder not to go again. You know that. Look after Ron, or Annie; look after the pub and the people that come to it. Damn you, it's not me; blame Higgins, blame those bloody journalists but don't blame me."

He put on his coat, and left her in the cottage. Outside, on the cliff path, were two strangers and as he left the door, one of them raised a camera and a flash light seared across the grass and rocks. Thatcher said nothing, just ducked against the wind-driven shower that had swept in, and walked quickly across the cliff path, towards the houses either side of the pub. He wanted to see the doctor; and to talk to Klaxon and Digger; he'd need to see the verger, not the vicar who came from up country somewhere. They'd tell Ron, but no need to disturb him. Not embarrass Gary, the local bobby, even though he was born on the Ford. Best not to use the phone. Word of mouth, and they could meet up in the top cottage by the path. He remembered it still had a porch with "Press Gang slits" in the walls. A small boy would have sat there, peering out for the press gangs and warning men in doors if they were in danger, so that they could escape across the clifftop. The Islanders just wanted to be left alone, always had. They had a sense of fair play and a sense of justice, and they did not need interference from outside to tell them how to sort out their own affairs. Their sense of justice was based on right and wrong, not on what was politically effective or most likely to benefit the ruling political party. They would help do right, and prevent wrong. These seemed to be ideas that the rest of the country had forgotten.

Brian called at the first house. Then he left, and five minutes later, so did the Doctor. Soon, the number of pedestrians choosing to walk in the driving rain seemed strangely high; but the streets soon cleared. One house seemed to be holding a party, or a meeting. It did not last very long, and the blaze of lights dimmed as blinds were drawn and lights turned off, and the top of the cliff became dark again.

It was very dark. The rain blew directly into their faces, and the squalls hit them horizontally, full in the face. The fronts of their coats were soaked, and rain rattled against them, and streamed off the skirts of the mackintoshes and waterproofs. Hats flew away. They walked frowning, heads down, feeling their way in the black night, but sure of every footstep.
The path curved along the top of the cliff, following the edge, and at one point was only inches from a steep drop. There, in daylight, could be seen a thinning of the grass fringe of the path, one that needed to be cut short because it was all that stood between the path and a fall. At this point, carefully identified, they gingerly left the path and slid some ten or fifteen feet down the grass slope, which quickly became greasy and muddied as

more and more men slid down it. Their feet made contact with a pathway only inches wide, left by sheep as they made their way along the very edge of the grass, and beyond which there was a great spoon shaped crater in the rock where a huge fall had thundered away from the surface of the cliff and which now lay in layers on the beach, hundreds of feet below. The path seemed to go nowhere. Leaning to their left, hands flat on the grass and inching along the stone path, they made their way to a step in the rock, and then another. In the dark, and with great difficulty even for local men, they managed to descend the slope until they were well under the lip of the old rockfall. There, the path flattened a little, and they could walk more easily down to the beach itself.

The wind was straight onshore, and spray was bursting up from the knee of rock at the base of the cliff. The old rails that had launched and recovered weapons were steep, but the channel between them served to funnel some of the spray directly into the mouth of the cave. It never would be submerged, but on such a night as this it ran and streamed with water and the noise was magnified inside the sloping archway. The old hut had been repaired, and the roof was in one piece; they had rigged a door across the opening at the side, and weighted it against the frame with rocks.

The men started to pull the rocks away from the door, and now they were out of sight, they produced torches and flashlights which they set up in the rock, to shine onto their work. There were not many rocks to move; and once they were out of the way, they could pull the door up and away from the frame, although the wind caught it and slammed it back against the wall twice or three times; and in the dim cave, amid the noise of the sea and the wind across the entrance, and the slamming of the wood against the frame, there came another sound in the night; not a cry, because the person making the noise could not cry; but a rapid snuffling breathing, wet as if with tears, choked as if with fright, and somehow, echoing with recognition; but the men, looking tired and stern, ignored the noise, and pulled with strong hands at the edges of the improvised door.

There was a sort of light, I could see it under the edge of the door. He was there, the bastard. I tried to edge into the corner and wrapped the blankets around me but he was always there, and the light would come on and stream under the door, and then the door would open and he would stick his head into the tall yellow oblong and whisper,
"Terry?"

The bastard. I would pretend to be asleep, and sometimes he would go away, but not often. He'd come in, and I would pretend to be asleep, right up to the end when he was punching the air out of me and the whole bed was rocking and my face was being driven into the thing so that all I could do was catch my breath, and remember the taste and smell of the foam mattress, and him, and he would grunt and mutter and his mouth was drooling, and it would be over. I would pretend to be asleep. I'd said something, once, tried to ask him to stop, and he'd beaten the shit out of me, the bastard, and so I knew better, I never said a word, I never made a noise. If I cried, he's start into me. If I made any noise at all, he'd belt me. I stayed quiet, made no noise. I never even flinched when sometimes he would try to speak himself, or put his hand on my head, or once I am sure, start to tell me he was sorry…nothing. Not a word, not a shiver; stay still, and wait for the bastard to go away.

I wish I'd been kinder to Philip.

I can see him so clearly. The day he first saw me. He'd been angry that his mother was going out with someone, and frightened, I suppose; and he'd been sitting in the garden digging and pulling out stones. I sat down beside him, and didn't speak.

And I'd seen the fern, in the stone. The top edge of it was exposed, and without telling him who I was, or saying anything, I'd taken the trowel he had been digging with and set its edge into the rock, and there was a half-brick in the border, used that as a hammer, crack!

It split open along the seam, and there was the whole fern, clear as glass.

Philip had washed it off, carefully, and listened as I'd told him what it was, and I felt ice in my stomach as I saw him gripped by the old feelings. He would never lose that, I knew. He was staring at the rock, at the feathery shape whitening as it dried, and losing himself in the vast, huge, ocean-wide sky-huge length of time that the fern has been embedded in the stone. Nothing mattered, nothing. On that carpet of time, you were nothing at all, not even a speck, just irrelevant. When the ship sat on its arse and struggled up a sixty-foot wave, then juddered at the top and then slid down until it fetched up with a crash of pots and broken helicopter engines, loose tools and stores not properly secured, you meant nothing and would sink no less quickly nor slowly than any other speck of flotsam, that happened to be on the surface of the sea; and so with the fossil. It would last, and when you were dust it would still rest in the stone, maybe unseen but still there, to be discovered or not. The fern was sublime, with an existence that needed no explanation or justification. Look at it if you wished to, or not.

He was mine, after that. Rocks, cars, models, boats. He laughed a little, then more. He forgot what had happened before, between his father and his mother, and he relaxed with us, as did his brother and sister. They stayed close to their mother, but not Philip. We went to rock pools, climbed cliffs, walked the beaches, went into the sea. The others stayed as a group, on the sand or at the water's edge, but we were the leaders.
I can't think about Philip.

When I do, my head grows tight, and I have to stop. As soon as the thoughts go, my head relaxes, and I can feel the scalp change shape, it relaxes. I could sleep, almost. I am so sorry, I was trying to read to him and I'd had that row with his mother, and he turned away from me. I tried to tell him that it wasn't like his father, that we had shouted but it was not for ever, it would soon go away and be as good as ever, but he pulled away and when I reached out to turn him to face me I felt the strength in him as his shoulder pulled out of my hand, sliding against the pyjama jacket as he pulled away and hit his head against the wall, not hard, but against the wall, not the pillow, and he cried. As I tried to comfort him, he cried, and then he screamed. I saw his face then, eyes blank, mouth open and gaping, slobber, just empty as if his soul had flown out of his mouth and was echoing around the room in the grief and screams coming from him. I tried to talk to him, then to hold him, but he would not be comforted and the noise grew and grew, and the irritation, the irritation grew and grew and welled up, damn the boy, damn the boy damn him why the hell wouldn't he just shut up and listen? I remember his thin arms and the elbows, and the rigid strength of the small body, and the noise. It had been loud before but nothing like as loud as that. The strength in his neck as I pushed his face into the pillow, oh my head I must stop thinking about

it, my head, stop thinking and feel the skin relax.
The rock behind my head is cool, it's wet. I can
rest my head against it for a while, it will help.
I wish, though.
That first time, when he smiled and saw the fern,
that was a warm, sunlit day. We sat in the
garden behind his mother's old house, and he
pretended not to watch as I opened up the stone,
and he saw it for the first time. He had stared
down at the fern and I held the two parts of the
stone in my hands as he stared at them. I
remember the smell of the fence, creosote, and
the way the wood strips overlapped, and the
grass of the garden with its small border edged
in triangles of half-brick; and the gnats, in a
cloud over the path, spotlighted in the sunlight
of the mid-afternoon sun. And Philip had looked
up, in the end, and I had looked down, and he
had pointed at the fern; and then he had smiled.
It was my smile.

I heard him.
"Terry?"
The same bloody whisper, the bastard.

I would be in the room, in the dark, and then he'd come home. If he was going straight to sleep he never turned on a light. He just made a lot of noise, and muttered a bit, and then it would be quiet, and then I'd hear him snoring. I'd sleep, then, because there was no chance that he'd wake again and he was always gone in the morning.

The other times, he'd turn on the light. I made sure the door was shut, when I went to bed. I would have to put something against it, but nothing heavy, I had learned that lesson. Something light. Clothes, anything.

Not often, but sometimes I had been asleep, and I would wake up when he turned on the light. It would be shining under the door, and around the edges. It lit up a crack in the wall by the bed, one that was shaped like a small man's head. I used to stare at it, imagining other shapes in the wall, other faces and shapes of animals; and then there would be the soft scraping sound as whatever I had put on the floor rubbed as the door opened and pushed it ahead, across the lino of the bedroom floor, the light spilling into the room.

Now, the door was banging against the frame, and there was light under it, and then suddenly light all around it, and I saw the light dim as something passed across it, and then it went out, and I knew he was bending over me but I stayed still, asleep. I am asleep. He can talk as much as he likes, I can't hear him I'm asleep, he can talk about what he bloody well likes but he'll not get a movement from me. He's talking now; he's with someone…they're talking about salt water. She's not there, I can't hear her voice and I can't feel the heat from the food, I can't smell, can't smell anything, can't smell the food she brings but I can feel the heat from it, and there's nothing like that, nothing.

"Never be able to prove a thing if they don't find anything in the cave. That's if they ever find the cave.." Man's voice, I don't know who it is. He sounds neutral, like a screw, just discussing arrangements, I think they have come to look after me, not like she does, not food; just to sort it out. It will be a relief to get it sorted out. It seems a long time since they brought me here, and what they hell they thought they were playing at, it's cold and wet, I know that, there's no way they're allowed to do that to me. She said a lot about it, but I can't remember much, not about that, just somewhere dry and warm would be an improvement. Bloody nerve, what about some proper treatment, I've never had any treatment for anything, just warm bottles and food, and these blankets which she keeps changing from dry ones. Do anyone's head in, that would, I could complain, write to the court or to the MP, see what they'd do when that letter dropped on the governor's doormat…
there's a strong light, now. The door's wide open and there's a scraping noise as it pushes across the floor, and the light's growing, I can't see much but it's lighter and I can feel it on my face, he's in the room and I can hear him, and feel him getting nearer, I'm not going to move, I'm staying still, I'm still, I'm asleep.

I wish I could speak. I have things to say. I think them, but they don't exist unless you say them. Or write them. Can't write, either. People burn. That came as a shock. They didn't teach us that at the fire school. We ran around in fearnought suits and covered fires in foam and others in water. We wore breathing apparatus, in the filth and smoke of the training units, and padded around using the backs of our hands to tap the bulkhead. Always the backs of the hands. If you touch a cable in the dark, and it's live, your hand will grip it and you'll stay there, dangling off the electricity, while your legs burn away from the fire. If you use the back of your hand, it throws you away from it if you get a belt. Interesting, the things they taught on the fire school.

We used to breath slowly. There wasn't much air, and so you try to use as little as possible, but the real reason was that breathing makes the demand valve hiss. It's deafening. If you're frightened, it hisses like a train, and they can all tell you're crapping hot conkers. So you have to be calm, long slow breaths, you do it out of pride. Daft, that you're walking around like a line of circus elephants, arms and legs clad in pounds and pounds of fireproof, soot-blackened water-soaked suit, blind as a bat, a huge air tank on your back and pulling a four-inch hose and surrounded with burning oil and smoke, and all you're worried about is that the others might think you're frightened. It wasn't frightening, just exciting. The glow of the fire through the black, through the smoke; and the warmth of it, through the suit, and for a minute, when you first find the seat of the fire, it's the same cheery feeling as when you're cold, and you walk into the parlour at home, and you're not expecting it, but someone's lit the fire. You know it's there before you see it. It's not the heat or the glow, but something else. It lives. Even behind a door, if it's there you know. If you are expecting a fire, and you turn the corner or open the door and there is nothing, just a cold grate or an empty compartment, cold and wet and full of smoke, it's a disappointment, somehow. There is nothing worse on a cold day, than an empty grate.

It was cold in the raft. One minute we had been burning alive, the next minute we were on the step, the wind blowing up the tails of our shirts and freezing the burns across our shoulders and backsides. Hardly got wet, stepping from the deck to the raft. The deck was streaming, then wet, then high again; and suddenly the ship's name plate was under three feet of clear green water, and it looked indecent. The water rose over the winch for the companionway, and the quartermaster's telephone. The stanchions were still bracketed to the screens, and the wood of the deck was almost black but there was still a grain in it and the caulking shone, and it surged up towards the surface again, but staggered, and fell away. The overhang of the torpedo deck loomed out over the life raft as she rolled to starboard, and we paddled like fuck to get away from it, and the wind did the rest. She drifted away, and the flight deck and the seven-Alpha passed close, and then she passed us by and seemed to head to port a little, her flight deck awash and the bows rearing up at an odd angle, the Lynx still fastened to the grid by the harpoon, and we drifted further away from her as she lurched and then suddenly rolled, a welter of noise and foam and the screws rearing out of the water, quite controlled but like a dream out of control, and the Lynx neat as all creation, tidily parked where it should be, but now on its side and soon to be under water, still parked, as if waiting for the Flight Deck Officer to signal start first engine, second engine, engage…

We weren't expecting it. One minute we were scoping happily away, plotting the air attack building up to the northeast and feeling glad we weren't on the outlying frigates. There had been a report of two pop-up contacts but they had been dismissed as spurious, and we had good tracks on the enemy aircraft patrolling north of the islands, well away from our position. The radars were working well, comms were clear as crystal, the officer of the watch was happy and it was one of those great days, when every button came to hand, the readings rolled off the tongue, ranges and scales seemed to be instinctive. Course to intercept? No trouble. Closest point of approach? Certainly, Sir. Radar was king, the sensors of the ship, keeping them informed and keeping us safe…there were ships everywhere, tracks to keep and contacts to avoids, with the whole group zig-zagging to guard against submarines, sinuating about the base course set by the zig-zag plan. It was the "Cruel Sea" and "In Which We Serve", we were at war and doing it well. We heard of the attacks on the landing group, and the Harriers' successes, and when ships were sprayed with gunfire or lost a helicopter. Glasgow took a bomb, in one side and out the other, it was a real war and we were keeping our section up to speed, and doing well. It was what we had joined for. We were mates. We were such friends. We were kind to each other. We worked and watched, and they

brought us kye and cluster buns to keep us going.
Then the crash, and nothing.

Deaf as a post, The radar was on my arm, and there were sparks from the electrical leads and cables, and blackness as the lights went off, and a feeling of air as if we were sitting at the edge of the fast lane of a motorway and an articulated lorry had just blasted past. Then there was a great belt of air, like a fist, and my head smashed into something behind me, and heat. I knew the anti-flash was smouldering, I could smell it, taste it. But I could see the others. Four of them on the far side of the table were running around, totally silent, not a sound; they were flapping their arms, mouths wide open and screaming but to me it was silent, and behind them their own shadows, in flame. They spread their arms and the flames spread, they fell and the flames fell with them. One man's arms dripped flame, and when he moved, large chunks of flame fell to the deck. Two others rolled him over onto the deck, and must have put it out because we couldn't see him anymore. Paint was on fire. Cables were melting and dripping down the bulkheads, and black insulation bubbled and streamed from the bulkhead connectors. There were fluorescent green arrows on the deck, and I kept my nose about an inch above them as I tried to find some clean air and all that time at Phoenix Fire School came back. I made it out of the Ops Room and to the Section Base, and suited up I couldn't hear much, but then I didn't have to. I knew what to do. The BA Controller was there, noted numbers, we went in to the room again behind a spray water wall and the others brought the jet. They started knocking down fire, soaking papers and kit which must have been isolated by then, the spray cleared the smoke like it always does and there were bodies and the foot of the ladder leading up to the bridge. It was black, and the curtain behind the door had burned away.

We made the ladder. There was a dull noise in my head, and someone was shaking my arm, and the others in the group had gone. I wiped the back of my glove over the faceplate and saw the next man, pulling at the suit. His mouth was working, but I couldn't hear. He was pointing up, towards the deck, and mimed someone swimming. They must have piped to abandon ship, but I couldn't hear much and I certainly never heard that. He must have thought I was stupid. Then he went, leaving me at the foot of the ladder, looking up at the door to the radio shack, which was shut. There was a light underneath it, though. A yellow line. The door was shut, but I could see a dark shadow, moving back and forwards along the line of light. It was odd. I felt a coldness grip my belly. I should have been on the other side of that door. I had been there often enough in the past. I knew how the person on the other side of the door felt. He could hear me, coming up the stairs, and he would be begging everything in his head to make me go away, to leave him alone, he's be shivering and face down, eyes shut, go away, go away… somehow, I was moving, the spray was still on, up three steps and keeping as low as I could, and the door was just an ordinary door, not a metal one. The handle felt hot through the glove.

It opened and I managed the spray even with my head turned away from the door. Must have been right. The fire arced over the top of the spray and lit up the deckhead of the Ops Room, bright as day for a minute, and then nothing. I turned into the room and the fire was already falling away from the table and the kid on it, although the manuals were on fire and the lad had been. He was slumped across the desk, and his feet had been against the inside of the door, he was kneeling on the deck and his chest, arms and head were across the desktop. He'd managed to drag himself half-up, but had scrabbled on the deck to push himself the rest of the way and hadn't made it. It must have been his steaming bats that made the shadows against the door. I looked at them. They were melting, at the edges. I sprayed them, and then the water stopped, and the ship lurched as if she'd been goffered for'ard, and he rolled to the side of the desk and then, as she recovered, back towards me. I managed the hook him up as he came towards me and then the ship dropped on a wave as I pulled at him and he weighed nothing, just flew up over my shoulder, and I braced to take his weight when the ship came up again. It was crushing. I could hear a bit, now, and the noise of the demand valve would have given me away as the biggest coward who had ever put on an ICABA set, but there was nobody there to hear me. He was in a bad way, but I couldn't give him my air. No BASCCA's, no smoke masks…what were they called? 5665 Pattern smoke masks…Breathing Apparatus Self Contained Compressed Air….funny. All that time, learning all those bits of kit. He was heavy, but we got out. I ran him up the starboard side ladder, remembering we were faced astern. It was as well I did. The ship was listing badly when we got to the boat deck. He rolled into the scupper while I fumbled and tore at the suit but the fucking thing would not come off, until I remembered the bottle. The harness. The mask was on the back of my head. Fumbling, excited, terrified now. Cursing. Screaming. I couldn't get the thing off, it weighed a ton and would drown me, I'd sink like a kitten in a bucket, and then it was free, and it was coming away from me on its own. They were standing on either side of me, soaking wet, cutting at the straps with rigging knives. There was a life raft alongside and they were shouting, but I couldn't hear them, they took the lad I'd carried out, and me.. they must have come back on board to get us, and I wanted to hug them, but they threw me off the step into the raft, a great breeze of freezing air, then the clammy, wet warmth of the inside of the raft. I fell down into a forest of hands, reaching out to pull me upright, sit me against the side of the raft, give me sweets, chocolate, water. He was burned, the lad I carried out. The side of his face, where it had been resting on the deck, was bad.

The hair had gone and the covering of the desk top had mixed with the skin of the his face, and had melted into the hair on the left side of his head, and then cooled and set. The hair writhed and curled among the strands of plastic. The side of his eye looked deep, a huge hole, and the edge of his mouth had been burned so far back that you could see his teeth. Very nice teeth. Very white and clean.

I was burned across my shoulders, where he must have pushed against the suite, and the backs of my legs but it always got you there. The suit worked best where it didn't fold, and when it was wet it passed a lot of heat through. My face was all right, though. I couldn't hear very well, but I had no burns on my face.

It doesn't hurt, when you burn your face. You are too busy watching the light around your eyes. There is a noise, as the skin burns. Your eyes feel tight, as if the skin is stretching backwards and your eyeballs are going to fly out. Your cheeks are stretched away from the bones under your eyes, and the hair crackles as it burns, and you can hear it, for a while. Nothing hurts, but your lips feel numb, and they tear when you open them, and when you breath it is so hot, and then searing heat branches down through your neck into your chest, and you know that you are going to be dead in a minute. The feeling is like nothing at all, unless you knew a similar feeling before you were born. It is a loss of sensation. No tears, no whiskers, no skin; no taste, no smell, no sight. Then pain, just pain.
I could see the paint curling towards me, and then the flame. That was the last thing I saw, I suppose. The heat came more from my hands than my head. The water was dark, bottle green. It seemed to be green. Then black.

They shouldn't have burned me, like that. Not after I got him into the life raft. Not after we got away from the ship so well. I never hurt the lad, he must have been frightened hearing me coming for him but I never hurt him, just picked him up as clean as a whistle and took him out of there. There is no need to worry in the ship. That sort of thing never happens in a ship. It never happens in a prison, unless you go looking for it. The best of ships, the best of prisons, they have rules and if you like them and want them, you can rest assured that you will be free from any sort of interference. You only have to worry about it when there is nobody telling you what to do. It doesn't matter in a prison.
Unless they find out what you have done, and then you might as well be dead. You'll wish you were dead. He'd have died. He must have felt so safe, when they took him into the life raft and then later into the sick bay on the Carrier. Not like it used to be for me. Not like it was for Philip.

The man started, suddenly, the burned mouth opened and sucked in a great breath, then sobbed, twice and around him the circle of men backed away a little.

I can hear the little noises. I know there's light. The bastard. I'm asleep. Bastard, leave me alone. Leave him alone. If only the sailor had made it alive; but he died. I'm asleep. I'm asleep. It doesn't work like it used to. Perhaps they're just bringing me some soup.

"We just need to make sure that they find him where they can believe he could be washed up."
"Poor bastard."
"Leave off, that. Just lay off."
Too late to apologise now, you bastard. Too late to feel sorry for me now. Just get it over with, and leave me alone. I'm asleep, I'm asleep, I'm asleep…

The biggest man of the group sighed, leaned forward, and using both hands, hit downwards with one of the smaller rocks that had been piled against the door. The body jerked and lay still, its breathing snorting and snuffling through the damaged face which now rested hard against the airbed. They took hold of the body, and carried it out into the cave, one of the group walking ahead, carrying the torch. They walked down the slope towards the mouth of the cave, where spray burst up from the sea below, and settled in pools among the rocks and in between the old iron rails. Where some of the rail had corroded away, there was left a long narrow strip of water about two feet deep, and into this they gently lowered the melted, burned face, and held the damaged back of the head down until the breathing stopped.

Chapter 16.

The weather changed. A warm southerly wind dried the rock until it changed colour from blue-grey almost to white. Brian rested his hand against it, and it was warm. Only a day or two ago, it would have felt wet and cold, as would the streets and the houses, and the people. Now, the rock started to warm; and the road surface steamed in the sun, and the prison took on a spring-like aspect as moss reflected sunlight along the joints between the stone blocks, as if the whole fort had been carefully grouted with seeds. The sea was still wintry, but it was blue, not grey; and now white foam hissed across the green blue tide race instead of grey foam and dull, sand-laden water.

The press had decided to ridicule the protestors. Editors could just as easily have praised them, and it would have been just as well received, but this time they had decided there was more mileage in the law and order lobby, and had spent the last four days proclaiming the importance of civil order, and how the democratic right to protest must be tempered by the constraints of respect for individual freedoms. They had decided that Mrs. Gibbs was the innocent victim of mob rule, and had tried to paint her in heroic colours, but she had refused requests for interviews and when, nevertheless, one paper published a largely imaginary human interest article about her, she wrote a long letter to the newspaper's rival in which she blamed it for inciting the mob to come to the Island in the first place, and then to behave in the way it had. She asked where had the banners been manufactured, who had distributed them, how had the photographers known where to stand when the demonstration became a mob. The rival had been delighted to print the letter and to add an editorial about responsible journalism. In the South of the country, a similar mob of paedophile-protestors mistook the address of a released sex-offender and burned the flat of an innocent and disabled woman to the ground. The woman was rescued by the fire brigade, and carried through a jeering crowd of arsonists and would-be murderers, confused by the severity of her burns, the violence visited upon her as if from nowhere, and the lack of sympathy she received as, choking and helpless, she was carried through a crowd of people chanting "Kill the bastard," "If you won't, we will," and so on. Outrage had ripped through the non-protesting population, and suddenly it was a bad idea for TV programme planners to give interviews to the nose-studded, hair-dyed leaders of the protestors. The whole idea of direct action against sex offenders had, it seemed, been shelved until the next time it could be dusted off and used.

It had been difficult for the press to keep up its story of a local community terrorised by the threat of an escaped sex offender on the Island. Television footage of the demonstration had been edited to show that the community was besieged by the press, not by criminals; and that they were more than capable of caring for each other. One newspaper experimented with the theme of a criminalised population, a community corrupted by its close association with the prisons set among it. The article had carried a large close up of the admittedly rugged face of Klaxon, and several smaller prints of the action as he punched three members of the crowd. There were other Island communities in Britain with prisons, however, and that theme did not prove popular.

Most of the journalists had left. Some of them felt they had fought for and won a great story, that they had unearthed something that would bear future examination. Some, more realistic newsmen simply regretted the loss of the compound overtime that they had been paid, especially the TV news teams, and they shrugged their shoulders and went on to their next story. None of them seriously believed that there was an offender stalking the Island. The search had been long and careful, and nothing had been found, despite the last minute flurry of excitement when a local man had remembered an abandoned and isolated torpedo recovery point, which had been missed by the searchers. The press and the police had approached the place with great caution, but it was abandoned and empty, its roof ripped away, the inside blackened by damp and fires, probably made by youths or beach fishermen. It had made great television, with armed police slipping gracefully down sheer slopes, apparently falling off the edge of a cliff, and then found by the camera to have dropped onto the narrowest of ledges. They had surrounded the empty hut, called out their warnings, burst into the doorway and stood, stiff-armed, pistols and carbines cocked and ready, all for nothing. It was as if that last raid signalled the end of the search. The Police vans had moved out, and that evening, so had most of the pressmen.

In the prison, security procedures were adopted that were nonsensical but which were insisted upon by the Home Office. The interior compounds were separated by security fences, extra locks and keys were issued so that cons had to queue to pass from one compound to the next and could only do so when let through by a key-holder. The prison tops were lined with illegal razor wire, and the Home Office paid the fine each year to the European Authority that banned such wire's use as inhumane; and the activities of any prisoner working outside a block were carefully monitored.

The cells, previously just rooms, were keyed. The snooker tables were initially removed, and then replaced. The education centre was congratulated on the role it had played in the temporary crisis and Higgins was selected for special praise for his television work, a commendation that cost the prison service nothing, as Higgins was a contractor working for the local college of Education. Higgins now presented to the world as a modest but efficient hero, good in a crisis and a man of the community.

Some of the prison officers shrugged their shoulders and had long, quiet conversations with the lifers and the long-term prisoners. Others swaggered more, wore aggressively creased and polished uniforms, muscled in on activity periods or handicraft workshops, and made rough and ready jokes about escape committees and tunnel checks, as they span the cells far more often than was necessary. Inside the prison, the cons carried on with their foolish posturing, and shouted and laughed as they made their remarks about Williams, and other nonces, and what they would do to any other Williams that might be hiding among them; and eighty per cent of them felt a quick flicker of fear, deep in their bowels, just in case they might be discovered. They then shouted insults at nonces, louder and filthier than the rest.

The prison officers, cons, even some of the locals, could not rid themselves of scanning the papers for the latest story about themselves. Most of them were disappointed to find none. Some of the locals, though, found it easier not to read newspapers. They found that when they did, they could not believe anything that they read. They talked matters over, in the pub or as they walked along the cliff top, or fished.

They talked a lot. Mrs. Gibbs seemed slightly more grim-faced, and performed her tasks with a dogged determination, that did not invite conversation. She would have a quiet time leaning against the bar opposite Brian, most nights, when he came in. She would smoke a cigarette, and have a drink. The conversation would be a series of statements, though, and no names were ever mentioned. Visitors thought it was simply some locals excluding them from any conversation.

"I suppose it was for the best, really."

"Sure it was."

"He'd not have been able to stand going back."

"He'd not have been left alone, not after that. No, for the best."

Nothing much was said. Often, Mrs. Gibbs would reach out and rub the back of Brian's wrist, roughly, affectionately, almost gratefully. She would look down at the thick wrist and the strong brown hand, and nod sadly. Then she would go back to work.

Ron and Annie talked to each other in the corner. He had slowly started to make more sense, and was able to speak slowly, for a while. He spoke mainly about Annie, paying her rough, childish compliments and unsteadily stroking her face or hair. The girl said little, but her eyes would be very bright, and if there was one signal of hope for the future in that pub, it was Annie's expression as she looked at Ron.

"It's just an old airbed, Sarge." Gary dragged the blue and red trophy out of the sea, and threw it onto the dock. The Sea Trout and Kingfisher danced at their moorings in the bright sunshine of a clear morning. The policeman stretched the material out on the top of the jetty. The black rubber interior was exposed in a three-inch triangular tear.
"Not very old, from the look of it."
The Sergeant shook his head.
"No. Amazing what people leave on the beach."
"Yes, but we haven't had any holidaymakers here since October. It's three months ago…"
"Chucked off a ship, perhaps? It's torn, look."
The two policemen turned the material over, and two newsmen who had started to walk towards them to look at the find, saw what it was, lost interest and moved away.
"There's something else there, Gary."
"Yes. An old blanket. I pulled at it when I got the airbed out. Loads of stuff there, Sarge; an old door, bits of wood, paper; this part of the coast has a break in the tide, it doglegs in to the cove and dumps loads of flotsam.."
The sergeant nodded. "Best you keep checking it, then. Come on. Let's see where those two are going."

Brian watched the last of journalists as well, from high on the cliff edge, just up from the cottage. His daughter was back at home, having spent a fortnight with Gary and Heather at the police house in the centre of the Ford. The newsmen were cooling off, now, and there were only four or five left in the area. He could see Peter carrying a rod and bucket, making his way to the old harbour wall, and the dog was prancing from smell to smell, as if seeing the path and its surroundings for the first time. There would be more of them, when the body washed in, he supposed. Brian sighed at the thought. One last invasion, and then the whole affair would be over.

Poor lad. What would he look like, when he was washed in. He would be. Just there, where Gary was pulling at old blankets and bits of wood. One morning there would be a shout, and what was left of the lad would be there, misshapen from the damage done by the waves throwing it against the rocks; and the lungs full of sea water. It wouldn't be much longer. The body would be pretty far gone, by then; if Digger and Klaxon had got it right. They had brought "Petrel" in to the old quay at high tide, and taken the boy out to the Green Grounds. There were three wrecks there, and they'd put him in one of them, weighted down so he wouldn't float away. Soon, after the sea had worked at him, they'd go out and slip the weight, and he'd wash in a couple of days later.

The Press would all come back, then, and film the place again. They'd find the locals quite willing to give interviews, and tell the watching public about their relief that there was no threat to their children, any more. There was, though; the threat to children never goes away. It is just that parents find it hard to think about, for a number of reasons, and only acknowledge it when something dreadful happens and makes the papers. Usually, of course, it will not reach the papers at all.

I could not do it any other way.

We are all capable of any crime. That tide is strong; the waves could be dangerous to anyone on the wall, if the wind was on shore, but it's not. Good day for bass, if he uses a spinner. Peter is outgrowing his clothes. Thin legs, huge knees, long feet that seem to flap but as sure footed as the dog. He can make light work of rocks and paths I cannot manage any more. Yet I remember them as a playground when I was a boy. Kids don't worry about obstacles, and they stop being obstacles. I suppose that's why a fall or a scrape comes as such a shock to a kid; they expect the best, they're optimistic. They shout at the time, but soon stop, and they have huge hearts that hope for the best and in bad times, that better things will soon come. We spend our time trying to avoid strains and injuries, and slow down as a result. We don't expect much; and that is usually what we get.

Is that why the papers concentrate on such stuff? As if they are telling us, it is bad for you but it's worse for others? Is that why we read it so carefully, treat it with such respect? People used to listen to the News because it affected them. Now, they listen out of interest, nosiness perhaps.

Young Terry didn't hope for much. He was content with a conversation with someone who didn't hit him, probably. He was good at rocks; didn't feel them. He never wore much on his feet; daps, or sandals, never had any decent shoes, but he went around the quarry like a goat. Very light on his feet. Like a deer.

He had the same way of looking at you, turning his head slowly, one huge eye and then both of them, grave, solemn. Occasionally he would smile, and the sun would come out, and be wiped away as quickly. You were staring into a soul, and seeing layers of pain, and now and again a glimpse of the core of a child's life, all the belief and the hope and promise.

Love, too. He must have been given love, somewhere along the line, for him to have that hope for love in the future. Or are you born with a desire to be loved? Terry looked for something he'd once had. I'm sure of it.

We knew his father was a shit. He'd come to Island to find work in the quarry. What sort of a man would do that? My father quarried rock, our parents all did; but they were born here. It's what we do. What we had to do. Islanders dug rock to throw at the Romans, they pulled it out of the ground to make shelters and houses; later we sold it for ballast and sent it for buildings and now it stands all around the world as cathedrals and capitals and palaces; but we only dug it for the money, the living, the food it bought and the clothes we wore; we did it for the Island, and made our place live by digging it up and selling it. Our land, our Island; to live, we had to give part of ourselves away. We did not live well, but they leant against their stone sills or climbed their palace steps, and had everything they needed, and we had the little we needed, but just slightly less of our own Island on which to live. It had always been like that.

One of the papers had been writing about them, and had said that "Hail Ford quarrymen lived and loved rock." Hail Ford quarrymen did not love rock. They loved the Island, loved the Ford. As soon as part of it was squared and lifted, it stopped being the Island. It was like selling a child for bread. It was obscene, and the sooner it was out of sight the better. Splinters of it, no good for ornament, were salvaged and re-set into the Ford, cemented into a wall of similar shards, or used as pavements, or if no good for that, shaped and sculpted and displayed as ornaments. But quarrymen; it was work you had to do.

Convicts made quarrymen, but convicts were destructive anyway. It was why they were in prison in the first place. They built the prison out of the Island, and then from it used to come streams of lanky, broad shouldered shaven headed men who would have destroyed the area anyway, but the state organised them to destroy it in an orderly fashion. The Ford accepted it. It was what the Island did.

But to come to the island and volunteer to be a quarryman! It was like visiting a house and volunteering to destroy the family. That was what Williams had done. Not the only one, of course; the quarry now belonged to outsiders; its original owners had become so wealthy on the backs of the Islanders the family now was one of the greatest in the land, the great Hailford dynasty, owning most of the region and half of the capital; but that did not seem to matter, it was the result of their way of life, not despite it. But for multi-national companies to come in, as they now had and strip away the very land from under the Islanders' feet to make gravel beds for roads in parts of Europe never even heard of, seemed the end of the way of life they had known such a short time ago.

Terry had loved rock, though. I gave him an old chisel, once, and a hammer. I remember once, he had found an ammonite and had chipped it clear and was squatting stroking it. He had crooned. Sung to it, as he wiped the white dust from the blue slate underneath the rock. He'd been singing, stroking the rock. He had loved the rock, caressing it as no one caressed him.

I never knew his mother particularly well; she was with us at the school, of course. Younger than me. Small, well-behaved girl, pretty in her way, and a lovely singing voice. I never noticed her at all until she took up with Williams, and then I was interested just to see what sort of person she was to go out with him. But she was normal. He'd been nice to her, and she was of that age. They had married and settled into a quarry cottage, like generations before them. It was just that he did not fit in, and she wanted to live a normal Island life; she would talk to her friends and relatives at the shop or in the village, and would go to church on Sunday as she always had, as we all did, because there was news to exchange and arrangements to make, and because Islanders don't live in houses, we live on the Island. We sleep in houses. We take our rest there, and have our meals, but we live among each other.

Williams was different, of course he was. He did not know anyone on the Ford at all, and news about each other passed him by, it was of no interest to him at all. He was glad to get in to his house. He wanted to get away from the Island, and into his home. He wanted to get away from work. He could not understand why his wife was so much happier than he was, and it first made him bitter, and then it made him bad.

She was pregnant, the first time he marked her.
We all saw. Not the first wife to be beaten on the
Island to be sure, but the first once such as she
was. She was a good girl. He had married one of
the best, steadiest girls we had, and he had
beaten her. He kept beating her, too. The boy
was early, and sickly for a while, and his mother
never complained, not out of courage but she
did not know how to put it into words, and we
would not have known how to reply. This man
was out of our understanding. I saw men like
him every day, in the prison, but I did not have
to understand them, and could not. I still can't,
today, and I've worked with them for forty
years. They are not a problem behind a wall; it's
when they are in front of it, living in a house
among your own community that they cause
trouble.

But then I saw her running towards me, one
evening, and the boy in front of her. She had her
arms out and the little lad ran ahead, looking
back at his mother and then ahead again, for all
the world like a chicken being chased by a dog.
She kept shouting, for the boy to run and then
she would grunt, and shout again, and I saw he
was running after them but kept stopping, to
pick up rocks. He was throwing rocks at his wife
and child, and she was trying to stop them
hitting the boy, and taking them all herself,
against her back, her head…

It was as if he was telling her to have her Island.
It would not accept him, so he threw it back at
her. He stooped and threw, then ran to catch
them up, and threw again. He even stooped to
pick up another rock after I stood behind his
wife and in front of him, and for a while his face
blazed at me and I thought he might have
thrown it at me. But he was a beaten man, a
coward. Only beaten men, beat their wives.
She came back, and leant against my arm.
"You will go," he said. I felt her shaking. She
looked around for the boy, but he had run off,
and gone home. I heard her say, "Terry?" but
he'd gone.
"You will go, and now. That is my cottage, my
son. I am the employee, and it's my home. You
will never set foot in it again."
I told him what he was, and he ignored me. He
was right, of course. The quarry supplied
buildings for its workers. She could have won
the child, but she was only a kid. She panicked, I
suppose. In a state, she went to her friends, they
looked after her for a week or two. She was lost
for her child, and he too, but neither of them
could do much about it and Williams knew how
to force his own way. She looked to us for help.
We couldn't help.
We did not know how to help.
Oh, hell…

Brian straightened up from the wall he had been resting against. He knocked out the pipe, and refilled it. He straightened up and stared out to the race, enjoying the clear air and the fine, black border that stretched between sea and sky and was only seen on the clearest of days. Peter was in full view, fishing. Thatcher walked steadily down the wide grass path, over the top edge of the beginning of the old quarry land. The main pit was well to his left, and where he walked was turf, with outcrops of white stone. He could still see, the boy of years ago, running, looking.

She met a steelworker, who was a tidy enough lad and came from South Wales, and she went off with him. Perhaps Williams had told the boy. Maybe he had just let Terry out at last, and the lad had run back here, the last place he had seen her. It was here, anyway, that I saw him that first time, running from rock to rock, searching.

I can still see the way he stood in front of me; hesitating. I nodded to him, I remember, and he nodded back, gravely. He'd not found her, but he'd found someone. I suppose he did not like men. Maybe the father had started on him already. Out of revenge? Loneliness? No, not Williams. Viciousness, more likely; taking it out on the boy because he could no longer get to the mother. He had his great triumph over her. He had made her part of him, taken her clean little life and Island ways and made them part of his own mucked up existence. Now he had the boy, all of her potential in the boy, all of his before life took him and spoiled him; so, instead of nurturing the child, he ruined him. It was mean, spiteful vengeance, mixed with his own perverted pleasure.

Brian shook his head, as if to dislodge a gnat. He inhaled on the pipe, and then withdrew it from his mouth and breathed in the smoke; held it for a while, and then let it out with a hiss. His left hand rested lightly on a rock pillar, and his fingers rubbed the end of a razor shell, buried for millions of years in its surrounding stone. His eyesight jigged and danced as his cardiovascular system rebelled at the inhalation and the nicotine. Then he walked on, and saw the road line ahead, and the back of Williams' old cottage.

I could hear the boy from the path.
I gave that chisel and broken pawl-hammer to him, and he spent most of his time on the rock. Funny that his father worked there and hated it, while his son took such delight in chipping at the same stone. His father created dust and filth, and tore blocks of the place away; Terry left his debris at the place where he found it, but he treasured the fossils, and stored them carefully away. He had carrier bags that he kept them in, he told me once, and I gave him a small set of drawers I had, a collection set. People used to have them for stamp albums, or coins. Nice little set of drawers. He had run back with them straight away, probably put them somewhere before his father had come home. Anyway, that was what the boy was shouting about, and what Williams was holding out of the window, when I walked up to the back of the cottage. Shaking them out of the window. Like a madman.
I could see the little pieces of stone raining out of the window, and then the wooden frame came out, and broke. The hammer landed quite near me. There was a side door to the cottage, no back door; and then the door at the front. I went to the side one. I could hear the boy being hit from outside the building. I thought I could. I pushed the side door open, and called up at him.
I don't remember what I said.

The boy was flat on his face in the back room, and his father was running for it, I suppose, but I still remember how hard he went down those bloody stairs, and how much it hurt him, and how much I enjoyed it. I wanted to do it again. I wanted to stamp and beat and kick the life out of him, and it was nothing to do with what he had done to the girl or to young Terry or the drawers; it was what he was, that I hated. What he did to the Ford. The way he lived. He should not have been there at all. He was just a bloody mistake. He was trapped and frightened, and strong enough from his work, but nothing much. I remember my hands. They're like it now, at the memory of it. I can feel it still. My heart's pounding! I hated him, I wanted to hurt him so much it made my fingers stiff…and I realised then how much I loved the boy.

I did not hurt Williams, but I wanted to, and he could see it. He knew what I did for a living. Later, when I'd told Gary about it, Williams was probably frightened he'd end up inside, but he knew what he owned. He owned the boy. He had come to a point when his future is uncertain, his past was a disaster, and he had to make certain of something. He had the job, the cottage and the boy, and he was ready to fight to keep them. They were his protection; shelter, life, pleasure. There was no love there, but a need for some sort of family. He had very little, but was going to fight to make sure he did not end up with nothing.

I don't think I hurt Williams. It was not viciousness, not revenge. It would have been unthinkable, to let him go on like that, and the lad deserved better than to be taken into care. Williams went, and the lad stayed with Ella and me. God, he loved Ella. He'd found his mother again. Same accent, same way of life, same friends. I left them to it. Ella was eighteen, she could more than handle Terry for me. We fixed his display, and found most of the fossils.

But Ella met a chap, and the boy went off on his own again. It was not so bad the second time; he was older, I suppose. And we only had him as a temporary measure, because the social had found his mother. She appeared, and took him off to Wales.

He stared at her, when she first came in. He stared, and wanted to run to her, I could see. She was the same, opened her arms, hesitated, shy. Closed her arms again, but not around him. She smoked, I remember. She hadn't smoked before. But the greatest shock of all was her voice. It had changed completely. She used to sound like Ella, but now it was harsh, the accent was thick as butter. The boy flinched when she first said his name. He just looked lost.

They patched some sort of love up, I expect. He went with her happily enough, and she chattered on about what he'd have, but she still sounded like a canary, when the boy wanted the soft, rounded, smooth voice he had remembered so long. Ella sounded more like his mother than she did. She picked her way towards the road and the bus stop, in her high heels and careful not to turn an ankle. He went off, though; looked back once or twice, a little wave, long, thin legs, big knees, effortless across the rocks and the grass path. Like a goat.

We have all been children. Innocent children. Massive potential for good or evil. We are all capable of becoming anything we like; good people or wicked. We are all capable of any crime, any level of saintliness or depravity. There would be no point in making crime illegal unless we were all capable of committing it; unless we had all wanted to commit it, at some time. I have. I have wanted to kill, to destroy. I know the love for a child, how it dominates you. I can imagine how easily it could become unnatural. If you have this huge need to give affection, but cannot do so, maybe you are not allowed to do so, I can see how it could become perverted. We are all capable of doing evil. Trouble is, the more often you do evil, the more normal it seems; and the more people around you that can be convinced to act in the same way, the less wrong it seems. Evildoers have a vested interest in getting others to act in the same way. Crooks recruit. Perverts need to pervert those around them, not as victims so much, but as fellow-practitioners.

They cannot sort it out. I watched them, week after week, come into the prison and queue up outside the reception centre. They are waiting for the first affront, the first insult. They are sullen with the officers and with each other, looking for what they know they will get. It is going to happen, soon, from somewhere. I get the impression that their whole life has been like that. Some lean against the wall, waiting to be told to straighten up. They are disappointed if you don't tell them to, and slow to respond if you do. You never do, not if you have any sense. It's not your wall. Ex-army types often tell them to stand up, out of habit probably, but it's a mistake. Never insult, never confront. Praise if you like, encourage. If you can stand the insults. Even if they want to accept your advice, they can't afford to be seen to accept it. Only the best keep offering. That's the thing, never hope for anything from a con, never trust a con, you won't be disappointed and any result is a bonus.

I've trained good bricklayers, good plasterers. Some of them have trained me, the tradesmen that end up inside usually take time to perfect their skill. They can shelter behind it, and it stops them having to let too much of themselves out. They become known among the other cons as someone with a skill worth learning. It's valuable, and can be exchanged for goods. They behave well, inside. They have no problems to solve. All they need to worry about is ensuring they don't upset anyone, officers or other cons. Keep their heads down, do their bird, find a bird killer, go to classes or learn a trade. They will be faced with drugs, have to come arrangement about tobacco, booze, sex, fear, assault, and that's about all. It is a relatively easy life, if you're reasonably fit and not frightened.

The bullies swagger, the cowards swagger. Idiots saunter, their underpants bright blue or red gingham check pulled high over their waist bands, the prison jeans, the yellow boots or training shoes, the maroon sweat shirts. They swagger with their arses hanging out, like baboons. Lifers slouch in their treasured duffel coats, racial groups form, many wear blue knitted hats and black gloves, like Clint Eastwood in the film about Alcatraz; and newly joined cons all have a walk, of some sort or another. They never walk normally, until they have been there a while. Then they relax. That's when they are most vulnerable. The initial fear has worn off, they have decided they can cope with the nick, that it's going to be easy. That's when they get sat on. The hard men take their soap, shampoo, tobacco. They are given tasks to do, and then these are added to, to see how far they can be pushed. They'll be attacked. The prison officers will start to ride them about cleanliness, spin their cells, nick them if they are late, see what they are made of.

He never relaxed. I saw him strutting, stiff-legged, stiff-armed, from block to workshop. It was a head down, shoulders-hunched walk and he did not look about him, just lowered his forehead and stared at his destination from under his brow; and people left him alone. He passed me in the block corridor, about two days after he came to Hail Ford, and he walked past me he hesitated, and slowed.

"Yes?" He looked up at me for a while, shifty but still, keen to pin down where he had seen me before.

"Yes, what's the matter. Who are you?"

"Williams, guv. "

"When did you get here?"

"This week, that's all."

"What do you want, Williams?"

"Nothing Guv. You spoke to me, that's why I stopped, that's all. Don't you want me for anything?"

"No." Then, stupidly, "Still like fossils, do you?"

"Fossils? Do my fucking head in, it will straight, one minute this and then…fucking fossils? Sorry Guv, you lost me…"

"Yes. On your way, then."

He stiff-legged away, muttering. He looked back, though, quickly and despite the fact he was not looking where he was going, his feet were sure and light on the corridor floor. Like a little goat.

Brian turned away from the back of the cottage and looked up at the high useless wall of the prison. It towered over an expanse of turf, containing ditches and mazes, the various perfections of the castle-builder's craft, and then a wide expanse of turf cropped short by the common's sheep. Turf stretched to the lip of the old quarry, a huge drop, the hole from which the rocks for the prison had been hauled. He walked towards the edge of the drop, and stared down into the jumble of rocks at its base. They were the result of a fall. The quarrymen had left it neat, scraped clean, a system of straight edges, steps and surfaces. Part of the edge had crumbled, after the quarry had closed. The rock there might have been weakened by blasting; great boulders and slabs of limestone, with smaller boulders sprayed across the quarry's floor. He could see the base of the quarry, and the far wall; on top of it ran the path, and then behind that, the cliff and it dropped down again, to the sea. It had never occurred to him before. The quarry floor must be at about sea level. Why did it not flood? And were there any workings that did flood? He must find out, one day. He could see on the far edge, where Gary's police van and the sergeant's car were parked, over the top path to the harbour where Peter would still be fishing, streaming for bass.

Thatcher stirred with alarm. If Peter were there when it was washed in, it would do the lad no good. Might be better for him not to go down there for a while; but you can't stop a lad from fishing. The police cars were moving, slowly, no blue lights. They could not have found anything, then. That's where it would wash up, Thatcher was sure of it. Sooner the better. He had been careful to remind Gary of that strange tidal swirl and the amount of rubbish that swirled in there. When it arrived there would be an end to it all. The newspapers would have a story, but not much of one, and they would be able to leave the Island in fear of the escaped paedophile. Nonsense, all rubbish. They would assume that the prison top had been washed up, found by a kid or a dog and dragged to where it ended up. They would see a decomposed body, its lungs full of sea water, perhaps they would see it had been burned and had head injuries, depending on what was left. They would assume that it had been hung up on a rock or in a cave, and finally washed out and into shore. See what they make of that, Thatcher thought.

He looked down into the quarry, and particularly at one corner of it, where the rock fall spread out from the base of the cliff. It would be about level with the harbour, at that point. The harbour, though, looked out on the great natural advantage that had compensated quarrymen for generations, the sea. It blazed with life and colour, and gave the food and riches but never failed. You could not dig a hole in the sea. It was where freedom curled and writhed and towered over the Islanders' boats, a place to work and fear but to play as well, to be able to stretch and breath and see the whole of the sky, not just a dark, shadowed circle. Deep in the quarry, the sun never reached, it was never warm, it was colourless and hard, a place of grit and sweat and pain. It was the right place for evil people, damned to such a life either through necessity or as the result of their own wicked actions. A quarry was the right place for evil men.

The sea, though, was for boys. It was full of all the life and adventure and love in the world, there for the taking, if you wanted it enough. The little lad Thatcher had known was out there somewhere; he had become buried deep in an adult's body, but the fears and wickedness that had collected around him over the years had been stripped off, and he was not far away, somewhere in the waves that Thatcher knew were rolling and surging, foaming and cascading droplets in the clean wind and the new-washed sun; and he knew that the boy, sure footed as a goat, hurt but still full of hope, would be making his way towards the love he had once known and then searched for, all the rest of his life.

Proof

Made in the USA
Charleston, SC
13 June 2011